RAVE REVIEWS FOR
FRANCIS RAY

ONE NIGHT WITH YOU
"The steam the lovers create is a pleasure to behold. Ray never disappoints!"

—RT Book Reviews (4½ stars)

WITH JUST ONE KISS
"Heartwarming and fun."

—RT Book Reviews (4 stars)

NOBODY BUT YOU
"A story that tugs at the heartstrings."

—RT BOOKreviews

"Fast and fun and full of emotional thrills and sexy chills. Everything a racing romance should be!"

—Roxanne St. Claire

"Not only does Francis Ray rock in this book but you also see a whole different side of racing that will keep you on the edge of your seat."

—Night Owl Romance

"A wonderful read."   *—Fresh Fiction*

UNTIL THERE WAS YOU
"Ms. Ray has given us a great novel again. Did we expect anything less than the best?"

—RT Book Reviews (4 stars)

"Crisp style, realistic dialogue, likable characters, and [a] fast pace."
—*Library Journal*

THE WAY YOU LOVE ME
"As always, Ray leads her readers on a mesmerizing journey of drama and love . . . *The Way You Love Me* confirms the fact that Francis Ray is, without a doubt, one of the Queens of Romance."
—*A Romance Review*

"A romance that will have readers speed-reading to the next tension-filled scene, if not the climax."
—*Fresh Fiction*

"Fans of Ray's Grayson and Falcon families will be thrilled with the first installment in the new Grayson Friends series. And this is done very well . . . told with such grace and affection that this novel is a treat to read."
—*RT Book Reviews* (4 stars)

ONLY YOU
"Francis Ray's graceful writing style and realistically complex characters give her latest contemporary romance its extraordinary emotional richness and depth."
—*Chicago Tribune*

"It's a joy to read this always fresh and exciting saga."
—*RT Book Reviews* (4 stars)

"The powerful descriptive powers of Francis Ray allow the reader to step into the story and become an active part of the surrender . . . If you love a great love story, *Only You* should be on your list."
—*Fallen Angel Reviews*

"Riveting emotion and charismatic scenes that made this book captivating . . . a beautiful story of love and romance." —*Night Owl Romance*

"A beautiful love story as only Francis Ray can tell it." —Singletitles.com

"Readers will find a warm and wonderful contemporary romance with plenty of humor and drama. Adding a fun warmth and reality to these characters and a plot that moves quickly add all the needed incentive to read this fun book."
—*Multicultural Romance Writers*

IRRESISTIBLE YOU
"A pleasurable story . . . a well-developed story and continuous plot." —*RT Book Reviews*

"Like the previous titles in this series, *Irresistible You* is another winner . . . Witty and charming . . . Author Francis Ray has a true gift for drawing the readers in and never letting them go."
—*Multicultural Romance Writers*

DREAMING OF YOU
"A great read from beginning to end, it's even excellent for an immediate re-read." —*RT Book Reviews*

All I Ever Wanted

FRANCIS RAY

St. Martin's Paperbacks

This is a work of fiction. All of the characters, organizations, and events portrayed in this novel are either products of the author's imagination or are used fictitiously.

ALL I EVER WANTED

Copyright © 2013 by Francis Ray.
Excerpt from *All That I Need* copyright © 2013 by Francis Ray.

For information address St. Martin's Press, 175 Fifth Avenue, New York, NY 10010.

ISBN: 978-1-250-02380-3

Printed in the United States of America

St. Martin's Paperbacks edition / March 2013

St. Martin's Paperbacks are published by St. Martin's Press, 175 Fifth Avenue, New York, NY 10010.

10 9 8 7 6 5 4 3 2 1

Lovingly dedicated to all of my loyal readers who waited so patiently for Richard and Naomi's story. I couldn't do this without your support and love. You are the best!

Acknowledgment

To Carolyn M. Ray for being so good at what she does.

Prologue

Long before dawn, Naomi Reese awoke in a panic. Cold sweat beaded her skin. Her heart pounding, her mouth dry, her one overriding thought was getting to her daughter, Kayla.

Shivering with fear, she fought back a whimper as she struggled to untangle her legs from the bedding. Seconds later her bare feet hit the carpeted floor. In two steps she was running.

Terror nipping at her heels, afraid she'd find the twin bed empty, she burst into Kayla's room next to hers. The butterfly night-light she always left on illuminated the bed. Seeing Kayla sleeping peacefully, her slim arm wrapped loosely around the waist of Teddy, her favorite toy and teddy bear, Naomi swayed, then briefly shut her eyes in relief.

Slowly, her fear receded. She moved closer to the bed to touch her daughter, to reassure herself that it had only been a bad dream. Her ex-husband wasn't in Santa Fe. They were still safe.

No matter how hard she tried to shake the fear

that he knew where they lived, she couldn't. Perhaps she should have moved when he found them the last time, but she had friends here. Good friends. They knew her worst secret and didn't think less of her.

But it was difficult not to think less of herself.

She'd been such easy prey for a sweet-talking man like her ex-husband. She'd swallowed every lie, believed his possessiveness was love instead of what it was, a way of controlling her. His overbearing ways became steadily worse after they were married. If she wasn't working, he wanted her home.

One night she'd wanted to go to a movie with girlfriends and he'd forbidden her to go. She thought he was joking at first. She quickly learned differently with his shouts and accusations that she was going to meet some man.

Insulted more than angry, she'd picked up her handbag and headed for the front door of their apartment, ignoring his orders for her to come back. She had few friends and was looking forward to a girls' night out. When she kept walking, he'd thrown the glass in his hand at her.

The glass shattered against the wall, missing her head by mere inches. Defensively, Naomi had covered her head with her arms and hands. The flying shards had cut her arm. He'd begged her forgiveness on seeing her bleeding arm. He'd had a stressful day at work. He'd been the first policeman on the scene of a horrible automobile accident. He couldn't stop thinking that the woman he'd been unable to save could have been her. She tried to understand as he bandaged her arm. She'd forgiven him that time and those times that followed.

Leaning over, her hands trembling, Naomi straightened the bedcovers, brushed her hand across her daughter's head, gently pressed her lips to her hair. Straightening, she wrapped her arms tightly around her waist and stared down at the most precious gift in the world to her. Her daughter. Safe. It had only been a dream.

Crossing the small bedroom, Naomi took a seat in the rocking chair. Last night she'd sat in the same chair, holding Kayla while reading her a bedtime story. Tucking her bare feet under her, Naomi pulled the long cotton gown over her legs and watched Kayla sleep. Naomi knew she'd put her daughter through so much misery because she had chosen the wrong man to love. She had been so blind and needy that she'd been easy prey for a cruel, deceptive man like Gordon Reese.

Her older parents were social butterflies and never understood their shy only child, who preferred to read rather than join school clubs or play sports. She'd always been a disappointment to them and something of an oddity.

She met Gordon when he came to her church to speak about safety. She'd been naive and flattered by the attention of such a handsome man. Her few friends and co-workers were actually jealous that she'd caught the eye of such an athletic, articulate man. She couldn't believe he wanted her when he could have had almost any woman. She'd never dated much and had turned him down twice when he asked her out. His persistence, his interest in her and how her day had gone as a fifth-grade math teacher, his easygoing manner, had won her over. He'd even agreed to wait to be intimate until after they were married.

Naomi closed her eyes and briefly placed her forehead on her updrawn knees. Their wedding night had been a disappointment for both of them. She thought he'd be just as patient and loving as he'd always been. Instead he was demanding and demoralizing. *Frigid* was one of the nicer names he'd called her.

Ashamed, with no close friends or family to talk to, she'd thought it was somehow her fault that she couldn't make him happy, just as she carried the burden that she couldn't make her parents love her.

To compound her untenable situation, her parents liked her ex-husband. When she tried to talk to her mother about his possessive outbursts, his unfounded jealousy, her mother immediately blamed Naomi. Her father agreed. She should try harder to make him happy. She never brought it up again, not even when he began hitting her. With nowhere to turn, she'd remained in the abusive marriage.

Things became worse when she became pregnant with Kayla. Naomi's eyes closed as she recalled becoming physically ill when he told her to get rid of the baby. He'd later said it was because he was afraid for her, but she hadn't believed him. After Kayla was born, he'd been jealous of the attention she gave their daughter, and even more jealous about Naomi as well.

When Kayla was two, fear for her daughter's

safety had finally given Naomi the courage to leave and file for divorce. The situation came to a head the night Kayla was crying and fretful because she had an ear infection. He'd complained that "the brat" was keeping him awake. Naomi should be in bed taking care of his needs instead of watching over a sniveling baby. He wished she'd never been born.

His cruel, unfeeling words still had the power to hurt. Tears glittered in Naomi's eyes, but none fell. Kayla deserved the love of both parents. Naomi's bad choice had taken so much from her daughter.

He'd never loved Kayla, had never been concerned about her. Instead he always considered her an inconvenience and ignored her unless Naomi was taking care of Kayla instead of doing something for him. She'd never been able to relax when he was around them. Naomi had hoped and prayed he'd change, but that night she'd accepted he was never going to love his child. She'd left him the next day and filed for divorce a few days later.

She'd gotten the divorce and full custody, but her ex had made her life hell, coming to her house at all times of the night, smashing her car windows, breaking into her apartment and stealing all her furniture. A couple of times she'd gone to the courthouse to have a restraining order issued against him, but his policemen buddies always called him and he'd show up, promising Kayla would pay if she "embarrassed" him in front of his friends.

One afternoon when Naomi had gone to pick up Kayla from day care, he was walking out the door with their daughter despite Naomi having told the staff that he was never to have contact with Kayla. She realized she had to leave San Antonio to be safe. Her parents had retired to Orlando, but even if they had been there, they wouldn't have helped. She'd been on her way to California when her car broke down in Santa Fe.

Untucking her legs and coming to her feet, Naomi neared the bed once again. They'd been homeless and sleeping in the broken-down car with nowhere to turn, no money. To this day she had no idea what would have happened to them if Catherine Stewart, now Catherine Grayson, hadn't befriended them. Even knowing she was lying about her identity, Catherine's future husband, Luke Grayson, had put her and Kayla up in a hotel, then helped her find a job as a receptionist with Luke's veterinarian friend Richard Youngblood. She smiled softly.

Richard was as much a part of the reason her life was turning around as Catherine was. He'd saved her when her ex-husband showed up at her hotel room, taking Kayla and ordering her to leave with him. They had only gone a few miles when they were stopped by a police car. Richard had notified the authorities and come for her and Kayla. His presence gave Naomi the courage to tell the truth, and obtain another restraining order against her ex.

Their life had been quiet since then. Still, the fear wouldn't stay away. She'd have weeks where she thought she was doing better, then something would trigger her unease. Perhaps this time it had been the story on the news of a woman in Santa Fe who hadn't been able to get away. She'd been severely beaten by her husband in front of her children. She remained in a coma: her children in foster care, their lives irrevocably damaged.

Naomi often wondered if she'd ever be truly free to live without fear, to live a normal life. Her ex was a cruel, vindictive man. He wouldn't want her to be happy. She worked hard to hide her nightmares that Gordon would return and kidnap Kayla, worked hard not to let her fear keep Kayla from being a happy, outgoing child.

Not for anything would Naomi have her daughter live in fear. Naomi just had to keep trying until it wasn't forced. Her daughter would have the happy childhood and life her mother never had.

Adjusting the covers again, Naomi promised herself that she wasn't going to let her fears ruin things for them. Straightening, Naomi left her daughter's room, praying with each step that this was one promise she could keep.

Chapter 1

Naomi couldn't sleep. She jumped at every sound, even ice falling from the automatic ice maker. Finally, around 7:00 AM Saturday, she couldn't stay in bed any longer. Throwing back the covers, she went to take a bath and get dressed.

In well-worn jeans and a T-shirt, she sat at the kitchen table and worked on lesson plans for the coming week for her students. She loved teaching and she loved her students. They eagerly returned the affection with hugs and smiles. They soaked up learning like little sponges.

She'd taught fifth grade in San Antonio, but at that age students could be defiant. After the past years dealing with her ex-husband, Gordon, she wanted as much peace as possible. She'd jumped at the chance to teach a lower grade level. Now, since Kayla was a kindergarten student, they were on the same hall and Naomi could watch over her. As expected, Kayla made friends easily and loved school.

As Richard had said when they first met, Kayla was a loving and affectionate child.

Naomi's fingers paused in making a notation. She often wondered if Richard ever realized the strong impression he'd made on Kayla. Almost from the moment they'd met, they'd become fast friends. Considering how her own father had yelled at her, it had surprised and pleased Naomi.

It was always Dr. Richard this and Dr. Richard that. Kayla had already decided to be a veterinarian and follow in Richard's footsteps. She liked Luke and his brothers, but her face didn't light up when she saw them the way it did when she saw Richard.

The phone rang on the kitchen counter. She tensed for a moment on seeing UNKNOWN on the caller ID, then chastised herself. Richard and Catherine both had unlisted home and cell phone numbers. "Hello."

"Good morning, Naomi. Is Kayla ready for her big day?"

Hearing Richard's voice, Naomi smiled and admitted her daughter wasn't the only Reese female who enjoyed being around Richard. "She's still asleep, which isn't surprising. She could hardly fall asleep last night because she was so excited about today."

"I wanted to be there, but I'm headed to a ranch thirty miles away. I don't think I'll be back in time."

Concern knitted her brows. Richard knew how much the day meant to Kayla. He'd be there if he could. "What happened?"

"A rancher's horse tangled with a mountain

lion" came the succinct answer. "He's usually a lev-elheaded guy, but he sounded frantic. I'm hoping it's not as bad as he believes. You know how own-ers can be."

"I remember." The people who brought their be-loved pets to the clinic were often overly concerned, but that was better than not caring at all. Richard understood that. His compassion and understand-ing were just two of the reasons he was such a great vet and in such high demand. He wouldn't leave the ranch until he knew the animal was all right.

"I'll be back as soon as I can, but I'm not sure how long this will take" Richard said. "Please ex-plain to Kayla."

"You know I will."

"Tell her to have fun. Bye."

"Bye." Hanging up, Naomi took her seat, leaned back in the cushioned, iron-backed chair and stared out the small window.

The morning haze had cleared and the sun was shining. Weather in Santa Fe could be unpredictable, but that was a small price for the beautiful scenery and the friends she and Kayla had found there. Kayla would be disappointed that Richard wouldn't be there. He'd come to mean a great deal to both of them.

She glanced at the clock. It was almost nine. She needed to wake Kayla, help her with her bath, then cook breakfast. They had a busy day ahead of them.

Standing, she heard muffled footsteps on the carpeted floor and smiled as Kayla hurried into the kitchen, her arm around Teddy's fat waist. Bending, Naomi kissed her daughter on the head, brushed her hand over Teddy's. The teddy bear had been her companion since Catherine gave her the stuffed toy shortly after they met. Catherine was also the reason her daughter liked butterflies. "Good morning."

"Good morning, Mama. The big hand is almost on the nine. Me and Teddy need to get our bath and get dressed so we won't be late."

"You won't be late," Naomi said, but she took Kayla's free hand and started toward her daughter's bedroom. Two months ago they'd moved from the second floor to the first floor because it was bigger, and Kayla had her own bathroom—which she loved. Naomi tried not to think that the back door also gave her ex another entry into their apartment.

"You can just run the water, Mama. I can do it by myself," Kayla said. "Teddy can watch me."

Kneeling on the rug with the butterfly appliqué next to the tub, Naomi turned on the water. "I know he can, but I'm sure he won't mind if I stay."

Kayla sighed. "I guess, but I can dress us by myself."

Testing the water, Naomi turned off the faucet and stared at her daughter. She was growing up and becoming independent much too fast. The need to cling was difficult to control. "After you take your bath, we'll see."

Sighing again, Kayla placed Teddy on the top of the commode, then reached for the hem of her nightgown. Naomi resisted helping when the neck opening hung briefly on Kayla's chin. Seconds later, Kayla's face popped though and she was smiling. "See, I can do it."

"I see. You did good." Naomi brushed her hand across Kayla's hair again. It was as thick as hers. "Richard called. He had to go out of town to take care of a sick animal. He'll try to make it, but he's not sure."

Kayla's head lowered briefly. "He told me that animals depend on him to help them get better. They don't want to be sick any more than people do. When I grow up, I'm going to be a vet and help animals get well, too."

No tears, no pouting, just simple understanding. Whatever she had done wrong by choosing the wrong man, having Kayla in her life had made up for it. "And you'll be very good at it, just as Richard is. Now, let's get you into the tub."

Naomi helped Kayla get settled, then picked up Teddy and took a seat on the commode top. Her baby was growing up. More important, she was growing up happy. "Teddy and I will be right here if you need us."

Thirty minutes later, Naomi was in the kitchen starting breakfast. After her bath, Kayla had wanted to pick out clothes for herself and Teddy. After her last birthday that wasn't a problem.

Of course Kayla had invited Richard and Catherine. He'd given Kayla the rocking chair in her bedroom so Naomi could read to her at night. From Catherine there were several outfits for Kayla with matching tops for Teddy, and a complete set of her published books for children. Luke had given Kayla the practical gift of a savings bond.

There were also gifts from other members of the Grayson family that Kayla had met through Catherine. There was no way Naomi could have refused any of the gifts. They loved Kayla. She'd be forever thankful that her car had chosen Santa Fe to break down in.

A knock on the back door startled her. Despite her earlier chastisement, fear had her gripping the spoon in her hand as she whirled from the counter, only to relax seconds later. Placing the spoon back in the pancake mix, she went to the door. Gordon's knock wouldn't be that light, and after the last time, he'd probably bang or burst in. Still, she looked through the peephole Richard had installed for her.

Seeing Fallon Marshall, Naomi smiled. Naomi had few female friends. They'd want to talk about their family, ask you about yours. She hated it when she had to lie, and she was tired of evading. Just saying she was divorced didn't always satisfy some women's curiosity. Fallon, a travel writer, had moved in the apartment next door a month ago. Like Catherine, Fallon didn't push or ask questions.

Fallon had knocked on Naomi's door the day she moved in to introduce herself. Naomi, usually cautious even with women, had liked the warm and friendly Fallon immediately. They'd begun their friendship over coffee and the freshly baked chocolate chip cookies Fallon had brought with her.

Opening the door, Naomi smiled and stepped aside. "Good morning, Fallon."

"Good morning," Fallon cheerfully greeted as she stepped inside. She wore a shirt with SANTA FE in colorful letters on the front, slim black jeans, and flip-flops. "I was hoping you were up and still here." She ruefully lifted her mug, decorated with a string of peppers, in one hand and a plastic cup in the other. Inside was a spoon. "Coffee, please."

"Help yourself." Naomi waved Fallon to the coffee carafe. One cup was all she needed. Like Fallon, she wanted cream and sugar in her coffee. Although she'd tried to dissuade Fallon from bringing her own, she continued to do so.

"Thanks. I was on a deadline and forgot to go to the store yesterday." Pouring the coffee, then adding the cream and sugar mixture from the plastic cup, Fallon took a sip, closed her eyes, and savored. "Good coffee. I finished the piece this morning and sent it off, thank goodness."

Knowing Fallon would need a couple of sips to be fully alert, Naomi continued stirring the pancake mix. The quietness in the kitchen didn't make Naomi nervous. Another thing she liked about Fallon—as with Richard and Catherine, she didn't need to fill the silence with conversation.

Fallon was easy to talk to and fun to be around. She and Kayla had hit it off immediately. Fallon had probably never met a stranger. It wasn't just the incredible, long-legged beauty and body to go with it that attracted people; she genuinely cared about people, and it showed. She probably knew everybody in their unit, whereas Naomi only knew the elderly couple on the other side of her.

"Can you stay for breakfast?" Naomi asked, already reaching for the refrigerator door.

"You don't have to ask twice. Thanks." Fallon topped off her coffee cup, added more cream-and-sugar mixture.

"We like having you." Removing the packages of pan turkey sausages and bacon from the refrigerator, Naomi added some to the skillet, then reached for the box of pancake mix.

"I'll say it again, you're my lifesaver." Fallon picked up the spatula from a spoon rest to tend the sausages. "My last neighbor was a man who wanted to hit on me on one side, and a jealous girlfriend living with her boyfriend who refused to pop the question on the other." She sipped her coffee. "The apartment gods were definitely smiling on me when I moved in next to you."

"It works both ways," Naomi said, adding more mix to her bowl. "I know they didn't mind keeping Kayla, but Mrs. Grayson and Catherine are busy. You take good care of Kayla for me when I have to work late at school. I didn't like having her stay at school with me. Now she doesn't have to, and I can volunteer at the Women's League."

"She's a sweetie and an asset to my business. That's why I pay her," Fallon responded with a grin, then tested the red potatoes frying in another skillet.

"The fun she has and the places you take her are enough. You don't have to pay her," Naomi protested, aware that it wouldn't do any good. Just like it didn't do any good to protest the coffee or food Fallon brought over. She said that way it didn't make her feel like a moocher when she showed up unexpectedly wanting coffee or a hot meal. Fallon always paid for Kayla's admission when required, purchased her food, plus gave her five dollars for each research outing.

Fallon shook her head, her long naturally curly hair brushing against her high cheekbones and slim shoulders. "My research assistant deserves every dollar. Because of Kayla, I'm able to write about local attractions for children. My travel blog got tons of hits and I sold more articles. One of these days in the far-distant future, I might have a little girl myself . . . after I snag a rich husband, of course," she said with a laugh.

Removing the sausages to drain on a paper towel, she didn't see the frown on Naomi's face as she poured pancake mix onto the hot griddle. Naomi knew she was kidding. Fallon wasn't the money-hungry type. Naomi just prayed that when she did find a man, he would love her and not use her as Naomi had been used.

"For now, I'm having too much fun traveling the world and getting paid for living my dream." Fallon stirred the potatoes again. "Santa Fe, the Sangre de Cristo Mountains, the nearby Native American pueblos, are a virtual gold mine for me. However, I plan to be in Aspen for the first snow, then in New York for Christmas Eve, before flying to Austin to be with my family for Christmas."

Naomi's frown cleared as she placed the pancakes on the platter. Fallon was too smart to let a smooth-talking man use her. Lots of men had tried to pick her up while they were out, and she always effortlessly brushed them off in a way that didn't offend them.

"We're ready," Kayla exclaimed as she rushed into the kitchen with Teddy under her arm.

"Good morning, Kayla. Teddy. He looks even more handsome this morning," Fallon greeted, bending down to eye level with Teddy to touch his red bow tie, then the red ribbons securing Kayla's two fat ponytails. "You both do."

"Hi, Fallon," Kayla replied with a big grin. "Me and Teddy have to look extra special because we're going to be on stage with Mrs. Catherine when she reads the book I'm in."

Naomi walked over to her daughter. She did look cute in the red-and-white sundress and red leather sandals. Teddy had on a red-and-white sweater. "She dressed herself and Teddy all alone."

"I'm a big girl just like the one in the story Mrs. Catherine is going to read," Kayla announced proudly. "She didn't have Teddy when she got lost, but she was brave when the gray wolf came to help her."

"You're brave as well," Fallon told her. "Who held my hand when the train at the fair went through the dark tunnel?"

Kayla's smile broadened. "Me and Teddy."

Naomi gazed lovingly down at her daughter, thankful that she was outgoing and ready to try anything. The book signing had been all Kayla had talked about for weeks. Catherine was a past UCLA professor of psychology, renowned child advocate, and *New York Times* best-selling children's author. She lectured all over the country on child psychology. "Let's eat breakfast."

Kayla took her seat at the small table for four and placed Teddy in the booster seat that Brandon Grayson, Catherine's brother-in-law, had given her along with a reloadable gift card to his restaurant, the Red Cactus. Kayla loved their hamburgers.

Naomi blessed the food then tucked a large napkin beneath Kayla's chin while Fallon placed food on her daughter's plate. "My nephew loves Catherine Stewart-Grayson books as well. He'll be happy to hear I'm a personal friend of one of the book's characters."

Kayla grinned. "My teacher and some of my friends from school are coming today."

"You and Teddy certainly look impressive." Fallon picked up her fork. "You deserve to be chauffeured, and I volunteer."

"That isn't necessary," Naomi said. "You must have things to do on a Saturday."

"Nope." Fallon forked in pancakes. "That's why I worked so hard to finish. I plan to go to the signing and get my nephew a copy of *The Guardian*."

"You can ride with us," Naomi offered, watching to ensure Kayla didn't pour too much syrup on her pancakes.

"Not on your life," Fallon said, taking a bite of her sausage. "You cook. I drive. House Rule."

Kayla offered a bite of sausage to Teddy, then took a bite herself. "Dr. Richard was coming, but he had to take care of a sick animal."

Fallon grinned. "Emmm. The good vet with the Y factor."

Naomi barely kept from squirming. The Y was for "yummy." "You know he'd be here if he could."

"I know. I just wish he was here with us."

Naomi wished he was there, too. His presence seemed to make everything easier. She wasn't as tense when he was with them. Not daring to look at Fallon, Naomi reached for her fork.

Richard loved being a veterinarian. It was the only thing he'd ever wanted to do with his life. Since he was single and not in a serious relationship, there were few times in his life when his profession had interfered with his personal life.

Today was one of those rare times.

He turned into the gate of the Bar S ranch and continued down the dusty road. He'd wanted to be there today for Kayla, but also for Naomi. There would be a lot of people at Catherine's signing.

The citizens of Santa Fe had embraced her not only because she had married into the beloved Grayson family and she was famous in her own right, but because they could tell she genuinely cared about children. More than once he'd seen a concerned mother approach her while she was eating to ask a question or get an autograph. She always responded with a smile.

One day he hoped Naomi would be that free and easy with a smile. She was doing better, but she still didn't like crowds. She had good reason for wanting to know who was near her. He hoped his presence helped. Until the unexpected phone call this morning, he'd thought he'd be there for her.

Seeing the ranch house, he continued around back to the barn. Several ranch hands were there. Their facial expressions warned Richard that Ted, the owner of the Bar S, might have reason to be worried. One came to the door of the truck before he stopped completely.

"The boss is inside with Foxtrot, Dr. Young-blood. He raised him from a colt. I'll show you."

"Thanks." Grabbing his bag, Richard followed the short, wiry man into the barn. Sunlight streamed through the hayloft opening, but it was still dim inside. A short distance farther on, he saw Ted and his signature black Stetson.

Opening the stall door, the ranch hand stepped aside. Richard's gaze went to the horse's bloody flank first, then to the worried eyes of the owner.

" 'Morning, Ted."

" 'Morning, Doc," the older man greeted, his voice thicker than usual. "Thanks for coming."

"Thanks for the extra light and the blanket." Placing his bag on the blanket, Richard snapped on a pair of gloves. "I'll try to be gentle, but this is going to hurt a bit."

Ted nodded. "Doc's gonna help, Foxtrot, so don't act up."

Richard probed the deep lacerations on the animal's flank, stopping occasionally as the horse shied away. Ted had been right. The lacerations would have to be sutured. There was no way he'd make it back to Santa Fe in time.

"Damn horse, she's too old to be so stupid," Ted growled, but his voice was as shaky as the hand that repeatedly brushed down the trembling horse's blazed face. "You should have picked up the cat's scent and run like the other horses."

Richard snapped off the gloves, then clasped the older man on the shoulder. "I'll be as quick and as gentle as I can." He placed the soiled gloves into a bag and reached into his open medical bag. "I'm glad you found her or those lacerations would have become infected. She's not going to like what we have to do, but she'll be all right."

The older man swallowed visibly. "You hear that, you old nag? Doc Youngblood is going to fix you up, and next time you better run."

Richard sanitized his hands, prepared a hypodermic needle, then put on a fresh pair of gloves. Some wounds were easier to treat and heal than others. He couldn't help but think of Naomi. He just prayed that one day she could put the past behind her and look at him as more than just a friend. He hoped it was soon. He wasn't sure how much longer he could hide his feelings for her.

He pushed to his feet. "Let's get this done."

Chapter 2

Later that afternoon, Naomi, Fallon and Kayla entered the famous La Fonda hotel in downtown Santa Fe. People with children in tow hurried past them. Kayla's hand firmly in Naomi's, they followed the signs and helpful people positioned in the hallways leading to the Conquistador Ballroom.

"This is one of my favorite hotels," Fallon said, looking at the overhanging balconies, wooden beams, and specialty shops. "I think I could happily live here. They picked a great locale for the signing."

"It is pretty," Naomi agreed, marveling that Catherine could return to the hotel where an embarrassing incident could have ended her career, if not for Luke's quick thinking. At the time, they'd just been dating.

"Looks like a line out the door," Fallon murmured. "Hope we can find a seat. No wonder they held it in a conference room."

"Mama, we can get in, can't we?" Kayla asked, worry on her face.

Naomi squeezed her hand in reassurance. "Catherine said she wanted you on stage. You know you can depend on her."

Kayla's arm tightened around the waist of Teddy. "She gave me Teddy."

"She certainly did," Naomi said, thinking she'd also given them hope and a chance to start over.

"Now, that is what I call a man," Fallon whispered in an aside.

Since her friend seldom noticed men, Naomi lifted her head to see who she was talking about and looked straight into the steady black gaze of Luke Grayson. She didn't drop her head as she had when they first met. He still made her a bit uneasy because of his height—well over six feet—and his brawny build, but she'd learned to trust him as she did few men.

"That's Luke Grayson, Catherine's husband," Naomi whispered.

"Then I'd say she's a *very* lucky woman," Fallon replied quietly. "Any brothers?"

"Three and all married," Naomi told her.

"I just bet they keep a smile on their wives' faces." Fallon laughed wickedly.

Naomi didn't know what to say. She knew Fallon was talking about sex. Naomi didn't like sex, dreaded the times her husband had reached for her. She was saved from commenting when Luke started toward them.

"Hi, Mr. Luke," Kayla greeted when he was at least two feet away. "Mrs. Catherine didn't forget about me, did she?"

"Ladies." Tipping his Stetson, Luke squatted in

front of Kayla. "How could she forget about you, the prettiest girl in the state and the bravest?"

Kayla grinned. "Me and Teddy wanted to look extra nice."

"I'd say you pulled it off." He straightened, tipped his Stetson again. "Hello, Naomi, miss."

"Hi, Luke," Naomi greeted, still holding Kayla's hand. "This is Fallon Marshall, my next-door neighbor. Fallon, Luke Grayson."

Smiling, Fallon extended her hand. "Hello, Mr. Grayson. Looks like your wife's signing is going to be a huge success."

"Looks like." The handshake was brief and firm. "Nice to meet you, Ms. Marshall."

Fallon tilted her head to one side. "How do you know it's not Mrs.?"

Luke smiled easily. "No wedding ring." He turned to Naomi. "I'm to take you to your seats."

Naomi threw an anxious look at Fallon. "We're together."

"I expected as much. Ms. Marshall can have my seat. It will save someone trying to look over or around me."

"With those shoulders and your height, you're right about that," Fallon murmured, then rolled her eyes. "Sorry. Sometimes my mouth gets ahead of my brain."

"That's all right. I know someone else just like you." He extended his hand toward the way he had come. "There's another door we can go in."

Inside the room, Luke beckoned a young usher. "These are Mrs. Grayson's special guests, Kayla and Teddy. Could you please take them to the stage?"

"My pleasure." The young woman reached for Kayla's hand.

" 'Bye, Mama." Kayla started forward, then stopped because her mother still held on. "Mama, you have my hand."

Naomi glanced around the crowded room. Her hand flexed, but she didn't release Kayla.

"I'll be close by and your seat is directly in front of the stage," Luke said softly.

Pushing the fear of the nightmare aside, Naomi kissed Kayla on top of her head and released her hand. Her daughter happily left without a backward glance.

"This way," Luke said, following the usher. "Afterward, we're all going to the Mesa at the Casa de Serenidad for an early dinner. You're both invited, of course. Kayla is a big part of today. We've outgrown the family booth at Brandon's restaurant since we're all married."

Fallon stopped and palmed her forehead. "Grayson. You must be Brandon Grayson's brother."

"Guilty."

Fallon laughed. "I'm a travel writer. I spotlighted his restaurant, the Red Cactus, in one of the first articles I wrote about Santa Fe. I didn't get to meet him the day I was there. The food was fantastic. He deserves the high reputation he's garnered."

"If you do meet him, don't tell him," a woman said with laughter in her voice. "His head is big enough already."

Naomi had been paying more attention to the usher guiding Kayla in the crowded room than to her surroundings. She recognized Luke's sister's Sierra's voice even before Naomi turned. With her were two men. Sierra was as beautiful and as well dressed as usual in one of the designer suits she favored, this one mint green and black. Both men with her were as broad-shouldered and tall as Luke. One wore a smile, the other a dangerous mystique.

"My sister, Sierra, her husband, Blade Navarone, and their friend, Rio Sanchez," Luke introduced. "Fallon Marshall, Naomi's friend and neighbor. She's a travel writer and she's joining us for dinner."

Greetings were barely exchanged before Fallon gasped, her hands reaching for the camera dangling around her neck. Her hand had barely closed over it before a larger hand covered hers. Her gaze snapped up to the man Luke had introduced as Rio. His gaze was flat, unblinking.

"No pictures, if you don't mind," Luke said. "This is a family outing."

"Of course," Fallon said, her smile returning as Rio moved back behind Blade in one smooth, graceful motion. "It was instinctive. I'm sorry."

"No harm done," Blade said easily.

Naomi had to admire Fallon. If Rio had approached her that way, she would still be shaking or running. Luke might not have smiled much, but at least there were emotions swirling in his intense black eyes. Rio showed no emotions, just emanated power and danger.

"Mr. Navarone, your properties are fantastic," Fallon continued. "I did an article on one in Playa del Carmen several weeks ago. I hated to leave."

"Thank you." Blade's grin was all male when he looked at Sierra. "So did we."

"Luke and Naomi mentioned all of the Graysons are married," Fallon said. "Seems like you have an interesting family."

"You can say that again," Sierra said, laughing. "You'll meet Brandon and his wife. Her family owns Casa de Serenidad, a five-star hotel. We're dining in their casual restaurant on the patio. Our brother Morgan will be joining us with his wife, the famed sculptress Phoenix Bannister. Pierce, the youngest brother, is married to Sabra Raineau, Tony-winning Broadway star. She also won an Oscar. Unfortunately for poor Pierce, he's in New York with Sabra, meeting with her agent and the director of the next movie she's starring in."

"Why unfortunate? If you don't mind my asking," Fallon said.

"Because my youngest brother will never get used to having his wife do romantic scenes in the theater or movies," Sierra explained. "He's forbidden to be on the set or backstage during those times."

"I can't blame him," Luke muttered, then looked at Catherine on the raised stage. "I'm glad she's an author and in academia."

"But you'd let her live her dream," Sierra said with confidence.

Luke smiled. "Yeah, I'm just thankful I don't have to go through what Pierce does."

"Same here." Blade turned his warm gaze on Sierra. "You might have to find another career."

Sierra lifted a brow. "I bet I could talk you into it."

Blade pulled her closer. "I'd enjoy you trying."

Sierra leaned securely into his arms. "I picked good."

Fallon frowned. "What?"

Luke just shook his dark head. "Inside family joke."

"We better find our seats," Rio said. His voice was quiet, yet somehow it demanded attention.

Naomi glanced at Rio. He was handsome enough to tempt any woman breathing. She had yet to see him pay the smallest attention to a woman or even smile. He had unflinching, all-seeing piercing black eyes. At least she sometimes forgot to be afraid and relaxed. He never seemed to. As the bodyguard of a billionaire, she guessed he had to be always on alert, but she couldn't help thinking there was something else that made him so vigilant.

"See you at the restaurant," Sierra said, her arm around Blade's waist, his around hers. They moved away with Rio close behind.

Naomi watched them leave, then looked at Luke, who was staring toward the stage. Catherine smiled and waved. He waved back. Love and devotion, you could almost feel it. The Graysons weren't so much interesting as they were blessed, Naomi thought. The strong family ties were obvious. That bond extended to their in-laws.

Naomi had been around them when they were all together, so she knew of what she spoke. How wonderful it would be to have an extended family that close who loved one another. She certainly hadn't had one, and sadly, neither would Kayla.

Her mother-in-law thought less of her than her

ex-husband. She was one of the reasons Gordon would never leave them alone. She openly goaded him about not being man enough to "control" his wife who had "shamed" him and, thus, the family. She hated Naomi. She wouldn't walk across the road to help Kayla. She was a mean, bitter woman and, because of her, Naomi knew that one day Gordon would walk back into her life and try to destroy her. His mother's anger and his wounded pride demanded it.

"Are you all right?" Fallon asked.

Surprised, Naomi glanced around. People usually tended to ignore her in a crowd, and that was exactly how she preferred it. She'd forgotten how observant Fallon was. She cared about people, had a close family. It was obvious from the way she talked about her family in Austin.

"Naomi?" Luke questioned, his full attention on her.

"I'm fine," Naomi answered, careful not to look at Fallon or Luke, an ex-FBI agent and now a private investigator. He might have been looking at his wife, but he missed little. "Shouldn't we take our seats as well?"

"This way."

Naomi followed Luke, thankful neither pushed for an answer. One day she really would be fine, she promised herself.

She just wished she knew when that day would come.

Richard called Luke on his cell phone as soon as he reached his truck. He had asked him to look after

Naomi even though he knew it wasn't necessary. Naomi was a friend of Catherine's and thus had Luke's protection.

Luke answered on the first ring. "Hello."

"How is she?" Richard asked, backing up his truck and heading for the front gate.

"Fine. Her neighbor Fallon is with her. Kayla, as expected, was a hit."

Richard was only marginally relieved. "Thank you."

"Not necessary," came Luke's easy reply. "Even if I didn't owe her, she deserves better than the hand dealt her."

Richard couldn't agree more. He pulled onto the two-lane highway and increased his speed. Neither Luke nor Naomi would discuss why he owed her. Asking again wasn't going to get a different response. "Is the book signing almost over?"

"Getting there," Luke said. "When Cath is finished, we're all going over to the Mesa for an early dinner. Naomi and Fallon are coming as well. I already told Faith you'd be joining us."

Richard chuckled. He might be embarrassed if it was any other man, but Luke knew what it meant to care for a woman. "Thanks. Is there room for one more? Lance is back in town."

"For good?"

Richard's hand flexed on the steering wheel. "We all hope so, but Lance can be unpredictable at best. He likes challenges, and unless he finds it in the auction house he just acquired, he'll eventually move on to the next challenge."

"There's always a reason for a man being so

restless. Something has ahold of him that he can't shake. Keeping moving is the only way to deal with it. Whatever Lance's reason, I hope he finds it this time," Luke said.

Luke was right, but Richard would keep Lance's secret. "I hope so, too. It will be nice having him back after all these years."

"Bring Lance with you. Faith won't mind the extra guest at the restaurant, and Mama always liked Lance," Luke said. "Come when you can."

"Will do. Thanks and bye."

"Bye."

Richard disconnected the call and placed the cell phone in the holder on his dashboard. Luke didn't know how close he was to the truth about Lance—or maybe he did. Luke was good at reading people and their actions. His uncanny perception was the reason Richard had asked him to look out for Naomi. Lance needed someone to look out for him as well, although he'd never admit it and would become angry if you even suggested that he share the heavy burden he carried.

Richard blew out a breath. Life; you never knew what to expect from one day to the next. You just had to be ready.

Topping the mountain, he saw Santa Fe in the distance. He'd lived there all his life except when he went to college, studying to be a vet. He never had a desire to live anyplace else. Unlike many, he didn't mind the influx of new people. Santa Fe had always been a haven for different cultures.

A mile out of town, he turned into a paved entrance and continued down the winding road. Just as he rounded a bend, a hacienda came into view. It was magnificent, with a fountain in front and a red slate roof. White stucco walls gleamed in the afternoon sun. Parking in front, Richard went to the recessed red door and rang the doorbell.

Almost immediately it was opened. A middle-aged woman in a black maid's uniform smiled up at him. "Good afternoon. May I help you, sir?"

"Good afternoon," Richard greeted, removing his hat. "I'm Richard Youngblood. Is Lance Saxton at home?"

"Mr. Saxton is not receiving guests."

Richard wanted to hoot at the *not receiving guests*. Lance had certainly come up from running barefoot through the woods when they were kids. "I'm his cousin. His only male cousin. I'm sure if you told him I was here, he'd see me."

She didn't budge. "I'm sorry, sir. Mr. Saxton was very specific—"

"Lance, get out here," Richard yelled, the sound bouncing off the walls of the barrel ceiling in the tiled entryway.

The woman's eyes rounded. "Sir!"

Richard grinned to put her at ease. "Uncouth, I know, but I couldn't think of any other way."

"Stop scaring my staff. That will be all, Carmen."

Richard looked up to see Lance coming toward him. Lean and trim, he stood six foot four and could be intimidating. He was used to giving orders and having them carried out.

They'd both come from humble beginnings, but it was Lance who had shot to the top and paid the price. His first cousin had been through so much within the past three years, and it wasn't over yet.

Pushing the unhappy thoughts away, Richard stepped forward, his hand extended. Yet when he was a couple of feet away, he saw the shadows in Lance's eyes and hugged him instead. "You look good."

Lance smiled. Dimples that had always made girls, then women, sigh, winked. "So do you. How's Aunt Stella and Uncle Leo?"

"Enjoying seeing the country in their motor coach." Richard grinned. "We keep in touch by text, Twitter, and Facebook. Who would have thought my parents would take to all things Internet so quickly?"

"And I can't even get Mama to accept a cell phone," he said.

Richard heard the disappointment, the mild anger in Lance's voice. His mother had remarried when he was ten. He and his stepfather never got along, and his mother always took the side of her husband. Too many times women he cared about had given him the shaft. From the sudden narrowing of his eyes, it appeared as if Lance was thinking the same thing.

Richard grabbed his cousin's arm. He couldn't do anything about the past, but he could see that Lance didn't bury himself in work while he was here. "Come on. Some of your old friends are having an early dinner, and we're invited."

Lance was already shaking his head. "I have a lot of work to do. Our first acquisition is scheduled in six weeks."

"And you'll be ready." Determined, Richard tugged harder. "Come on. You'll get to meet Luke, Morgan, and Brandon, and their wives. Pierce is out of town with his wife. Sierra will be there. You once thought she was hot, but I would advise you not to look too hard or you'll find her husband in your face."

Lance frowned. "I couldn't believe she married Blade Navarone. He seemed too intense."

"Believe it," Richard said. "Neither of them goes to any social engagements without the other. You're getting a chance few people have in Santa Fe, and I can promise the food will be delicious—Henri, Casa de Serenidad's executive chef, is cooking for us."

Lance eyed him. "And why are you going? You spend your free time at your ranch since you seldom have any."

"Follow me and find out."

"A woman." Lance grinned and slapped Richard on the back. "You never mentioned her."

"That's because there's nothing to mention." Richard went to the door. "Coming?"

"You betcha. This I have to see."

Chapter 3

Richard finally got a break. The attendant at valet parking for the Casa de Serenidad had barely driven away with his truck when he saw Fallon's rental pulling up. What made his heart glad was the smile and wave Naomi sent him. He'd try not to be greedy for more, but he wouldn't bet on it.

While the two valets reached for the two front doors, he opened the back door for Kayla. Her eyes rounded with happiness.

"Dr. Richard! You're here!"

Laughing, he swung the little girl up in his arms. "Hi, pumpkin. Sorry I missed everything, but I heard you and Teddy were great."

With one arm locked around Teddy's waist, her grin widened. "My friends in my class wanted me to sign their book. Mrs. Catherine said it was all right."

"I know a famous person." He smiled, then turned as Naomi emerged from the front passenger side of the car. After all this time, her shy smile still got to him. Just as Catherine had first described her to him, she looked like a china doll with huge black eyes. She was beautiful in all the ways that counted.

"Hello, Richard."

"Hi, Naomi. Fallon," Richard greeted as she came around the car.

"Hi, Dr. Youngblood." Fallon grinned, her sunglasses resting on top of her curly black hair. "Did you know you're holding Santa Fe's latest celebrity?"

"I heard." Richard placed Kayla on her feet. "I get to say I knew her when."

"I think you forgot about me, cuz."

Richard ignored the teasing that twinkled in Fallon's eyes and faced his cousin. "Sorry. This beautiful young lady is Kayla Reese, her mother, Naomi, and their friend and next-door neighbor, Fallon Marshall. My cousin, Lance Saxton."

"Pleased to meet you," Lance greeted, his gaze lingering on Fallon.

As long as Lance wasn't turning his considerable charm on Naomi, Richard didn't mind. Maybe it was time for Lance to think about a woman and not just business. Richard was just glad that woman wasn't Naomi. After being patient with her so long, he wasn't ready for his good-looking cousin to swoop in and take her from him.

"Let's go in." Richard reached for Naomi's arm and Kayla's hand. He didn't have to look around to know Lance would probably take Fallon's arm. Lance enjoyed beautiful things. It was past time he began to enjoy beautiful women again. In a strapless floral sundress that complemented her caramel-colored skin, showing off her long legs and laughing black eyes, Fallon might be just what Lance needed to pull him out of his funk.

Lance had noted his cousin's possessiveness with Naomi. She seemed shy and sweet and exactly Richard's type. Lance had always gone for cool beauty and sophistication—and look where that had gotten him. With ease of practice, he pushed the unhappy memory away. "Shall we?" Lance asked, extending his arm.

"Why not?" Smiling, Fallon hooked her arm through his.

"Are you a native, Fallon?" Lance asked as they went through the archway to the restaurant on the terrace.

"No," Fallon answered, wondering if she should take Lance up on the signals he was sending. He definitely had a high Y factor. "You?"

"Summers only with Richard and his parents until I went to college," Lance said as they entered the restaurant.

"Are you back for good or a visit?"

"That depends."

Intrigued by the sudden narrowing of his midnight-black eyes, Fallon was about to ask more about his reasons for returning until she heard them being greeted by those already there. She looked around at the men there and blinked. She'd never seen so many gorgeous, physically fit men in one place. The women weren't shabby, either. And best of all, they were secure enough that they genuinely welcomed her and Naomi. Fallon prepared to enjoy herself and possibly indulge in a little light-hearted flirtation with Lance. It had been months since a man had remotely interested her.

After greetings were finished, Naomi found herself seated between Kayla and Richard. Sitting beside him, their shoulders almost touching, she couldn't imagine that at one time she'd been afraid of him. Usually she was leery of strangers. And with Richard there, his cousin hadn't bothered her.

"How did things go on the call?" she whispered. She didn't want Kayla to hear in case things hadn't gone well.

"Good. I might have known you'd remember," he said, leaning closer.

For some odd reason, her heart rate increased. She felt a bit breathless when he stared at her for so long. Flustered, she turned to check on Kayla.

To Richard's immediate left sat Fallon and Lance. From the first, it was obvious he was more interested in Fallon than he was in Naomi and Kayla. For once, Fallon seemed interested as well.

On Naomi's immediate right sat Kayla, Catherine, and Luke. His mother, Ruth Grayson, and fellow Women's League member Amanda Poole were seated at the head and foot of the table, respectively. On the other side were Rio, Sierra and Blade, Morgan and Phoenix, and Brandon and Faith.

Ruth Grayson came gracefully to her feet. Today she wore a beautifully cut teal suit instead of her usual casual attire. The men started to stand, but she waved them back to their seats. It was as clear as it had always been to Naomi that Ruth Grayson was loved as well as respected by her children, in-laws, and friends.

Quietness settled around the table. "I'm pleased you could join us this afternoon to celebrate another successful fund-raiser for the Women's League, thanks to Catherine and Kayla."

"Mrs. Grayson, don't forget Teddy." Kayla held up her bear.

Momentarily embarrassed, Naomi reached to push Kayla's hand down, but applause erupted.

"Go, Kayla!" Richard shouted.

"Go, Teddy!" Catherine said.

"Go, Cath!" Luke yelled.

"And Teddy," Ruth amended, smiling warmly at her daughter-in-law and Kayla. "I can't thank you enough. We'll be able to help more women in need because of your generosity and talent." She turned to Faith. "Thanks to my other daughter-in-law for providing a lovely place for us to eat and wind down. "

"Go, Faith!" Brandon shouted; then he kissed his blushing wife on the cheek as more applause erupted.

"Now that the Women's League has surpassed its budget expectations quite nicely, I'm turning my attention to another project."

Groans were heard around the table, especially from the Grayson men. "Mama, no," Luke said. "Not again."

Naomi's gaze swung to Richard. He was looking at Ruth with affection. Most of the residents in town knew of Ruth Grayson's successful matchmaking efforts. Despite her children's resistance, she'd found the perfect person for each of them—with the exception of Sierra, who was always quick to point out that she had picked Blade herself. Mrs. Grayson had even helped a few of their friends find love. Was Richard on her list? Naomi didn't know why she felt a mild sense of panic at the thought.

"Not *that* kind of project," Sierra said with a laugh. "This one is to raise funds for the music department she's chair of at St. John's. I'm helping."

More groans from the Grayson men and mutters about the "little general" and smiles and offers to help from their wives. Sierra sipped her sparkling cider and winked at Catherine.

Blade chuckled. "I'll do my best to restrain her."

His announcement didn't seem to satisfy her brothers. Even Naomi knew Sierra wasn't afraid of the devil. She always did what she wanted.

"Phoenix, I'm delighted you were able to come," Ruth said to her other daughter-in-law as she took her seat. "I realize you were busy getting your sculpture pieces ready for your gallery showing in two weeks."

"Thank me." Morgan kissed his wife on the cheek. "I have ways."

"You certainly do," Phoenix quipped with a grin.

All the adults laughed except Naomi. They meant intimacy; intimacy meant degradation. She never wanted that in her life again.

Faith signaled the waiters to serve the family-style dishes. Naomi lifted her head to help Kayla with her napkin and food, but Catherine was already helping her settle Teddy in the high chair Faith had thoughtfully placed just behind Kayla's chair. Then she tucked her napkin in the front of her sundress.

It struck Naomi again how good and patient Catherine was with children. "You're going to make a great mother."

Catherine's smile slipped just for a second. She almost looked . . . bleak. Naomi remembered how she'd thought Richard had insulted her when he'd complimented her as a mother. Panic seized her. Catherine was her best friend, her confidante. She wouldn't hurt her for anything. "I meant it as a compliment."

Catherine reached across Kayla and gently touched Naomi's trembling shoulder. "I know. You couldn't have given me a greater compliment." She glanced tenderly down at Kayla. "Kayla is blessed to have you."

"Cath, you want chicken or beef fajitas?" Luke asked.

"Surprise me," Catherine said, turning her attention to her husband.

Naomi didn't know why, but she couldn't shake the feeling that somehow she'd wounded Catherine. She'd suffered too many times because of her ex-husband's cruel words to ever want to do that to anyone else.

Glancing around, Naomi saw Luke staring at her with the hard frown of disapproval he'd worn when they first met. Something cold settled in her stomach. Then Catherine briefly leaned into him. The harshness vanished instantly. He smiled and kissed her on the nose. When he lifted his head, the frown was gone.

Naomi breathed a sigh of relief. She'd imagined things. Catherine had everything.

"You'll upset Faith's executive chef if you don't eat," Richard told her. "Chicken fajitas with extra peppers and onions."

Naomi looked at her prepared plate, then at Richard. "You take care of me as well as you do of Kayla."

"She's eating, you're not." Richard bit into his fajita.

Hearing Catherine laugh, Naomi fully relaxed and rolled her flour tortilla. The taste was as good as she expected. "Fantastic."

"I agree," Richard murmured around his food.

"Yes, but—" Brandon began, but Faith held up her hand, palm out.

"But—"

"No," she said emphatically, staring at him.

He opened his mouth, then closed it when his wife continued to stare at him. "A chef should be able to take criticism."

There was choked laughter around the table. Brandon stared at his family. "Funny."

Naomi, like his family, knew that Brandon was sensitive about his cooking. He had a right to be. She had eaten some of the best meals she'd ever had at his restaurant.

"If Henri came to the Red Cactus and tried to tell you how to cook, you'd toss him out," Richard said, finishing off his fajitas.

"That's because my food is the best. Perfection can't be improved on. Let's ask an unbiased person." Placing his food aside, Brandon's settled his midnight-black gaze on Fallon. "Fallon, thank you again for the mention in *Travel* magazine. Now that you've had a chance to eat here and the Red Cactus, which food is better?"

"Don't answer!" several people shouted.

Fallon looked at Sierra, one of the people who had shouted. "I see what you meant earlier."

Faith shook her head. "He and Henri butt heads about once a month. It's a good thing I love them both."

Brandon turned to her with a confident grin. "You love me more."

"True, and you had better be glad or you wouldn't like the conversation we'd have when we get home," Faith said.

Brandon straightened and looked worried.

"Plead momentary insanity," Morgan, his brother the lawyer, advised.

Brandon grinned, then kissed Faith on the lips. "I won't have to because she knows how much I love her right back."

"Yes, and that's why you're going with me to thank Henri before we leave," Faith said sweetly. "Aren't you?"

"I guess, but you'll owe me." Brandon picked up her hand and kissed it.

"Sounds fair to me," she said, grinning up at him.

Naomi found herself smiling as well. She'd slowly learned that some men didn't mind their wives arguing with them. Her smile died. She'd just picked the wrong man. And what did that say about her judgment? Since she never wanted a man in her life again, that was one less worry she had.

"Welcome back to Santa Fe, Lance. Glad you could join us," Luke said, his arm curved possessively around Catherine's shoulders.

"Thank you, Luke." Lance tipped his dark head. "Thank you, Mrs. Grayson and Mrs. Poole, for allowing me to come unannounced."

Amanda waved his words aside. "We're proud to have you. I'm glad you're back, as well."

"When is your first auction?" Morgan asked.

"Six weeks. The entire estate of Herbert Yates will be sold to satisfy creditors," Lance explained. "With over eight thousand square feet of living space, the task is going to require some hard work and long hours."

"It's unfortunate it had to come to that," Mrs. Grayson said. "I wish there had been another way. He was a good man."

"Whose apparent philosophy was, you can't take it with you," Lance said slowly. "He spent lavishly. At least he wasn't married and didn't have any children."

"Would it have made a difference?" Fallon asked, hoping her voice wasn't accusatory. Her good mood had vanished the instant she heard Lance worked with an auction house.

To think she'd actually given a great deal of thought to going out with Lance. He was handsome and charming enough to interest her, and had a lazy, sensual smile that had probably led a lot of women astray. His voice had just enough growl in it to imagine it whispering naughty things in her ear before biting her earlobe. She never stayed in one place long enough to have a relationship. It helped that very few men made her want to get to know them romantically. Looked like her record was going to stand.

The unscrupulous owner of an auction house had conned her mother into signing over papers to let him liquidate their estate when her father became ill. He'd given them pennies on the dollar. They had lost their home along with irreplaceable antiques handed down through generations. When her mother complained, he'd threatened to call the police. Because of his dishonesty, they'd lost everything

Lance turned toward her. "No. I have a job to do and I do it."

So had the bastard who had cheated her family. Her hand clenched on the stem of her glass of wine. She had her answer. She was seething, but she wasn't going to let it ruin the day for Kayla or the people who had invited her. But if she didn't get out of there in a hurry, she'd dash the excellent Bordeaux in Lance's too-handsome face.

Subtly shifting away from him, trying her best to keep a smile on her face, she carefully placed the flute on the pristine white tablecloth and made herself relax. She had a quick temper, but this special event was no place to let it get the best of her.

"Naomi, are you ready to leave?"

"I—" Naomi stammered, throwing a furtive look at Richard.

Seeing the uncertainty in Naomi's eyes, Fallon

could have kicked Lance for putting her in a position to leave when it was obvious Naomi wanted to stay. And who could blame her? Unlike his scum cousin, Richard was a great guy.

"Naomi," Richard said as he turned to her. "I was hoping we could take Kayla to the new Disney movie. Or, if you'd like to stay longer, I'll take you and Kayla home when you're ready."

"Kayla, how about going to a movie?" Naomi asked her daughter, already knowing the answer.

"Yeah!" Kayla shouted. "And I get to hold the popcorn."

A shy smile on her lips, Naomi said, "Fallon, thank you for the ride. We're staying."

"I'll catch you later." Fallon pulled her matching robin's-egg-blue leather wallet out of her hobo handbag.

"Not necessary," Luke said to her, waving away Lance with his billfold as well. "My invitation. My treat. I'm glad you could come and bring our special guest."

Aware she wasn't very good at hiding her emotions, Fallon kept her gaze on Luke. "Thank you," she managed, then she spoke to the other women. "Mrs. Grayson and Mrs. Poole, thank you again. Catherine, my nephew is going to love his book you signed. I had a wonderful time. Faith, the food and atmosphere were superb. You gave me another story." She came to her feet as the women thanked her. The men stood with her. Trying to keep the smile on her face, she waved them back into their seats. "Good-bye."

"I'll walk you to the valet," Lance said quietly.

Fallon gritted a smile and turned toward the arched entryway of the restaurant's courtyard. She could feel Lance beside her. He emanated a presence, a power that she'd never felt before. He would be a man to be reckoned with. It might have been fun to test her will against his—if he weren't the scum of the earth.

She waited to speak until they were outside under the portico of the hotel. "I'm going to save us both time and aggravation. It's not happening. I loathe people in your profession. They have a smile on their face and a hatchet behind their back."

Lance's brows shot together. She'd laugh at the shocked look on his face if she weren't so annoyed. He probably hadn't been turned down since he was in third grade. "Do both of us a favor and forget we ever met."

Long-fingered hands slipped into the pockets of his sinfully tight jeans. "Was it you, a family member, or a friend who didn't handle their finances properly?"

She gasped, and clutched the strap of her handbag to keep from punching him. He'd press charges and she'd end up on the losing end. Again. "So now it's everyone's fault but the vultures that prey on them. Figures." Her gaze hardened. "Stay out of my way and I'll stay out of yours." With one finger she dropped the sunshades on top of her head over her eyes, then continued to the front of the hotel for valet service.

Lance stared after her. She was stunning and pissed. For the first time in months emotions stirred inside him he'd long thought dead. He wasn't sure what it was—passion, intrigue—but he planned to feel it again, and find out why the very beautiful Fallon wanted nothing to do with him.

Changing her mind would take hard work, but he had a feeling the rewards would be well worth the time and aggravation. And just maybe he'd stop thinking of another woman's unimaginable betrayal.

Hands still deep in his pockets, Lance started back to the restaurant to say good-bye. He'd take a cab home so Richard wouldn't try to be noble and take him home. He had work to do. Despite Fallon's poor opinion of him and his profession, he had a job to do and he had every intention of doing it well. He'd failed once. Never again.

Naomi watched Lance return, a hard frown on his face, and wondered what had happened. Fallon had stopped smiling the moment they began talking about Lance's job. Since Naomi didn't want people asking her questions, she didn't ask any of her own.

"I just came back to say thanks and good-bye." Lance placed his hand on Richard's shoulder. "Check you later. I'm taking a cab home."

Richard protested, along with the Grayson men who made offers to take him home. Lance refused each of them. "Stay here and enjoy yourself. It's good seeing everyone again. I'll see you around." Waving good-bye, he walked away.

"I hope he stays this time," Ruth said. "I've a feeling he could find what he's searching for here."

"Mama, leave the man alone," Luke said.

Ruth smiled and picked up her glass of sparkling water. "I haven't done anything."

"And please leave it that way," Morgan said.

Ruth looked over the rim of her glass at both of her sons. "Which would you choose—the life before or now?"

Luke, Morgan, and Brandon said nothing, simply looked at their wives with such boundless love and affection that Naomi glanced away—and straight into Richard's gaze. Her stomach dipped. The reaction was so unexpected she pressed back in her chair.

"You all right?" he asked, placing his hand on her arm.

He'd touched her lots of times, more lately, but this time it was somehow different. She shook her head at the crazy thought. It was just because there was so much love and happiness around them. The Graysons had what she'd always wanted and was destined never to have.

"I'm fine."

"You wished to see me, Faith?" Henri, all five feet of him, in his chef's hat and spotless chef's jacket, looked formidable and austere.

He had an air about him that made you forget his size and think of his keen intelligence and culinary skill instead. He also had an ego as big as Brandon's about his artistry as a chef. Brandon might have trained in France, but Henri was fond of saying he *was* French.

Henri stopped by Faith's chair. She sent Brandon a stern look and stood. He came to his feet as well.

"Thank you for the excellent meal," Brandon

said, then coughed and reached for his glass of sparkling water as if the words had stuck in his throat. Faith crossed her arms and narrowed her gaze at him.

Henri was unfazed. He simply lifted a thick brow in that superior way of his. "That cough is probably due to the high fat content of the food you prepare."

A low growl came from Brandon, a smothered laugh from his wife. He whipped his head around to stare at her.

"Brandon, you know Henri was just teasing you," his mother said. Then she stepped forward to profusely thank the chef for their excellent dining experience.

"You and your guests are welcome," Henri said. "We pride ourselves on the pleasure of our guests from the moment they enter Casa de Serenidad, the house of serenity."

Faith beamed proudly at her executive chef.

Brandon had recovered by then. "My wife and I are going home."

Henri had caught Faith's hand and kissed it before Brandon could pull her away. "If you must. I'll see you tomorrow." He'd bested Brandon again, and Brandon knew it.

Blade had to hold Sierra to keep her from falling out of her chair, she was laughing so hard. Blade's lips twitched. Obviously, he was having a tough time not joining his wife.

Brandon's attention snapped to Sierra, who quickly straightened and wiped away the moisture from her eyes. "You know I'm on your side."

"Because your chef isn't flying back from vacation until Monday and neither you nor Blade can even boil an egg," Brandon said. Then a gleam entered his dark eyes. "And I had some nice salmon ready for you to take back to the castle."

"I also have salmon," Henri said, then added, "but when food is prepared with love, it tastes better." With a curt nod, he left.

"I think he definitely won that round." Luke slapped Brandon on the back. "But you have Faith."

Brandon instantly brightened. "Come on, you can go with me and make sure I don't put anything vile in my favorite's sister's food. I think we might be out of dessert."

"Brandon, you might not have Faith if it wasn't for me," Sierra said, seemingly not worried. Especially since she was his only sister and all her brothers spoiled her. "In any case, did I tell you about this gadget Rio has? It can ring a phone every ten minutes."

"Phones can be unplugged," he came back.

"Faith likes being available to her employees." Sierra's smile was sweet. "Besides, like Henri said, food tastes better when it's prepared with love."

Brandon shook his head, laughed, then slung his arm around Faith's shoulders. "Bested twice in one day. That's a record I hope never to repeat. Good thing I sort of love you, too."

"And I love you right back."

Ruth Grayson had looked at her children with a smile, then she sniffed. "I wish your father were here."

All of them, her guests, her children, her daughter-in-laws, and Blade moved to her. When the crowd parted, Ruth stared straight into Rio's unblinking eyes. He didn't move.

Then he came to his feet in one fluid motion. "I'll go get the car." Long, graceful strides carried him quickly from the terrace. There was total silence for four seconds, then everyone erupted into laughter.

"Mrs. Grayson, I believe you're the only person on this earth Rio might be afraid of and can't figure out," Blade said.

"One day I hope to change that."

Naomi frowned, wondering if Mrs. Grayson planned on finding a wife for Rio. If so, she certainly had her work cut out for her.

Chapter 4

Thirty minutes later, Richard stopped at the concession counter of the movie theater for their usual: a large box of popcorn, Milk Duds, and soft drinks. Naomi didn't think he should buy her or Kayla food because they had just eaten. He reminded her that it was almost five and gave his order to the cashier, well aware that she never stayed cross with him for long.

Richard wasn't sure if that could be said of Fallon's feelings for Lance, since they'd just met. He'd returned from seeing her to the valet looking none too happy. Apparently he'd struck out with Fallon. A rarity for him. More so since she was the first woman Lance had taken an interest in since the incident.

However, aware of his cousin's tenacity when he wanted something, Richard knew he hadn't given up. It might be interesting to see the two get together. In the meantime, Richard was working on his own romance. He put the popcorn box in Kayla's waiting hands and glanced at Naomi. He certainly knew what it was like to want a woman and not have her.

"Your diet soda," he said.

Shaking her head, Naomi accepted the large drink. "You know I'm weak when it comes to sodas and popcorn."

He wished she'd add his name to her list of weaknesses.

Kayla sipped the soft drink she held in one hand; her other arm was curved around the giant box of popcorn. "Teddy would, too, if he wasn't asleep."

"That he would." Richard ushered them from the lobby. On their first movie outing, Kayla had learned that she couldn't hold Teddy and the popcorn. She enjoyed being a part of the group and sitting in the middle. Since he was crazy about her, he didn't mind her being with them.

"I wonder how Brandon is doing?" Naomi asked.

"Fine, since Faith loves him," Richard assured her. "A couple arguing doesn't always mean they don't love each other."

"I know," she said. "None of the Grayson women seem to have a problem standing up for themselves, but it can be different for other women."

Since it was the truth, Richard didn't argue. He just handed the attendant their tickets. They'd only gone a few steps when he said, "I hope you know you can disagree with me."

She lifted her soda and angled her head down at Kayla. "For all the good it does me."

Baby steps. Naomi was learning how loving

couples treated each other. He couldn't think of a more loving or diverse family than the Graysons. Ruth had certainly hit it out of the park with her selections for her children.

"It's not really a movie if you don't have food," he told her. If Richard thought Ruth could help him move from friend to lover and beyond with Naomi, he would have asked for her help long ago.

Ruth had helped Richard once with Naomi, but he hadn't been interested in her romantically—at least he'd told himself that at the time. In any case, he thought as he followed Naomi and Kayla into the row of seats, those Ruth had matched hadn't asked for her help. He idly wondered if she was serious about helping Lance.

If anyone needed to move on, it was his stubborn cousin. So it looked like he was on his own. Ruth's instincts had been dead-on with his friend Brandon, who had been enjoying his bachelorhood. He was passionate about his food, but he was even more passionate about Faith. Richard looked at Naomi and knew just how his friend felt. But Brandon had his woman; Richard wasn't even close.

Kayla scooted back in her theater seat, her arm wrapped firmly around the popcorn, her drink in the cup holder. She liked going to the movies with her mother and Dr. Richard. It was almost as if they were a family.

She didn't remember her father much except that he yelled at her all the time and made her mother cry. Kayla didn't like to remember the awful time when he'd come to Santa Fe for them. He'd taken her from her mother and gotten in his big car. Kayla had been crying and begging for him to let her go back to her mother, but he wouldn't listen. Crying, her mother had gotten into the car as well. Kayla was scared, and just held on to her mother while her father drove.

She could tell time now, but then she hadn't been sure how long they were in the car before she heard a police siren. Dr. Richard had come with the police to get them. He'd held them while her mother cried. Only this time Kayla knew they were good tears, not the bad ones of before.

Kayla looked at her mother smiling and sipping her drink. She always smiled when they were with Dr. Richard. Sometimes she'd look worried and scared and squeeze her eyes tight—her fists real tight, too. Those times made Kayla sad. She wished she knew how to make her mother smile all the time.

Kayla tried hard to be good and take care of herself so her mother wouldn't have so much to do. She'd heard the mommies at her school talking about how tiring it was to take care of their children and work. One mommy said she couldn't wait for summer to send her children to their grandparents.

Kayla tucked her head. She had grandparents, but her mother didn't talk to them. Kayla guessed they didn't want her coming to visit.

"You all right, pumpkin?"

Kayla looked up to see Dr. Richard smiling down at her. She liked that he had a special nickname for her. He'd started calling her that after he'd helped her carve a pumpkin for the school competition and she'd won the first prize for her class. "Yes, sir."

"Just checking on the celebrity." He picked up a few kernels of popcorn and tossed them into his mouth. "You're the only person I've ever met who's a character in a book. Catherine was right to choose you."

Kayla felt the warm glow she always did when he praised her. She might not have grandparents to visit, but she had Dr. Richard, Mrs. Catherine, Mrs. Grayson, and now Fallon.

She dug into the popcorn with her hand, munched, and looked around the theater. Like always, there were lots of mommies, but few daddies. She didn't tell her mama that she wished she had a daddy. One who smiled and gave her lots of hugs, not one who yelled and said bad words.

She looked up at Dr. Richard and leaned closer. Almost immediately he hugged her. She wished he was her daddy. As the lights dimmed, for a little while she could pretend he was.

They arrived back at Naomi's apartment shortly after eight. They'd stopped for ice cream and a walk in the park. Richard carried a sleeping Kayla to her room and gently placed her in bed. "She's worn out."

Naomi slipped off one of Kayla's sandals. "She had a wonderful ending to her memorable day, thanks to you. Although we both eat too much when we're with you."

"You need a break from cooking. I'll wait for you in the living room, if it's all right."

Feeling nervous for some reason, Naomi tucked her head and reached for the other sandal. "Of course."

Naomi lifted her head once she heard Richard moving away. She did all right when others were around, but just the two of them made her . . . restless for some reason.

Kayla tucked in, Naomi pressed her hand over her dress, took a deep breath, and headed for the living room. Passing her bedroom door, she found herself going inside to check her hair. The other women at the restaurant had looked so nice. The odds were none of them did their own hair as Naomi did. It couldn't be helped. She needed to cut corners and save when she could. After combing her hair, she returned to the living room.

The moment she stepped into the room, Richard looked up from the magazine he was flipping through and smiled. Her stomach got that free-falling feeling from the warm way he looked at her. It amazed her that around other people she might not be noticed, but Richard always seemed to be aware of her.

Her steps were slow as she crossed to the sofa where he was sitting. She admitted to herself that she hadn't thought about how beautiful Fallon was until she'd introduced her to Richard. He'd been cordial, but even Naomi with her limited experience with men could tell he wasn't romantically interested in Fallon. Fallon later told her how yummy

Richard was, and that Naomi had good taste. Naomi had responded that they were just friends. Fallon had just smiled.

"Would you like something to drink?"

"Nope. I've reached my limit," he said.

Naomi sat on the other end of the sofa, her hands folded in her lap. "Thank you again for the movie, and ice cream. Kayla had a wonderful time."

"What about you?"

Her head snapped up, her eyes widened in surprise. "Of course."

"Just checking," he said easily.

She relaxed. Richard liked to tease her at times. He was a good friend. "I wanted to talk to you about something."

He was instantly alert. He reached for her, then clenched his hand. "Is everything all right?"

"Yes," she assured him, thinking it might have been nice if he had touched her. Her emotions were all over the place where he was concerned, but she felt safe with him. Not for anything would she tell him about her nightmares. She'd burdened him enough with her problems. "I'm thinking of buying a house."

"I think that's a great idea," he said.

The tension eased. She'd been half afraid that he'd think it was a terrible idea. She should have remembered, her ex might have always told her what she couldn't do, but Richard never doubted that she could do anything. "I've been saving since I was hired. I want Kayla to have a backyard. Maybe the puppy she talks about," she told him. She didn't mention that a house would also make her feel more secure. The apartment was located in a good neighborhood, but people were going and coming at all hours at the apartment or to the little store behind the complex.

"Sierra helped you find this apartment; she can help find you a house," he told her.

She shook her head. "When she helped me, I didn't know she sold property listed in the millions. And that was before she married a billionaire. Now she's even more out of my league."

"That hasn't changed Sierra and you know it," he told her. "Dinner this evening should have convinced you of that."

Sierra was friendly, but Naomi didn't want to impose or make Sierra feel obligated to help because Naomi worked at the Women's League or was friends with Catherine. "I'll think about it."

"If you'll let me, I'd like to help as well," he told her.

"I'd like that." She folded her hands in her lap again. "I don't know anything about buying a house, and your place is beautiful."

"Thanks. You and Kayla should come out tomorrow and we can go riding," he said.

She wrinkled her nose. "I'm terrible at it."

"You're getting there. Riding isn't as easy as it looks."

"Kayla rides better than I do." Naomi smiled. "She took to riding as she does everything with you."

"I'm here for you as much as for her," he said softly, his gaze direct. "You should know that."

Naomi was captured by the intensity of his gaze.

Her stomach got that fluttery feeling again. Unsure of herself, a bit embarrassed by her reaction to him, a reaction that was happening more and more, she glanced down at her hands clenched in her lap. She wanted Richard's friendship, but even thinking about anything more made her uneasy. She wasn't good in a relationship. Her ex-husband's degrading comments had taught her that.

Richard barely kept from sighing. As much as he wanted to, he wouldn't push Naomi. She wasn't ready for anything more than friendship. However, it was becoming more and more difficult not to reveal how much he cared. Two steps forward and three back. At least he didn't see fear in her eyes.

He came to his feet when what he wanted to do was unclench her hands, gently place them on his chest, and kiss the lip tucked between her teeth. "I better be going."

She stood as well, relief in her expressive brown eyes that kept slipping away from his. "Thank you again."

"My pleasure," he said and watched her gaze skitter away again. Moving around the coffee table in the opposite direction of her, he went to the front door. "Good night."

"Good night. Drive carefully."

He reached for the doorknob. "Don't forget to think about asking Sierra to be your Realtor. She's honest and she knows her stuff."

"I will. Thank you for wanting to help. It means a lot."

He'd do that and more if she only gave him a

chance. Her ex had taken a sledgehammer to her self-esteem and self-confidence. Until she believed in herself as much as he did, she'd never be completely happy or the woman he knew she could be, not just for him, but for herself.

"Talk to you later." He went out the door, closing it after him, then waiting until he heard Naomi slide the two dead-bolt locks into place. It hurt his heart to know she didn't feel safe. With domestic violence of men against women rising, she had good cause. He just hoped she eventually learned not to let the fear dictate how she lived.

Continuing to his truck parked in front of the apartment, he climbed inside. After checking the rearview mirror, he backed out and headed for his ranch fifteen miles out of town. He might be prejudiced, but he agreed with Naomi that he had a beautiful home.

There were only fifty acres, but the land was as rugged as it was beautiful, with the Sangre de Cristo Mountains in the distance. The eighty-year-old home had belonged to his grandfather. His parents had begun the renovations that he'd completed two years ago.

He turned off the main highway. A short distance farther he saw the peak of his house, then he saw the barn that held his horses a short distance away. Beautiful and peaceful and he had no one to share it with.

Putting the truck in the two-bay garage, he headed along the stone path to the back door. His ranch hand would have cared for the ten horses he owned. Four were Arabians, two Thoroughbreds; the others had no pedigree, and that was all right with him.

Entering the back door, he flicked on the light. The phone on the counter rang. He crossed the room and picked it up, noticing the unknown caller. "Dr. Youngblood."

"Richard, it's Lance."

"Is everything all right?"

"Yeah," he quickly said. "I called you on another matter."

"All right?"

"What's the story on Fallon?"

Since Richard was having his own woman problems, he wasn't going to tease his cousin. They were the only sons of only sisters who were as different as humanly possible. His mother was outspoken and self-assured, while Lance's mother was meek and needy. He and Lance were just as different. Richard had returned to Santa Fe to set up practice after graduating; Lance had left his hometown in Oklahoma after graduation and seldom returned.

"If you're asking why she obviously went cold on you and shut you down—if the expression on your face was any indication when you returned to the table and your quick departure afterward—I don't know."

"She told me the reason. She loathes people in my profession," Lance explained. "I thought you might know why."

"Not a clue." The phone in one hand, he opened the fridge door for a bottle of water. "You'll have to find out on your own."

"Easier said than done, since she wants nothing to do with me."

Placing the phone between his shoulder and ear, Richard opened the bottle of water. "Since when have you let a no stop you?"

Lance chuckled. "I knew there was a reason you were my favorite cousin."

"That's because I'm your only cousin."

"There is that. 'Night."

" 'Night." Richard hung up and continued to the bedroom, and his solitary bed. He'd tried not to fantasize that Naomi was there with him, but it was impossible when he saw the wide expanse of the bed.

Placing the bottle of water on the coaster on the nightstand, he unbuttoned his shirt and accepted that he'd probably dream of her again. The dreams were sweet, torrid, playful. He wanted to give her the pleasure of his body as much as he wanted to give her dreams without fear.

One day, he promised as he pulled off his boots, he would.

Chapter 5

Sunday afternoon, Naomi took Kayla to Fallon, who was going to babysit for her. Kayla was excited because they planned to go to the park. Still, Naomi had packed her new favorite book, *The Guardian*, a *Finding Nemo* DVD, and snacks before driving to the Women's League office near downtown Santa Fe. After kissing Kayla good-bye, she got into her SUV. It was ten years old, but it had low gas mileage and maintenance records from the very first trip to the service center.

She pampered the four-wheel-drive Toyota as if it were a Ferrari. She knew how dependent on others you were if you didn't have a car. Plus she felt safe driving it no matter the weather. She hadn't had to worry much about snow in San Antonio. She'd jumped at the opportunity to purchase the car from one of Richard's clients. The car was one more step to independence, and best of all, she'd done it on her own. Richard hadn't been pleased that she hadn't let a mechanic look over the car, but she had trusted Mrs. Carson who was moving into a retirement home and didn't need the car any longer. It felt good to trust.

After parking, Naomi went up the curved walkway, past the blooming pink and red roses, the well-manicured lawn. If you didn't know it, you wouldn't think of the bricked building as a place where people with broken dreams came to begin to heal.

Naomi had been one of those people. She pressed the buzzer to be let inside. Before the sound faded, she heard the click of the lock disengaging and opened the glass door. "Hi, Marie."

"Hi, Naomi. I heard you have a celebrity in the family."

Naomi smiled and stopped in front of the elegant French-inspired desk. The office looked beautiful and stylish, with large, healthy potted plants and artwork. Ruth said she wanted the people who came here to know they were valued and had worth. She'd achieved that and more. "Kayla is still walking on air."

"I would be, too, if I was spotlighted in a book." Maria came to her feet. She was five feet of bubbling energy with an engaging smile. "My life is too dull for anyone to ever want to write about me."

Be thankful, Naomi almost said before she caught herself. "You have a wonderful husband and three beautiful children. I'd say your life is far from dull."

"They drive me crazy, but I'd be lost without them." Maria opened the hardwood cabinet in the corner and removed her purse. "The oldest has a soccer game this afternoon. Her team hasn't lost a game."

"I'd say you have some celebrating of your own to do," Naomi said. "That's wonderful."

"We kind of think so." Maria shoved the thin leather strap over her slim shoulder. "Dan and the other two girls are picking me up on the way to the game."

"Have fun, and tell Paula I said good luck."

A car horn interrupted what Maria had been about to say. "That man. He used to drive my mama crazy honking that horn instead of coming in for me. He does it now just to get a rise out of me."

Since Naomi had seen Maria and Dan together, she wasn't concerned. He outweighed Maria by eighty pounds and was a good foot taller, and he treated her like spun glass. "He likes to tease you."

Maria shook her dark head of hair as the horn sounded again. "Sixty-two and he still acts like a kid at times."

Naomi couldn't ever remember Gordon being anxious for her. Impatient and annoyed, yes, but never anxious. "You go on. I'll take it from here."

"Things have been quiet," Maria reported, heading for the front door. "You're closing at six."

"Yes, this will be my first time." Before, she hadn't wanted the responsibility of closing or being out late. Baby steps, Catherine called them. Placing her handbag in the cabinet, Naomi took the seat Maria had vacated. "You better get out of here before Dan comes to get you."

"I'm going. Bye."

"Bye," Naomi said, watching the heavy door swing shut. Uneasiness momentarily swept through her. She was alone. If she needed help, there would be no one. *Stop it,* she mentally chastised herself. She was safe, the door locked, the glass in the front door unbreakable, the alarm system the best available, camera on the front and back doors. She didn't even have to pick up the phone. All she had to do was push the button Rio had installed and an alarm would go straight to the police office.

She'd asked Mrs. Grayson how she'd managed to have that installed and she'd just smiled. Naomi imagined with a billionaire son-in-law, wealthy relatives, famous in-laws, influential friends, and protective children, most people didn't say no to Ruth Grayson.

She looked sweet, but on a couple of occasions when an unruly boyfriend or husband had tried to coerce a woman into leaving the center, Ruth had stepped into the conversation.

Their harsh words and threats hadn't fazed her. She hadn't used her connections or her sons—who would have torn the men apart—just her unflinching courage and desire to help others. The men had backed down even before the police car had pulled up. Not long after, so had Luke and Brandon. Her other children had been out of town or Naomi was sure they would have shown up as well. Ruth Grayson was a phenomenal woman. Naomi would settle for waking up without fear. One day she'd get there.

Entering her password, she brought up the log for the day and entered her name. The Women's

League wanted accurate records. Unfortunately, they might be needed in legal cases. Naomi's hands flexed as she recalled the woman in the coma. She hadn't been a client of the Women's League.

Naomi had overheard women at her job and in line at the checkout counter at the grocery store saying that they didn't see why the woman hadn't left. Some even blamed her for the abuse. They had no idea how you could be beat down, cowed. They took their safety and the love of a good man, their ability to stand up for themselves, for granted. They didn't see it as a blessing like Naomi did.

She looked over the calls for the day in case anyone called again and wanted additional information. From experience, Naomi knew that making the call was the first and most difficult step of admitting you were abused and needed help. Women could come into the office for assistance daily. Although there wasn't a place to stay, the league could provide hotel accommodation, if necessary.

Working there for the past month, Naomi had learned that she wasn't the only one who'd had a knock on the door and received the gift of new clothes, and, more important, the gift of self-worth when you felt you couldn't make it a day, an hour longer. She wanted to help others who found themselves alone and feeling hopeless as she had.

The buzzer sounded. She looked up to see Sierra holding a stuffed plastic garment bag with the name of a local department store. Two men stood a few steps behind her. Each held a large handled shopping bag in his hands.

Naomi hit the buzzer to unlock the door and

rushed around the desk to help. One of the men reached around Sierra to open the door.

"Thanks, Aaron." Sierra stepped inside. "Hi, Naomi."

"Hi, Sierra," Naomi greeted. "Let me have that."

"Got it, thanks." Laughing, Sierra glanced over her shoulders at the two men who had quietly entered behind her. "You might want to help Paul and Aaron."

Naomi might have hesitated, but the men stepped around Sierra and extended the bags in their hands. She took the ones from the man nearer to her. The others were set down beside her. Once the bags were relinquished, the men smoothly stepped back behind Sierra, their motions in sync, their faces pleasant but unsmiling.

"I found a fantastic sale and couldn't resist," Sierra said.

"Thank you." It was well known Sierra loved clothes and shopping. The clothes closet in the league was often the beneficiary of her enjoyment. Her yellow spiked heels matched the beautiful lemon dress that stopped a couple of inches above her knees.

Still bubbling, she glanced behind her at the two men. "We had a good time, didn't we?"

They simply stared at her. Laughing, Sierra turned back to Naomi. Leaning over, she whispered, "They're my shadows. I can take care of myself, but it makes Blade feel better. Rio heard me mention shopping and chickened out."

Bodyguards, Naomi realized. Blade wanted his wife safe and made sure of it. The door swung shut behind one of the men before Naomi realized he'd moved.

"I'll help you put everything up." Sierra reached for the other two bags. The remaining man stepped around Sierra for the bags, startling Naomi. She gasped and stumbled back. The man froze.

Naomi didn't know what to say. She felt heat flush her cheeks. There had been no threat to her.

"I got it, Aaron," Sierra said easily. "Naomi, you lead the way."

Naomi turned, then swung back to the silent, watchful man. She would not hurt someone's feelings because she was learning to live without fear. "It's not you."

"No problem, Mrs. Reese."

Surprise widened her eyes that he knew her name; then she realized that they had to know the family's close associates to be effective.

Sierra must have noticed her surprise. "They even know my hairstylist, although she tried to flirt with them."

Naomi understood Sierra was trying to make her feel better and lighten the mood. While grateful, Naomi wished for the day people didn't have to be cautious or make excuses for her. She wanted a normal life for her and Kayla. She'd already decided that didn't include a man. "This way."

The "clothes closet" was a room with revolving racks of women's and children's clothes from floor to ceiling, with full-length mirrors and private dressing rooms. No one saw the sense of leaving with clothes that didn't fit. Naomi reached into her bag to find toiletries. She began placing them in the designated bins. Out of the corner of her eyes, she saw Sierra on the short ladder, hanging up the clothes she'd purchased.

"That's a pretty dress."

"I thought so." Sierra smiled and pulled out the full hem of the white sundress with pink piping. "The saleslady must have thought I was crazy to buy the same dress in three sizes, but it was too cute to pass up. A new outfit can make the day brighter."

Naomi wasn't surprised Sierra understood. She might be wealthy but, like her family and in-laws, she wasn't stuck up or pretentious. She understood that hard times could make people feel worthless and make them give up hope. Naomi was proud that she was able to give back just a little of what had been given to her.

Perhaps she could do even more. Her hand closed tightly around the bottle of shampoo. "If—if you need help with the fund-raising for Mrs. Grayson's music department, I'd like to help."

Amazed delight swept across Sierra's beautiful heart-shaped face. "Thank you, Naomi. Blade's event director is flying down next week for a fact-finding and planning meeting. I'll let you know."

Nodding, the tension easing out of her, Naomi went back to emptying the bags. She hadn't been rejected or made to feel as if she were worthless. She hadn't let fear rule her. She just had to keep reminding herself that she had something to offer. She almost smiled. She couldn't wait to tell Richard.

Finished, they folded the empty paper shopping

bags and put them in the stack. They saved the bags for women to carry away their items.

"Thanks again for the donations," Naomi said.

"I had fun," Sierra said. "I have to admit, there's also a couple of outfits in the car for me. Besides Blade, clothes and food are my two weaknesses."

Once it might have been hard for Naomi to imagine a woman smiling about a man being her weakness, but she'd been around the Graysons and their spouses long enough to realize that loving the right man was a good thing. The trouble was finding him.

Watching the younger woman, who had such a zest for life and was in such a good mood, Naomi thought it was the perfect time to bring up her request. "Sierra, if you don't mind, could you please recommend a Realtor?"

One perfectly arched brow lifted regally. Sierra folded her arms and simply stared at Naomi. Her easygoing demeanor and smile were gone.

Naomi swallowed and rushed to explain. "Richard said to ask you, but I can't afford the homes you list. I didn't know when you helped me find an apartment that you handled only upscale properties, and now you're married to a billionaire."

"And you think that changed me?"

"No." Naomi quickly shook her head. She always messed things up, just like her ex said she did. "You're always nice to me and Kayla."

Sierra's arms unfolded, her face softening. Reaching out, she gently touched Naomi's arm in comfort. "Then you don't want to hurt my feelings, do you?"

"No. You've been wonderful to me. Your whole

family has." Half the things in her kitchen and home were housewarming gifts from Richard and the Graysons. It wasn't just the gifts that they gave her, it was their friendship and acceptance that counted for so much more.

"Good, then I'm your Realtor. I need to go to the car, but I'll be back." Sierra headed for the front of the building.

Naomi followed Sierra out to the reception area. She saw Aaron open the door just before Sierra rushed through. A man emerged from the driver's side of the black Lincoln parked at the curb and opened the back door. Bending to reach inside, she emerged with something in her hand and hurried back. Aaron opened the door again and followed her inside. Naomi saw that Sierra had an iPad, her slim manicured fingers moving quickly over the screen.

"Why don't we step into one of the counseling offices? Aaron can watch the front, if that's all right with you." Sierra lifted her head and waited for an answer.

She was giving Naomi a choice and privacy. She understood Naomi's need to have both. Richard had been right about choosing Sierra. "All right."

This time it was Naomi who followed Sierra into one of the offices, but neither sat in one of the comfortable chairs. "What kind of house are you looking for? What neighborhood?"

"Something I can afford, with a yard for Kayla to have a swing, maybe a puppy later on."

Sierra's fingers paused over the keyboard. She looked up. "What about what *you* want?"

"To be safe," Naomi answered before she thought and wanted to tuck her head in shame, but Sierra's gaze was already on the screen as she resumed typing.

"Then we'll look in those neighborhoods where you will be. To ensure your safety even more once you have your house, I'll ask Rio to put in a security system."

As much as she liked the idea, she knew she couldn't afford the type of system Rio would probably install. "That will cost a lot of money. Maybe I can get something cheaper." At Sierra's raised brow, Naomi quickly amended her words. "Less expensive."

"Amounts to the same thing." Sierra continued talking when Naomi opened her mouth. "I wouldn't be surprised if Rio already has the equipment. You'll just need an alarm company to monitor it."

"Won't they want to install their own equipment?" Naomi asked.

Sierra flashed a quick grin. "You'd be surprised by the things people do when Rio asks them."

Naomi didn't doubt her for a second. Rio was a formidable man. Then there was Sierra's husband, and her older brother Luke. She certainly wouldn't like saying no to any of them.

"Now, back to basics," Sierra said. "What price range? How much can you afford to put down?"

Naomi swallowed, barely kept from fidgeting. "Six thousand down. I'm not sure what price range. It can be small. We just need two bedrooms."

Sierra nodded and entered more data into the iPad. "You'll want the payments in line with your apartment rent. You haven't paid utility bills so you'll have to factor that into monthly expenses. Yard upkeep. Incidentals."

Cold fear knotted Naomi's stomach. "Maybe I should stay in the apartment."

Sierra's head came up, her gaze curious instead of accusatory. "Did you have a house before?"

Before. Naomi barely kept from looking away in embarrassment and shame. Before meant before she came to Santa Fe after running from her ex-husband with little more than the clothes on her and Kayla's backs. "No."

"First-time homeownership is always daunting, but you have to be sure it's what you want. You won't be able to call the apartment manager if the plumbing backs up or the central air goes out," Sierra told her.

With each statement, Naomi's eyes widened. She hadn't thought of all those possibilities.

"Luckily for us, I know honest repairmen. But more important, before you sign any contract, the house will be thoroughly inspected. I also know a home warranty company that won't rip you off. And I imagine Richard will want to take a look before you purchase."

Naomi felt her face flush, but she also felt relief that she had Richard. "He said he wanted to help."

"Thought so." Sierra closed the leather case over the top of the iPad. "I'll start working on it tomorrow. I have your phone number. I'll be in touch." She started from the room.

"Sierra?"

"Yes?" She glanced back over her shoulder, her long black hair swinging down her slim back.

"Thank you."

"Thank *you*. I love finding just the right house for a client. Since you're a friend, it will be that much more enjoyable." Sierra started for the front again. "I better go before we have company. If it wouldn't upset Blade, I'd ditch them."

"You can't do that. Some men don't respect women."

Sierra stopped and placed her hand on Naomi's trembling arm. "I won't."

In trying to help protect Sierra, Naomi had revealed too much, but she didn't feel the humiliation she once might have. Sierra didn't think less of her, and she was tired of thinking less of herself. "I won't keep you."

"We'll talk later this week." Sierra stepped into the reception area. "Aaron, please call Paul from the back and let's go."

"Already done when I heard your heels."

Sierra lifted a perfectly ached brow. "Why didn't you call him the first time?"

"You wore the same excited expression on your face when you were searching for clothes," he said easily. "You were on a mission. You weren't leaving."

"I'll have to remember that."

"Thought you would. I'll wait outside."

"They seem very efficient," Naomi murmured.

"They have to be to get Blade and Rio's okay," Sierra confided. "Good-bye, Naomi."

"Good-bye." Naomi followed Sierra to the door.

Aaron opened the back door to the shiny Lincoln. The windows were tinted so she couldn't see inside. On the front passenger side stood Paul. Closing Sierra's door, Aaron went around to the other side. Both men got inside at the same time. The car pulled smoothly away from the curb.

Naomi stared after the car. Sierra had found a man who valued her and wanted her safe. She was a lucky woman. For a second Naomi thought of Richard, then pushed him from her mind. He was just a friend and that was the way it was going to remain. The last thing she needed or wanted was a man ordering her around and messing up her and Kayla's lives again.

Once was more than enough.

As the day lengthened, Naomi expected a call from Mrs. Grayson or Richard to check on her. Until today she'd always had the early-afternoon shift. That way Ruth or Catherine could keep Kayla for a couple of hours. She'd never closed the building by herself. As the clock moved closer to six, she finally accepted that they weren't going to call. Initially she wasn't sure how she felt about that, then she decided it showed they had confidence in her to handle whatever came up.

And she had. There had been calls seeking information about the league as well as call-backs, as she'd thought.

Although the calls had brought back painful memories of her abusive marriage, they also gave her a greater insight into what the caller was going through or how to be of assistance to a relative who

wanted to help a family member in an abusive relationship who wasn't ready to leave her abuser. For
her there had been no relative, no one she could
turn to . . . until she came to Santa Fe.

When the antique clock on the wall read five
fifty-eight, Naomi pulled her purse from the cabinet and powered down the computer. Exactly at
6:00 PM, she set the alarm, left on the lamp on the
front desk to signify that help was always available, and walked out the door.

The air was crisp and clean. As the evening
lengthened, the temperature would drop, but by
then Naomi would be home, getting her and Kayla
ready for school and work tomorrow. Walking to
her car, she looked around as the defense course
had taught her, checked the backseat, and unlocked
the door. As Luke had said during the course he'd
taught the workers and clients of the league, it was
better to be careful than a victim.

She got into the Highlander, and the motor
started instantly. Backing out of the parking lot,
she realized—not for the first time—she had so
much to be thankful for. Her life could have taken
a much different direction. But she and Kayla were
safe, and if all went as planned, they would be
homeowners soon. She realized something else—if
she kept looking over her shoulder waiting for her
ex-husband to show back up, she'd never have the
kind of happy life she wanted for them.

Stopping at the entrance of the parking lot, she
put the car in park, picked up her cell phone, and
called Fallon. It was past time to take another step.

"Hello."

"Hi, Fallon. How is Kayla?"

"Wonderful as usual," Fallon reported. "We're eating pizza and watching the Discovery Channel."

"Do you mind keeping her for a bit longer? I want to drop by a friend's house."

"Is it too much to hope that the friend is Mr. Yummy?"

Naomi didn't know why she felt like tucking her head. "It's Catherine."

Fallon's sigh came through loud and clear. "One day you're going to give me the right answer. In any case, take your time. We saved some pizza for you."

"Thanks. I appre—"

"Stop there or I might think twice about coming over in the morning for coffee and cereal. I'm out of milk and too lazy to get dressed and go to the store and buy any."

Naomi often wondered if Fallon, who was as intelligent as they came, really forgot on purpose so she could come over. Naomi knew what it was like to be isolated and lonely. Fallon had family, but they were in another state. Naomi didn't mind. She liked the company and was grateful Kayla had a wonderful sitter. "I shouldn't be long. Give Kayla a hug for me. Bye."

"You got it. Bye."

Hanging up, Naomi punched in Catherine's number. She refused to live in fear.

"Hello."

"Hello, Catherine. It's Naomi," she said, unsure

of how to proceed. She always expected Catherine to have all the answers. How could she this time when Naomi wasn't sure of the questions?

"Hello, Naomi. How did it go today?" Catherine asked.

"Fine. I—" Her hand clenched on the cell phone.

"Naomi, are you all right?" Catherine asked, her voice concerned.

"Yes. No." Naomi blew out a frustrated breath. "I just need to talk to you."

"Are you at home? I can come right over."

No question, just an offer to help. Catherine had been that way since they met when Naomi fainted from hunger and exhaustion in front of her. "I'm just leaving the Women's League office. Fallon is keeping Kayla. If it's all right, I'd like to come by there . . . if you're in the city." Luke had a mountain cabin they often stayed in, and when they did, they liked being left alone.

"We're in the city. See you soon."

"Bye." Naomi hung up the phone and pulled into traffic.

Chapter 6

Less than ten minutes later Naomi pulled up in
front of a beautiful ranch-style home in a gated
development. Roses and a profusion of flowers
snaked around the house. Two elms stood sentinel
on either side of the large yard. A block away to
the left lived Ruth Grayson. To the right was Morgan and his wife, Phoenix. Naomi didn't think it
was by accident that the two oldest sons lived near
their mother.

Getting out of the car, Naomi went up the
curved walkway bordered by liriope and daisies.
On the wide porch was a wheelbarrow with dark
purple petunias trailing over the side. She rang the
doorbell.

The door opened. She was caught off guard
when Luke, tall and imposing with his hair hanging
straight down his broad shoulders, answered the
door. Unlike the signing when he had greeted them,
he wasn't smiling. Again, she got the impression

that somehow she might have unwittingly hurt
Catherine's feelings.

"Hi, Naomi."

"Hi, Luke."

"Come on in. Cath is on the phone with her
mother." He stepped back.

She hesitated, then chastised herself and stepped
inside the foyer. When he went to walk away, she
touched his arm. She was as surprised as he appeared to be by the instinctive move. She kept her
distance from men, but especially those over six
feet and broad-shouldered like Luke was.

"Yes?"

She could tuck her head as had been her habit at
the direct stare or try to repair whatever damage
she had inadvertently done to their friendship. "I
love Catherine. She's my best friend. She gave to
me and Kayla without us asking because she knew
we were in need and I was too afraid and too
proud at the time to ask. If I said or did anything
yesterday to hurt her, I didn't mean to. I'll apologize to her when I see her."

"No," he barked out, then raked his hand
through his thick black hair. He seemed unsure of
himself. Never in a million years would she have
used that word in connection with Luke Grayson.
"Forget about apologizing, and don't mind me."

"But you're upset with me," Naomi said. "I
know that look."

He bit back an expletive. "Then I apologize. I'm
nothing like your ex-husband."

"No, you're not, and I apologize if you thought
that's what I meant." She tried again because they

both loved Catherine. "I just meant I know when someone is upset with me. Catherine will know as well. She loves you, so it will upset her."

"It's not you," he said slowly. "But if you love her, forget yesterday and move on. Promise me. Promise me now. She's coming."

"I promise," Naomi quickly said, not really sure what she was agreeing to or understanding, but the relief in Luke's face was enough.

"Hi, Naomi," Catherine greeted, hugging Naomi, then hooking her arm through hers. "Sorry to keep you waiting."

"Luke kept me company," Naomi answered.

Catherine's gaze went to her husband. Smiling, he kissed her on the lips. "See, I can be of use."

"How well I know." If the expression on Catherine's face was any indication, she knew that fact very well.

He brushed his finger down the bridge of his wife's nose, then let his attention switch to Naomi. "Bye."

"Bye, Luke."

He walked off, his moccasined feet soundless on the wooden floor. Catherine's gaze followed for a long moment before she gave her attention back to Naomi. "There's lemonade in the kitchen and we can talk."

Naomi allowed herself to be led to the spacious kitchen with a barrel ceiling, recessed lighting, and cream-colored marble countertops. "I love your kitchen."

"Thanks. I do, too." Catherine waved Naomi to banquette seating for at least eight people. Clearly, it had been built with the large Grayson family in mind. "Although neither Luke nor I can cook very well. I'm not sure what we'd do if Brandon didn't take pity on us."

Naomi took her seat. "What about Henri?"

"Bite your tongue." Catherine laughed and poured Naomi a glass of lemonade with strawberries floating in it. "Brandon is territorial."

"Just like some men," Naomi murmured.

Catherine finished filling her glass and set the pitcher down. "The difference is, Brandon would never hurt one of us."

Naomi's hands circled the glass. "I don't want to live in fear. I thought I was doing so well until I read in the newspaper about the woman's husband beating her unconscious. I felt for her and her children."

"It made you remember and realize that life can change in an instant."

She might have known Catherine would understand. "Yes. My ex-husband is a cruel man. I can't forget his saying I was his wife no matter what."

"And that's just what he wanted you to remember," Catherine said with feeling. "You're living your life, a good life you've made for yourself and Kayla. Don't beat up on yourself when you have moments you're not as strong as you want to be. It's a process. I was scared once."

"And Luke helped you."

Catherine smiled. "Yes. He's my strength."

Naomi had heard Luke say the same thing about Catherine. She had what Naomi had believed she had in her marriage, a man who loved her unconditionally. Instead, he'd abused her, made her weak. For some odd reason, she thought of Richard, a man who helped her, encouraged her.

Naomi wasn't sure she was ever the strong woman Catherine was, or ever could be.

"I don't want to live in fear, not only for Kayla's sake, but mine as well."

"You're talking about your fears, admitting them," Catherine told her. "It helps when you aren't alone. You're getting there. You're going to win this battle."

There it was again, the faith and reassurance that had helped her though so many times when she'd doubted herself. "Thank you. I'm glad I have you."

"Same here. Is there anything I can do?"

"Being my friend and confidante is enough," Naomi said, sipping her drink. "I just wish I knew he was still in San Antonio."

"That I can help you with." Catherine rose from her seat and walked to the door. "Luke, I need you."

Naomi almost choked on her drink. She didn't even have time to shush Catherine before Luke appeared. "Everything okay?"

"Naomi needs your help."

Black piercing eyes turned on her. "For what?"

If nothing else, Luke was direct. She could do no less . . . at least with Catherine standing there to encourage her. "Could you please check and see if my ex-husband is still in San Antonio?"

"Do you have a reason to think he might not be?"

"No, I just . . ." How could she explain?

"I'll check and let you know."

Like Catherine and Richard, he hadn't demanded an explanation, because she was Catherine's friend. "Catherine always said I could trust you."

"You can."

"I know. Thank you."

He didn't move. "If you feel anything is off, call the police."

"Then call me and Luke."

His arm curved around Catherine's waist. "Just call me."

Catherine made a face, but she didn't correct Luke. Naomi came to her feet. "If we could set up a payment—"

"I don't recall asking for money," he said.

"Thank you." Naomi stood, accepting that friendship counted more than money. "I feel better already."

Stepping away from Luke, Catherine took Naomi's arms. "We're here for you. Remember that."

"I will. Good-bye."

"I'll walk you to the door," Catherine said.

Naomi glanced over her shoulder. The harsh expression was gone from Luke's face. If a strong man like Luke Grayson could be afraid, she didn't feel so bad that she was afraid at times as well.

Richard pulled up in front of Naomi's apartment Sunday night and turned off the engine of his truck. He simply stared at her front door. Before Naomi came into his life, he would have sworn that he was up to any challenge, that he'd always prevail once he made up his mind.

After all, he'd been pushing limits and breaking barriers all his life. No one outside his family and a few teachers expected a child who didn't walk until he was two and talk until three to graduate valedictorian of his high school class and in the top 3 percent of his graduating class in veterinary medicine at Texas A&M. He'd simply seen no reason to do either with such doting parents. As the boy his father had hoped for, a child his mother had longed for, his every wish had been catered to . . . until his wise paternal grandmother had put a stop to it. Her Lab, Caesar, had been his first patient when he'd opened his clinic.

But in school and college he'd been dealing with hard facts, not fragile emotions. Naomi had come a long way in the time he'd known her, but he had to reluctantly admit she had a long way to go. She was less uneasy around men but at times, if she was caught unaware, those big vulnerable eyes would widen and she'd go stark still or shrink back.

His mouth flattened into a grim line. He wished he had punched her ex in the face when he had the chance. However, as satisfying as that might have been, the police he'd called to help get Naomi and Kayla would have had no choice but to arrest him. In jail, he would have been no help to them.

Still, those times pierced his heart, more so if it had been him who had frightened her. He wanted her to be as carefree and as happy as Kayla.

His somber expression morphed into a smile.

Precocious, energetic, and smart, Kayla embraced life. He didn't think Naomi had ever been that lighthearted. His smile vanished at the thought.

Naomi was a good mother, a good friend. She deserved love and was so afraid to reach out and take what was in front of her . . . because she had tried once and reaped horrible consequences.

She would, though. He'd promised himself that long ago. For now, he had to be satisfied with just helping her realize that she wasn't alone. He was there and so were others. She just had to open her eyes.

Opening the door, he got out of the truck. He was bone-tired from dealing with a herd of calves that had to be vaccinated. However, he hadn't been able to keep going when he neared the exit for Naomi's apartment.

This was as big a day for her as Kayla's had been yesterday. He hoped it was another indication that she was capable and smart. He'd wanted to call a dozen times but he recognized that it was important for her to know they trusted her, that they weren't checking up on her.

He knocked on the door, well aware that her face showed her every emotion. The moment he saw her, he'd know how the day had gone.

Out of the corner of his eye, he saw the curtain at the window move. Moments later, he heard the double locks he'd personally installed, disengage. He wasn't aware of the tension coiled within him until he saw her shy smile.

"Hi, Richard," she greeted, opening the door wider and stepping back.

"Hi, Naomi. Hope it's not too late to stop by."

"Kayla's bedtime might be at eight, but I stay up a little later," she said, closing the door after him.

Richard grinned. She seldom teased. It was another indicator that her volunteering stint had gone well. He took a seat on the end of the sofa. He'd learned not to crowd her. "How long did it take tonight to get her to stay put?"

"Since she was anxious to see her classmates and talk about *The Guardian,* she only got up once to tell me something she'd forgotten and get a drink of water." Smiling indulgently, Naomi took a seat in the middle of the sofa.

Richard liked being with Kayla, but he was beginning to realize that she was a buffer at times. He and Naomi needed to be alone. "If their response Saturday was any indication, she is going to be the talk of her school."

"Catherine did that for her." Her smile dimmed. "She's done so much for us. I'd never do anything to hurt her."

Richard frowned, almost reaching out to pull her into his arms. "Of course not. What made you say that?"

Her eyes widened. "No-nothing."

She wasn't telling the truth, but if there was something going on with Catherine, Luke would move heaven and earth to fix it, just as he once had, just as Richard would do for Naomi. "You thought any more about the house?"

Her smile blossomed, and Richard wondered if she had any idea how pretty she was when she smiled. "You were right again. Sierra came by the

Women's League with donations today and I asked her for a Realtor's name. She quickly set me straight and agreed to help me." Naomi shook her head. "She's as formidable as her mother."

Richard heard the longing with tinges of envy in her voice. "She grew up with a family who didn't believe in any other way."

"And they all married people who are just as uncompromising," Naomi said softly. "They'd never let . . ." Her voice trailed off; her hands clenched in her lap.

"It's what they learned, just as Kayla is learning to be warm and loving because that's what you taught her," he said. "She's smart and determined, and already showing her independence. I know she says she wants to be a vet, but I haven't a doubt that she'll succeed in whatever she decides. You're the one stable factor in her life."

Her head came up. "And you."

Finally, he was getting someplace. "It's easy to love her." The words were barely out of his mouth before he realized that included the mother. This time he was the one to look away. She'd slam the door on their friendship if she had any inkling he wanted more. He'd made that mistake when they first met. Never again.

"Would you like something to drink or a cookie?" She smiled. "Kayla and Fallon stopped at the bakery on the way back from sightseeing. She's really been a help. I'll hate to see her leave."

"She's leaving?" Lance wasn't going to like that.

Naomi slowly nodded, apparently not pleased, either. "In five weeks—when school is out, she's leaving. She travels a lot. She loves it, but I want to plant roots in one place."

He was glad the place she'd chosen was Santa Fe. "For you and Kayla."

Longing entered her dark eyes. "I had a few anxious moments at first when Sierra mentioned some of the homeowner's responsibilities that I didn't have to worry about while renting, but I think having our own place outweighs those possibilities. Plus she said it would be inspected first."

"And don't forget I want to take a look as well."

"I didn't." She tucked her head for a moment. "Sierra already guessed that you want to help. You're a good friend."

He worked hard to keep the pleasant smile on his face, and not grit his teeth. "And I always will be."

Her face grew serious. "I haven't mentioned it to Kayla yet, in case Sierra doesn't find anything I can afford."

"With the housing market the way it is, and Sierra for a Realtor, I don't think finding a home will be a problem," he told her. "It might be a good idea to consider a house that needs a little work to get a better price. I'm pretty good with a hammer."

She was shaking her head before he finished. "I couldn't ask you to do that."

"You're not asking. I'm volunteering. Now I better get out of your way." Reluctantly he pushed to his feet, when what he really wanted to do was to hug and reassure her that she could do this.

She came to her feet as well and stepped forward to show him to the door, expecting him to move. He didn't. For a long moment they simply stared at the other. She studied him, trying to figure out why his gaze was so intent. It troubled her that he was worried about something and she couldn't help when he had always been there for her.

She was about to ask him if he was all right when his gaze dropped to her lips. Her heart skittered the crazy way it did at times when he looked at her a certain way. Her skin felt hot, tight.

His hand lifted toward her face. She stumbled back, tripping over her feet and almost falling backward. She gasped, not sure if it was because of the near fall or because Richard caught her arms, drawing her securely to him. She felt the muscled warmth of his hard body against hers, smelled his cologne. Her heart thumped even harder.

Not for the first time when he'd held her, she wasn't sure if she wanted to lean in or pull away. She trembled as indecision held her still.

"Are you all right?" Richard asked, concern in his face and voice instead of annoyance. He wasn't a threat to her.

"Yes." Her cheeks heated with embarrassment. She hadn't expected him to reach out to her, and had instinctively reverted to the days when a male hand coming toward her meant pain and humiliation.

Releasing her, he stepped back. She missed the warmth and comfort. "Well, good night. Call when Sierra has a listing and I'll go with you."

As always, he'd forgiven her. His kindness made her feel worse. She didn't want to keep hurting the people she cared about. First Catherine and now

Richard. Both had helped when she had nowhere else to turn, asking nothing in return.

Yet unlike Aaron at the Women's League, she couldn't apologize as she followed Richard to the door. Somehow she knew an apology would only make him feel worse. It was there in his miserable expression.

"Good night. Tell Kayla to have fun at school tomorrow."

She wanted so badly to reach out and touch him, to take the unhappiness from his eyes that hadn't been there before her silliness. "I will. Good night and thanks for stopping by."

Turning, he started for his truck parked in front. Aware he expected her to be inside by the time he was at the vehicle, she slowly closed the door, locked it, then leaned against it, briefly closing her eyes. How could she have reacted that way to him? Annoyed with herself, she opened her eyes and straightened.

Richard had been there for her, encouraging her, helping her, and she'd repaid him by acting like a scared rabbit. The reason was a complicated one. Although he had caught her unaware, she also had to finally admit that she knew he wanted more than friendship from her. When he reached for her, her reaction was not from her fear of him so much as her fear of altering their delicate balance.

To her shame, she hadn't done anything to dissuade him, just kept taking his friendship that had come to mean so much to her. Without her becoming aware of it, she had come to depend on him. He was steady, dependable, and he made her feel as if she could do anything. He had given her so much, but she couldn't give him what he wasn't able to hide that he wanted: a woman in his bed.

Naomi flushed at the thought as her mind scampered away from the visual images of herself and her ex, his taunts, her tears. She couldn't be the woman Richard deserved. He was everything any woman could wish for. She'd stopped wishing for a man long ago.

Pushing away from the door, Naomi went to check on Kayla. Opening the partially ajar door farther, she saw Kayla on her side, asleep with Teddy. Despite the tension in her, her uncertainty, Naomi smiled. Kayla was the best part of her, the best part of her hellish marriage.

Turning away, Naomi went to her room intending to get ready for bed, but when her hands reached for the buttons of her blouse, they stilled. She could still recall the hurt on Richard's face, the dejection.

Her hands slowly lowered to her sides. She glanced at the clock on the nightstand. Eight thirty-three. Usually she'd call Catherine when she was troubled, but even if she hadn't already intruded on her once today, Catherine didn't answer her phone after 8:00 PM. That was family time.

Naomi tried to think of how she might have inadvertently hurt Catherine and came up blank once again. Whatever it was, as Richard had said, Luke would fix it. She couldn't keep hurting people because of her own insecurities.

As if she were standing right there, Naomi could hear Catherine's words of that afternoon: *Prob-*

lems are easier when they're shared with someone. Going to the phone on the nightstand, she picked up the receiver and dialed.

"Hello," Fallon answered with her usual cheery voice.

"Fallon, it's Naomi."

"Everything all right?" her friend quickly asked.

"I need to talk to someone. I'd come over, but Kayla is asleep."

"I'll be at the back door in ten seconds." The line went dead.

Naomi left the bedroom and went to the kitchen. By the time Fallon knocked, she was reaching for the door. "Thank you."

Fallon stepped inside and held out one of the two pints of ice cream she'd brought. "You sounded as if you might need this. Have a seat and I'll get the spoons."

Naomi took the ice cream and the spoon Fallon handed her. When she didn't move to take off the lid, Fallon removed it for her, then took her seat.

"Problems always seem easier when I have a pint of blackberry cobbler." Fallon dug into her ice cream. "Since you were all right earlier, would I be wrong that this has something to do with Dr. Yummy?"

Naomi spooned into the peach cobbler—her favorite flavor—before she spoke. "Richard is a wonderful man."

"Agreed," Fallon said.

Naomi poked her spoon at the peaches in her pint. "He's always been patient and kind to us. I don't know what I would have done without him."

"I hear a *but*."

Naomi's head came up. She leaned back against her chair. She wanted to look anyplace but at the steady gaze of Fallon, but she realized that was what she'd always done when faced with difficulty. "My first marriage didn't work out. I'm not ready for another relationship. I—I think Richard wants more."

"From the way he looks at you, I'd say you were right." Fallon spooned in another bite. "I say go for it."

"No." Naomi jabbed the spoon into the ice cream. "I just want his friendship. Nothing more."

"At the risk of starving, I'm not sure you're being completely honest with yourself."

Naomi's eyes widened. "You're wrong."

Fallon shrugged. "You're happier, less uptight, around Richard."

Naomi didn't know what to say because it was the truth.

"From what I've seen, Richard is a man any woman would jump to have. He takes time with Kayla and is patient with you. Most men move on when there's no s-e-x."

Naomi blushed and ate more ice cream.

"At the risk of being redundant, I say go for it."

And disappoint and embarrass both of them— if it got that far. She'd been a dud in the bedroom. "I'm not as outgoing as you are."

Shadows darkened Fallon's eyes. Naomi wondered if there was something painful in her friend's past as well. "I wasn't always. I just had to learn to live my life instead of going through the motions.

Give Richard a chance to move from friend to something more."

"Are you going to give Lance a chance?" Naomi countered.

"Not my type," Fallon responded, eating more ice cream. "Besides, I'm leaving in five weeks."

"Don't remind me. We'll miss you," Naomi told her, ready to drop the conversation. She didn't like being reminded of another inadequacy.

"I'll miss you and Kayla as well." Fallon smiled. "For the first time in a long time, I'll be sad to move on. You're a good friend and mother. So give yourself and Richard a break."

The prospect of intimacy made her stomach roll. She capped her pint of ice cream. "Thanks for coming over and for the ice cream."

Fallon wrinkled her nose and replaced the top on her own pint. "I think you've made up your mind, and it's not in Richard's favor."

"Some things are just not meant to be." Naomi placed both pints in the fridge.

"I'd argue if I thought it would do any good." Fallon came gracefully to her feet and went to the back door. "Just remember, it's a woman's prerogative to change her mind. 'Night."

" 'Night," Naomi said, then watched until Fallon let herself inside her apartment. Quickly stepping back inside, she closed and locked the back door, painfully aware that she wasn't brave enough to risk her daughter's happiness or her own fragile self-esteem if she were less than what Richard expected.

No matter how much Richard had done for her and Kayla, Naomi didn't want to be that vulnerable again. It wasn't fair to Richard to keep taking up his time when she knew she couldn't be the woman he deserved. She never knew how to act when he looked at her as if he wanted more than friendship, more than she was capable of giving him. She wasn't a whole woman.

Flicking off the light, she went to her bedroom to get undressed. The phone rang just as she stepped out of her shoes. Thinking it was Fallon, she reached for the receiver. "Hello."

Expecting to hear Fallon's voice, she frowned, then stiffened, her gaze going to the caller ID. She heard the dial tone the instant her gaze saw the blank readout. The caller had hung up. Her hand gripped the phone, then eased. She replaced the receiver and continued to undress.

Her ex had made her life miserable enough. He was not going to control her future. He might have had friends in the police department to uphold him in his wrongdoing, but she had friends now as well. Luke was checking on Gordon, and Luke was the best. Until she knew something differently, she was living her life the way she wanted. With one exception.

Richard wasn't going to be a part of her life any longer.

Chapter 7

The next day at work should have been one of the best ever for Naomi. Instead she was just as restless and as on edge as she'd been the night before. Kayla was the star, not only of the kindergarten wing, but of the entire school. She had the biggest grin on her face when they turned the corner Monday morning into their hallway and saw a giant poster of the cover of *The Guardian*.

However, instead of the little girl standing with her back to you and the wolf by her side as depicted on the cover illustration, they both faced forward. The art teacher had expertly captured Kayla's happy face. There was even a morning announcement on the PA system about her characterization in *The Guardian*. The unnerving part had come shortly before lunch when a reporter from the local newspaper had arrived to do a story on Kayla.

Naomi hadn't known anything about the school principal's "surprise." She'd actually thought of refusing to let Kayla be interviewed despite Principal

Crenshaw's enthusiasm. Naomi might have if Catherine and Luke hadn't shown up moments later.

Despite Naomi's talk of conquering her fear, she didn't want any mention of them in the newspaper. Catherine Stewart-Grayson was nationally known. Once her name was attached to the story, Naomi didn't have a doubt the story would be picked up by other media outlets.

The possibility of her ex or someone he knew seeing the article was too great a risk. He'd be enraged to see they were happy and doing well without him. She'd said as much to Catherine after the introductions.

"Look at Kayla," Catherine had said quietly from beside her.

Naomi had followed the direction of her friend's patient gaze. Kayla, a proud smile on her face, was talking to the reporter about the book and the little girl's courage not to fear the wolf.

"Animals are our friends," Kayla said. "They're afraid of us because sometimes we don't treat them as we should or because they aren't used to people. You aren't supposed to play with animals you don't know, but this time it was okay because the wolf didn't growl or try to hurt her."

The woman reporter, hunched down with a mike in her hand, smiled. "Did you learn not to play with animals from the book?"

"Dr. Richard," Kayla told her. "He's a veterinarian. Sometimes he lets me help feed and take care of the animals at his clinic. I'm going to be a veterinarian, too, when I grow up."

The reporter straightened, the mike from her

tape recorder moving to Catherine. "I'd say you picked the perfect little girl for your book."

"I couldn't agree more." Catherine held out her hand and Kayla grasped it without hesitation. "Not only is she courageous, she's kind and has a generous heart."

The reporter held the mike out to Naomi. "As her mother, what do you think of all the attention your daughter is receiving?"

Naomi could feel all the people standing around the hallway looking at her. Help came from Catherine's reassuring hand on her arm, and oddly Richard's comment long ago about her being a good mother.

"Kayla is the gift I never expected. I treasure her as any parent would." She'd placed her hand on Kayla's head. "I'm proud to be her mother."

Luke applauded; others joined in. By the time the applause had quieted, he was by Catherine's side. "Ms. Franklin," he said to the reporter. "I'm sorry to rush you, but we're going to have to cut this short. Cath has another engagement. I think a group photo in front of the artwork would be perfect."

Naomi was so relieved that the attention had shifted from her that she almost didn't see the mesmerizing effect Luke had on the reporter. For a moment, she didn't seem to be able to take her eyes off him. True, he was handsome, with broad shoulders and a muscular build, but those were the very attributes that made Naomi wary. His hands could easily inflict pain. Richard was lean and trim; his fingers narrow and gentle. Her mind jerked away from that line of thought.

"What a wonderful idea, Luke." Catherine motioned for the principal. "If you have signed permission slips from parents for photographs, I think it would be a good idea to have her classmates. Kayla is the star of the book, but each child is just as important."

"We certainly do," Principal Crenshaw quickly answered. "I include the form with each enrollment just in case opportunities like these come up. Ironically, Kayla is the only one without her permission slip signed. But since her mother is here, that shouldn't be a problem."

Naomi hadn't signed for this very reason, but one look at her daughter's face and she knew saying no was impossible. "It won't be a problem."

"Ms. Franklin?" Catherine asked, her grin all teeth.

The oblivious reporter finally stopped drooling over Luke. She didn't even have the grace to look embarrassed. "They're not part of the story."

"I beg to differ," Catherine said. "In the story, Kayla was trying to find her way back to her family and friends. Her classmates or the other staff members aren't in the book, but they'll shape and mold Kayla just the same. More important, her classmates shouldn't feel left out because they aren't in a book. They're just as important." Catherine glanced down at Kayla. "What do you think?"

"They're my friends," Kayla said softly. "Some of them came Saturday to see me. I'd like them to be in the picture."

"Ms. Franklin, I wouldn't mind stepping over to

Kayla's classroom and asking the teacher's assistant with them to let them join us," Luke said.

The reporter's frown morphed into a smile. "Would you, Mr. Grayson?" she asked, her voice dropping a husky octave, her hand on his muscled forearm. "It appears Mrs. Grayson has good instinct in other matters as well."

Luke turned away without comment. The woman's hand fell away, but her eyes stayed on him for seconds too long before she moved to the waiting photographer. If the woman had seen the expression on Catherine's face, she would have run for her car.

Instinctively Naomi placed her hand on Catherine's arm to soothe her. Luke loved her. They made a good team. Together they had effectively put the spin on the article they wanted: that all children mattered. Catherine knew better than anyone that Luke wouldn't cheat.

Naomi wouldn't have minded if her ex had cheated. That meant he would have stayed away from her.

Catherine leaned over and whispered, "She bats those eyes at him again, and I might not be responsible."

Naomi didn't know what to say. Catherine was always so calm. Naomi would have never thought she'd be possessive—least of all over a man. Catherine must have read her thoughts.

"There are men, and then there are those who pretend to be men," Catherine said softly. "Some you thank God daily for placing in your life; others you thank Him that they aren't."

Naomi shivered. She knew about the latter group all too well.

"You've had the bad," Catherine went on to say in a soft whisper. "Open your heart to the possibility that there are good men out there."

Naomi didn't answer as Kayla's classmates, with huge grins, came out of the classroom down the hallway in single file. However, this was one time she had no intention of taking her friend's advice.

She didn't want a man.

If that meant cutting Richard out of her life, so be it. She'd just have to deal with the loneliness that she already felt the best way she could.

Naomi's intent to end her friendship with Richard came at half past five that night. As soon as Kayla had eaten her dinner and finished her homework, she'd asked to go next door to tell Fallon about her day at school.

"When I come back, I'll call Dr. Richard. It's almost closing time at the clinic and he's always the busiest now," Kayla explained, proud that she remembered so much about his schedule.

Naomi might have been equally proud if the situation were different. She didn't have a clue how to tell her that they'd be seeing less of Richard, so she'd walked her to Fallon's apartment, then returned. To keep her mind off Richard, she called Sierra. She punched in the phone number without taking her seat.

"Hello," Sierra greeted, laughter in her voice.

Naomi wrapped an arm around her waist and

hoped she wasn't interrupting anything. "Hi, Sierra. It's Naomi. Did I catch you at a bad time?"

"Hi, Naomi," Sierra greeted, then asked a question of her own. "You haven't changed your mind, have you?"

"No." That was the one thing she was certain about. "I'd like to look at homes that need minor repairs. Maybe I could get a better deal," she said, trying not to recall that it was the idea of the man she planned to cut out of her life.

"Excellent idea. When Luke and Daniel's cabin was being built in the mountains, I helped," Sierra said. "A woman can build or repair just as well as any man."

Naomi thought she heard male laughter in the background. Probably Sierra's husband, Blade.

Regrettably, Naomi wasn't one of those women, but it was too late to think about that now. She'd never done any household repairs or renovations except paint Kayla's room when she was a baby. Her ex had gladly pointed out the glaring spots that needed another coat of paint when the paint dried, *and* the waste of money.

"I'll have you know that Aunt Felicia, Mama, and me nailed the last nails on the porch and put up the two lanterns on either side of the front door, so there," Sierra said with a laugh. "Excuse me, Naomi, my husband was trying to be funny."

More laughter and a woman's playful squeal, and something like "You'll pay for that" from Sierra.

Naomi's hand flexed on the phone. They were having fun, enjoying each other. She and her ex had never been that way. Without thought, a picture of her and Richard at the circus, laughing and having a good time with Kayla, popped into her mind.

"I'll add that to my data search. Anything else?"

"No." At least nothing she could think of.

"All right. I'll call you when I get a lead, but if you'll remember, I like to show clients more than one option at a time so they can compare. It might take several days," Sierra reminded her.

It had been the same way with her apartment search. It was easier to judge and make a decision when you saw one after the other. You didn't forget as much. "That's fine."

"Good. I'll make the appointments after six so Richard can come with us."

Naomi moistened her lips. "That's not necessary. I'm doing this on my own." There was a long pause. Naomi steeled herself for the inquisition.

Sierra spoke her mind. "You're the client."

The relief she expected to feel at not being questioned didn't come. All she felt was an aching loneliness and a sense that she'd betrayed a good friend. "Thank you. Good night."

"Call anytime. Good night."

Naomi placed the phone in the holder, easily seeing Blade and Sierra in each other's arms. They had each found that one person who loved them. Not every woman was as fortunate. She and Kayla were safe. Gordon was out of her life. She wouldn't be greedy for more. She'd be crazy to even think of letting another man into her life.

She started for the chair at the kitchen table to

finish grading papers. There never seemed to be enough time to do everything at school. The ringing phone stopped her. Her pulse raced on seeing YOUNGBLOOD'S VETERINARY CLINIC on the readout.

She wanted to ignore it, but that was what had landed her in the present predicament. Her hand trembling, she picked up the receiver. "Hello."

"Hi. How did your day go?"

Naomi's gripped the phone, started to ease into a chair, then straightened. She was too nervous to sit still. "Fine."

"I realize it's early, but does Sierra have any leads?"

"Not yet," she answered, reminding herself to keep her answers short.

"She will, and when she does, I'll help you check the places out."

Just thank him for his help in the past and tell him you don't need any assistance, she told herself, but she couldn't say the cold words aloud.

"How was the celebrity's day at school?"

"Wonderful. Thanks for calling, I better get back to grading papers."

There was a slight pause. "Sure. I'll call you tomorrow."

Here was her second chance. "I might be busy."

"Is everything all right?"

Naomi bit her lower lip, shoved her fingers though her hair. She was trying to push him out of her life and he was worried about her. She didn't want to hurt a man who had the bad judgment to see her as a whole woman, but she didn't see any other way. "Yes. I really have to go."

Another pause. "Good-bye. I'll call you tomor-row."

"Like I said, I might be busy."

"I'll call. Good-bye."

"Good-bye." Naomi hung up. He wasn't going to take the hint and back off. As long as he thought there was something wrong, he was going to be there for her. It didn't matter, she wasn't going to change her mind. This was for him. She couldn't be the woman he needed.

This was his fault.

Eyes closed, Richard leaned back in his chair behind his desk in his office. Last night he'd scared her. For that one critical moment he hadn't been able to keep his emotions under control. He'd let her see his desire for her, and it had cost him.

What the hell had he been thinking?

Too upset to sit, he pushed away from his desk and stood to pace his office. The receptionist had gone and he was alone. He stopped. But how much more alone was Naomi?

He shoved his hand over his head. He couldn't even be annoyed with her. Her reaction was in re-sponse to his. She wasn't ready to think about a man in her life. The problem was, he wanted so badly to be the man she ran to, the man who ban-ished her fears, the man who loved her so com-pletely she was never afraid for herself or Kayla again.

Love wasn't always enough. He only had to look at his cousin Lance to realize that. But sometimes it was. He'd been friends with the Graysons almost from the time Mrs. Grayson had moved with her five children from Oklahoma to teach at the university. He and Brandon had been in the same grade. Now all of them were married and as happy as they could be.

He recalled Naomi being concerned about Catherine but, as he'd told her, Luke would find a way to help her, just as he'd helped her care for Hero, the hybrid wolf she'd discovered near his cabin in the mountains. When the animal had been wounded, they'd brought him to the clinic. Coincidentally, their coming had also led to him meeting Naomi.

And now he'd lost her. *Only if you give up,* a small voice chided.

Richard pulled out his cell phone and looked at his contact list. Finding Sierra's number, he dialed and listened to her outgoing voice message. He tried her private number and listened to another recording that it had been disconnected. He should have guessed as much. Since her marriage to Blade, access to her wasn't as easy. Now that he had come to a decision, though, he wasn't giving up. He punched in another phone number he knew by heart.

"The Red Cactus," answered a cheerful voice.

"Brandon, please. Richard Youngblood calling."

"He's in the kitchen, Dr. Youngblood," came the quick response.

In the kitchen meant he wasn't to be disturbed. He might be cooking something you could pull him away from or he might not. Brandon could be temperamental at times, unless it was with Faith. "Never mind, good-bye."

Disconnecting, he called Casa de Serenidad. The

phone was picked up on the second ring. "Faith Grayson, please."

"May I ask what this is in regard to?" came the response.

"It's personal. Please just tell her it's Richard Youngblood. I was one of the guests Saturday afternoon at the restaurant for the Women's League."

"Please hold, Mr. Youngblood."

If Faith wasn't available, he wasn't sure of what to do next. He supposed he could drive out to the castle, as everyone referred to Sierra and Blade's home, and ask to be admitted, but security there was tighter than at the White House. It was iffy at best.

His last resort would be Mrs. Grayson. He didn't think he could sleep without knowing there was still a chance for him and Naomi. Showing up unannounced on her doorstep wouldn't help.

"Hi, Richard."

"Faith." He rounded his desk and picked up a pen. "I need Sierra's personal phone number, please."

There was a slight pause. "We were instructed never to give that out, but if it's important, I can call her."

"It is." He rubbed the back of his neck. "I called Brandon but he was in the kitchen. I didn't even think of asking them to disturb him."

Faith laughed softly. "Good thinking. It would have been bad for all parties. I'll call Sierra. Should she call back at this number?"

"Yes."

"All right. Bye."

"Bye." Richard disconnected the call and paced

some more until his office phone rang less than a minute later. Caller ID read UNKNOWN. "Hello."

"Hi, Richard, what's on your mind?" Sierra immediately asked.

He was just as forthright. "I want to be there to help Naomi find a house."

"Naomi said you were no longer involved," she said.

Richard hadn't thought it would be easy. Sierra wasn't a pushover. With her family background and married to a real estate mogul, she had to be her own woman. "She needs my help. I want to check out the house for her, make sure everything is on the up-and-up."

"That's what I and my top-notch inspector will be doing" was her crisp response.

He wasn't sure if he had insulted her or not. Sierra had a way of cutting a person down and they didn't even know it until later. "I'm not insulting your capability. It's just . . ." He blew out a breath. How to explain it? "I just want to help her."

"I have to adhere to my client's wishes."

His hand flexed on the phone. He'd call Mrs. Grayson. Perhaps she could persuade Sierra to help him. Mrs. Grayson had helped him once with Naomi, but at the time she'd also made it clear the reason wasn't because of him. She'd assisted Naomi and Kayla through the Women's League because they were in need.

"However, if I were to call you and tell you where I'd be and you just happened to drop by, that would be an entirely different matter."

Relief coursed through him. "Thank you."

"If I hadn't seen you with her and Kayla, I wouldn't be helping," she said. "Sometimes people need a little help in seeing what's in front of their eyes. Another lesson I learned from my mother. Good night."

"Good night, and thanks." Richard disconnected the phone and took a seat behind his desk. He hadn't missed the reference to her mother's matchmaking skills. Ruth Grayson had married off her five children just as she'd planned. He'd take all the help he could get. He still had a chance with Naomi, and this time, he'd make it count.

Naomi turned at the knock on the back door. Looking through the peephole, she saw Fallon and Kayla. Reluctantly, she opened the door. Kayla had a one-track mind when it came to something she wanted.

"Hey, you two." Bending, she kissed Kayla. She had a no-good man for a father, and the man she looked up to, she couldn't see again—all because of her mother's incompetence.

"Mama, I can call Dr. Richard now. His clinic is closed." Kayla started for the phone on the kitchen counter.

Naomi caught her by the arm before she had gone two feet. "You haven't said good-bye to Fallon or thanked her."

"I did, Mama, before she knocked on the door," Kayla replied, staring up at her mother with impatience. "We gotta call him. I want to tell him about today and ask about the puppies."

Naomi's hand flexed. Shoving Richard out of

her life also meant shoving him out of Kayla's. Why did her daughter have to pay again for her mother's mistakes?

"Kayla, you were going to show me the drawing you did in class," Fallon said in the ensuing silence.

"I almost forgot. I'm going to give it to Dr. Richard." She took off running for her bedroom.

Naomi didn't even think of reprimanding her for running in the house. Instead she shut her eyes in gratitude for the brief reprieve.

"From the look on your face and not wanting to call Richard, you've made up your mind," Fallon said softly.

"I have. It was doomed before it began."

"Not if you don't want it to be, Naomi. Give Richard a chance."

"It's better this way," she answered. Richard would soon forget her. One day they might even be friends again. This way was better for both of them. He'd never realize she wasn't a whole woman, and she wouldn't have to live with the disappointment and distaste on his face.

She heard the sound of running footsteps, then Kayla's excited voice. "Here it is! You think Dr. Richard will like it?"

Fallon squatted down to eye level, then carefully took the tablet offered her to study Kayla's pencil drawing of the cover of *The Guardian*.

'It's not the best one in my class, but my art teacher said the meaning and the heart in doing artwork is just as important," Kayla pointed out.

Naomi felt the lump in her throat just as she had the first time she saw the painting. In *The Guardian*, a male member of the search party looking for the lost little girl in the Sangre de Cristo Mountains was the one who'd found her. In Kayla's drawing, she'd added a man holding her hand with the wolf in the bushes watching them.

Naomi didn't have to be a psychiatrist to realize Kayla wanted a father, and had placed Richard in that role. That wasn't going to happen. Naomi would just have to fill Kayla's life with so much love that she wouldn't miss Richard.

"You did a great job, Kayla. He'll like it," Fallon said before pushing to her feet and going to the door.

"Wait for me," Naomi instructed Kayla before joining Fallon. "Take care and thanks for everything."

"We can finish the ice cream after Kayla goes to bed, if you'd like to talk," Fallon offered.

"Some things just aren't meant to be," Naomi answered.

Mouthing *I'm sorry,* Fallon left.

Naomi took her time locking the door to give herself a few moments to compose herself before facing her daughter. A lump formed in her throat. She accepted that it was because of the realization that Richard was no longer going to be a part of their lives, and what it would mean to her daughter.

Not for the first time, she wished she had been strong enough mentally to hit back at her husband at least once, to let him know what it felt like to be hurt. But she'd been a coward and was paying the price. Again. And so was her daughter.

"Hurry, Mama. When I finish telling him about

my day at school, do you think I should tell him about my drawing or wait until he comes to get me to go see the puppies?"

Kayla was so excited her words tripped over each other. This was going to be even harder than Naomi had imagined.

Sitting in one of the kitchen chairs, Naomi opened her arms. "Come here, sweetheart." Her daughter's hesitation was brief and telling. As soon as Kayla reached her mother, Naomi picked her up and hugged her.

"Do you think I could have one of those puppies? I'd take real good care of it."

Naomi grabbed at the reprieve. She sat Kayla away from her and stared down into her face. "The apartment doesn't allow pets, but I have a surprise for you. Sierra is going to be looking for a house for us. If she finds one, you'll have a backyard and a swing set. I'll think about getting you that puppy."

Her eyes rounded. "A house for real?"

"For real."

Kayla threw her arms around her mother's neck. "You're the best mother in the world."

She was trying to be the mother Kayla needed, Naomi thought. However, there were times like now when she had no idea of what to do or say. She searched her mind to find a way to tell Kayla, who had excitement dancing in her eyes, that they wouldn't be seeing Richard. She loved Richard, included him in her nightly prayers. Naomi knew he cared about Kayla as well. All but once—when she wanted to surprise Kayla with her own bedroom furniture—Kayla had been with them when they went anyplace.

"Mama, can we call Dr. Richard now?" Kayla asked impatiently.

Both of them had gotten used to speaking with him almost daily. "Not now, sweetheart. He's a busy man. We shouldn't take so much of his time."

"But he doesn't mind," Kayla insisted. "You remember he told us that he was never too busy if we needed him. Just like Miss Catherine told us."

Naomi wished for Catherine's expertise as a child psychologist now. She relied on love as she stared down into her daughter's expectant face. "I know, sweetheart, but we shouldn't be selfish. Other people need him as well."

Kayla's lowered her head, her chin almost touching her chest. "I guess."

Her heart breaking for her daughter, Naomi tried to smile. "Since you're finished with your homework, we can watch one of your favorite movies."

Kayla lifted her head, but her eyes remained sad. "Dr. Richard likes *Finding Nemo,* too."

Naomi's hands trembled. Although the Disney movie was an old one, Kayla's kindergarten teacher had showed them the film. Kayla had immediately fallen in love with the father clownfish searching for his son Nemo, and Nemo trying to find a way home. Despite her father's emotional abuse or perhaps because of it, Kayla wanted a father who would go to any lengths to find her, love her. Her drawing of Richard said as much.

It wasn't going to happen.

"I love you, Kayla."

Kayla's arms immediately went around her mother's neck. "I love you, too, Mama."

But she wasn't enough. Fighting the aching knowledge and the misery, Naomi stood with Kayla in her arms and started for the living room.

Chapter 8

Wednesday afternoon, Sierra knocked on Naomi's door precisely at six thirty as they'd agreed. Naomi stood in the middle of the living room, her stomach in knots. Homeownership was a huge step. As much as she wanted a house for her and Kayla, a nagging doubt that she wasn't ready for all the responsibilities it entailed kept circling her.

"It's Mrs. Sierra." Kayla straightened from shoving the curtain away from the front window. "She's here to show us a house. I could get a puppy if we have a house."

Her daughter hadn't forgotten about the puppy, but at least she was smiling today. She'd moped around the house and at school for the past two days. She missed Richard. If Naomi were truthful, she'd admit to missing him as well.

Richard was rock-steady and had a way of making her feel she could do anything. With her heart beating out of control, she could certainly use some of his encouragement now. It wasn't going to happen. She was on her own. She had to stiffen her spine and take control of her life.

Her shoulders straightening, she took a few calming breaths. It was past time she learned to stand on her own.

"Open the door, Mama," Kayla urged. Since her father's attempt to kidnap her, she no longer rushed to open the door—unless it was Catherine or Richard.

Naomi rubbed her damp palm down the side of her simple white sundress and finally opened the door. "Hi, Sierra."

"Good afternoon, Naomi, Kayla," Sierra greeted. "It's a beautiful day to go house hunting."

Kayla came to stand in front of Naomi. "When we find one, Mama says I might be able to have a puppy. Dr. Richard would help me find one." Briefly she tucked her head. "I don't think he'd be too busy."

All Naomi could do was place her hand on her daughter's shoulder. Somehow she'd make it up to her.

"Neither do I," Sierra said. "Richard is the kind of guy who would always be there for his friends." She caught the initial excitement of Kayla but, on the other hand, her mother looked scared to death. With any other person Sierra might have reached out to reassure her; she wasn't sure how Naomi would react. In her association she had seen the woman relax only a few times. And always Richard had been there.

"Did you change your mind about Richard coming with us?"

Naomi's big brown eyes widened. "No. He's busy."

"But I told you, Mama, he said if we needed him, he'd come."

Moistening her lips, Naomi caught Kayla's hand. "Kayla, we're not going to have this discussion again."

The young child tucked her head. "Yes, ma'am."

Naomi lifted hers, swallowed. "We're ready when you are."

"We'll take my car." Sierra stepped back outside. "There are three houses I want you to look at."

Naomi released Kayla's hand to lock the door, then tested the locks to ensure they were secure before turning to Sierra. "I know real estate is expensive in Santa Fe even with the recession. Like I told you, we don't need much, but I want Kayla to have a backyard with a swing."

"And a puppy." Kayla's head came up.

Sierra laughed. "It's on my list. This way. I couldn't find a spot closer."

"That's all right," Naomi told her. "Residents and guests disregard the parking policy all the time."

They were several feet from Sierra's BMW SUV when a black truck pulled into the parking lot and came to a screeching halt behind Sierra's vehicle. Before the driver could get out, two men came out of nowhere. One stepped in front of Sierra, the other converging on the driver's side of the Dodge Ram.

Naomi sucked in her breath, grabbed for Kayla, but her daughter was already moving toward the truck. "Dr. Richard!"

Sierra rolled her eyes, and tried without success

to step around Aaron's wide frame. "Paul. Aaron. You know Richard and his truck."

"He blocked you in. There could be someone crouched in the front seat or backseat."

"Aaron—"

"We stand or I call Rio."

Sierra blew out an irritated breath. And he'd call Blade. "Then check it out before you frighten my newest client."

"Sorry, Mrs. Reese," Aaron said, but he didn't sound sorry. "Paul?"

"Clear," the other man yelled.

Richard came around the front end of the truck, a hard frown on his face. "Sorry."

Sierra noted he had eyes only for Naomi. He didn't look any sorrier than Aaron had sounded. Richard she'd forgive.

"Dr. Richard." This time Kayla managed to pull free and, with her arms already open and upraised, ran to him. His face changed in the blink of an eye, warmth and love filling it.

"How's my best girl?" he asked, scooping up Kayla in his arms, the motion easy and practiced. Sierra smiled secretly. She just loved being right. Her mother wasn't the only matchmaker in the family.

"I told Mama you weren't too busy to come see us," she said. "See, Mama."

Naomi didn't know what to do or say. Her heart rate shifted into overdrive. She didn't want to care for him, get used to him. She didn't want him to want her. Caring about a person too much meant being vulnerable. She was doing this for both of them.

"Hello, Richard," Sierra greeted cheerfully. "I

guess you were in the neighborhood and decided to stop by."

"Yes. Hello, Naomi."

Hearing her name on his lips shouldn't make her want things better left unsaid. Naomi wanted to look away from him, but somehow she couldn't. She deserved his condemnation, yet that wasn't what she saw in his eyes. It was bewilderment, hurt. He should know better than anyone that she couldn't be what he wanted.

"You just caught us," Sierra said. "We were about to go look at houses."

Naomi's gaze jerked to Sierra. He'd want to go. He couldn't.

Richard hated the fear and uncertainty in Naomi's eyes. What gave him hope were the unguarded moments of happiness, and the frank female interest he'd seen in the past when she forgot to be scared and just enjoyed life. Those moments were precious few, and that's why he treasured them so much.

Her bastard of an ex-husband had abused her, made her afraid to trust, but Richard was a patient man, perhaps too patient. He usually backed down when she was unsure because he didn't want to make her uncomfortable, but those days were long gone.

"I'm glad I caught you," he said. "I told Naomi that you were the best."

"I try," Sierra said, then laughed.

Naomi swallowed. Her heart was thudding in her chest. She clenched the leather strap of her purse. Sierra and Fallon relished life while Naomi ran from it.

"Mama, you forgot to say hi to Dr. Richard," Kayla chided, one arm around his neck, the other holding Teddy.

Naomi felt her face heat. "Hello, Richard."

"You were going to let me go with you when Sierra took you to look at houses," he reminded her. "Looks like I arrived just in time."

Naomi's gaze darted to him then away. The disappointment in his voice was worse than if he'd yelled at her—something he'd never do. But better that than either of them wanting something that could never be. "Kayla and I have taken enough of your time. I didn't want to bother you."

"Have I ever given you that impression?"

The hurt in his voice was so unexpected her head came up. "N-no."

"And I never will." He turned to Sierra. "We'll follow you in my truck." Setting Kayla to her feet, he reached for Naomi's arm, his hand gently closing on her forearm.

He could blame Sierra's bodyguards or her ex, but Richard was afraid this time the blame rested squarely on his shoulders. And it made his heart clench to know Naomi was afraid of him, even if it wasn't physical

Her eyes widened, but she allowed him to take her arm and gently lead her to his truck. Feeling her shiver, he wanted to curse again. If he ever saw her ex again, he was taking a shot at the bastard.

Sierra turned to Aaron. "Mentioning Rio was low."

"And effective," he said, his expression unchanged.

Sierra's eyes narrowed. She'd push, but the results

would be the same. They didn't want to have a "chat" with Rio, and she didn't want to have one with Blade. "I don't suppose it would do any good to tell you to back off since Richard is going."

"It's nice you know us so well, Mrs. Navarone," Aaron said.

Sierra's brow arched. They might call Blade by his last name, but she preferred to be called Sierra, which they usually did. Addressing her as Mrs. Navarone was a none-too-subtle reminder of whom she was married to. She'd never forget that she was blessed to have the one man she'd love through eternity, but she did enjoy having her way and calling the shots.

"And since Dr. Youngblood will be following you, I don't suppose you'll go through any lights on caution," Aaron went on to say.

Sierra stuck her tongue in her cheek. "Just keeping you on your toes. It must be boring guarding me."

Aaron grunted. So did the man standing a short distance away.

Laughing, Sierra got inside her SUV. Richard backed up for her to pull out, but she waited until her two shadows were in the Mercedes. She never thought she'd get used to men watching her every move, but if it made Blade's life easier, she'd do it. And have a bit of fun in the process she thought, already planning to "test" her bodyguards before she returned home.

"I did a drawing for you, Dr. Richard. It's in my art book."

"You did? Thanks, pumpkin. I'll look at it when I take you and your mother home," Richard said. Out of the corner of his eye, he saw Naomi start.

"That isn't necessary," Naomi said, staring straight ahead at Sierra's SUV.

"I think it is." He glanced at the Mercedes keeping pace with him. He'd forgotten about the bodyguards. All he'd been thinking about was keeping Naomi from leaving him.

"How was school this week?" he asked.

"It was the best," Kayla said. "A lady came to the school to interview me and took a picture of me and my classmates and everything. I wanted to call and tell you about it."

Naomi threw a glance at Richard, swallowed and looked away. Kayla was innocently revealing her mother's lies.

"I read the article," he said, signaling to turn behind Sierra. "You did a good job on the interview. I was proud of you."

"Fallon helped me cut out the article. I saved it for you. I just knew that you wouldn't be too busy and come back."

Naomi had always wanted Kayla to be open, proud of her intellect and vocabulary. She hadn't thought it would come back to haunt her.

Richard glanced over to see Naomi's fingers digging into the purse in her lap. He had to grip the steering wheel to keep from reaching over and placing his hand on hers, telling her it would be all right.

"How are the puppies?" Kayla asked.

"Getting fat," he said, pulling up behind Sierra.

Her bodyguards' car pulled in front of her. She started to get out, but one of the man reached her first. He could see her roll her eyes when Aaron held out his hand. After a few seconds, she placed something in his hand.

Going up the cracked sidewalk, he opened the front door and went in. The other man hung back on the sidewalk. They weren't taking any chances.

Richard didn't mind the wait while they checked out the house. "With your mother's permission, you'll have to come see them."

"Mama said if we get a house she'd think about letting me have a puppy." Kayla unbuckled her seat belt and scooted forward. "I told her I'd take real good care of it."

"Like Teddy, a puppy would be happy to come live with you."

Aaron came back to the front door, handed Sierra the key, then stood to one side of the wide porch.

Unbuckling his seat belt, Richard opened the back door and helped Kayla out. Naomi was already standing on the sidewalk.

"This is the first of the three houses today," Sierra said as she met Naomi on the sidewalk. "It's a three-bedroom, one-and-a half bath, Seventeen hundred square feet. It's in need of the most repairs, but it's the least expensive."

Naomi could feel Richard watching her. Usually he wasn't so obvious.

"Let's go see, Mama."

"I like a woman who knows what she wants," Sierra said with a laugh. "Come on, Kayla. Let's go see if you and your mother like this one." Kayla and Sierra disappeared inside the stucco-and-wood house.

Naomi started after them, very much aware that Richard was behind her. She should be excited about the house, but what kept coming back were the lies she'd told her daughter.

"I think we're falling behind."

She turned. It had to be said. He could have outed her and he hadn't. "Thank you."

"I want what's best for you and Kayla. Remember that."

"Come on, Mama." Kayla came back to the front door. "There's a fireplace in here."

"We could roast marshmallows," Richard called, stepping around Naomi and going into the house.

Standing there, she wasn't sure why she felt so alone. This was what she'd wanted.

"Coming?" Richard asked, one foot on the porch, and one on the cracked sidewalk.

"Yes." Naomi hurried into the house.

None of the houses was what Naomi was looking for. She almost hated to tell Sierra. She just had a vague idea of what she wanted. She was horrible at decorating so she couldn't visualize how her furnishings would look or how to turn the place into something warm and inviting, like Catherine's house. "I'm sorry, but none of them seem right. They're in my price range, but . . ." Her voice trailed off.

"Don't worry about it," Sierra said as they stood in front of the last house. "You'll know it when you walk inside. Sometimes it's fast, but it could take months. We'll find the house. I want you to find a house that you and Kayla will love, not one that you'll regret buying."

"And a place for a puppy," Kayla interjected.

Sierra smiled. "You remind me of me when I was your age."

Naomi was a bit startled by the compliment. Her facial expression must have showed it.

"She isn't swayed from what she wants," Richard explained.

"Exactly." Sierra hugged her iPad case to her chest. "I had a lioness for a mother and four strong brothers. As the baby of the family, I had to assert myself."

"You were headstrong and would dare the devil if I remember correctly," Richard reminded her. "You still are."

"Yes, I was and look how fantastic my life turned out." Sierra bent to eye level with Kayla. "Always go after what you want. It makes life more interesting."

"Yes, ma'am," Kayla said.

Naomi wasn't sure if she liked the advice Sierra gave her daughter or not, but considering how Naomi had tried to please everyone at the expense of her own happiness, perhaps Sierra's way was the best. More than anything, Naomi wanted her daughter to be happy.

Sierra straightened and turned to Naomi. "I can take you back to your apartment."

"Thanks—"

"No, Mama," Kayla interrupted, no longer smiling as she stared up at her mother. "Dr. Richard is going to take me to see the puppies. Remember?"

"I can't compete with that." Sierra laughed. "Good-bye."

Naomi watched Sierra walk down the sidewalk. All she had to do was say something. She couldn't. Kayla wasn't going to suffer because of her mother's insecurities.

"Come on, Kayla." Richard held out his hand. Kayla immediately grasped it. "Let's get you buckled up."

Once again, he walked away, leaving Naomi behind. Slowly she followed, trying to figure out why he was keeping his distance from her. Worse, since that was exactly what she wanted, why was it making her so unhappy?

Opening the front passenger door, she climbed inside. He seemed more interested in Kayla than her. He'd moved on. She should be glad, she thought as he pulled away from the sidewalk.

Somehow, she wasn't.

Richard was totally aware of the furtive glances Naomi keep throwing at him, her furrowed brow, as if she was trying to figure him out. Good. Perhaps giving her the space she obviously wanted was making her realize that that wasn't really what she wanted. Hovering over her certainly hadn't helped.

Unlocking the door to his clinic, he snapped on the light and shut off the alarm. Kayla had eagerly followed him. Naomi looked as if she wasn't sure what to do next.

"You can wait here, if you want," he told Naomi.

"Don't you want to see the puppies, Mama?"

Kayla asked. "You could get one, too, so it would have someone so it wouldn't be lonely when I'm at school."

A small smile curved the corners of Naomi's mouth. She stepped inside and brushed her hand across her daughter's head. "The puppy isn't definite and I think one is enough—if I decide to let you have one."

"Yes, ma'am." Kayla's head fell.

"It wouldn't hurt to go look, I suppose," Naomi said.

Kayla's head lifted. She grabbed her mother's hand. "Mama is going with us, Dr. Richard."

"This way." He went to the back were the animal cages were kept. He didn't have any animals boarding at the time. Opening the door, he turned on the lights. "The mom and her litter are in the second cage."

Releasing her mother's hand, Kayla rushed to the cage, her eyes wide as she sank to her knees. "Oh, Mama, aren't they beautiful?"

Naomi edged closer. "And just as fat as Richard said."

She'd said his name. *Progress.*

The five mixed-breed puppies were snuggled against their mother, sleeping. He'd told Kayla about the puppies, not that the mother had been tied to the front door of his clinic in labor. It was well known around town that he'd take in pets the owner no longer wanted. The inhumane treatment of humans of one another and of animals never ceased to amaze and anger him.

"Can I hold one?" Kayla asked.

"When they're older. Now it's best that they're handled as little as possible."

Kayla turned her attention back to the puppies. "They don't have a daddy, either."

Naomi gasped, bit her lower lip. It took considerable control for Richard not to pull her into his arms. He knew, more than anything, she blamed herself for marrying the wrong man. She believed that she'd failed Kayla as a mother.

"They don't need a daddy when they have a good mother. She loves and takes care of them," Richard said.

"Just like me and Mama." Kayla said, then stared back at the puppies. "Can I come see them again?"

"Anytime," Richard said.

"Kayla, we need to go so you can get to bed." Naomi held out her hand. Kayla was slow in getting up to take it.

"We're ready to leave," Naomi said quietly.

"I'll follow you to the front and set the alarm." Richard watched Naomi hurry to the front. She was backing away again. It wouldn't do her any good. He had no intention of letting her push him out of her or Kayla's life.

As soon as Richard stopped his truck in front of her apartment, Naomi unbuckled her seat belt, got out, and opened the back door to get Kayla. Her hand firmly in her daughter's, she hurried to her door and unlocked it. "Thank you, Richard. I need to get Kayla her bath and into bed for school tomorrow."

"I'm not sleepy," Kayla wailed.

"You will be." Naomi said gently urging Kayla inside, then turning to face Richard. "Good night."

"It's not over," Richard said, then he returned to his truck.

She gulped and hurried inside. By the time she heard his engine starting, Naomi was halfway across the living room with Kayla.

"I wanted to show him the picture I drew," Kayla protested.

"You can when you see him again," Naomi said.

"When is that?" Kayla wanted to know.

"I'm not sure. Now let's get your bath and into bed." Naomi was relieved Kayla didn't ask any more questions, because she didn't have any answers for either of them.

Naomi had another restless night. She might not want Richard in her life, but her subconscious certainly liked having him around. She freely admitted as the day wore on that forgetting Richard was going to be more difficult than she had imagined. She decided work would help and kept busy during the day at school.

Naomi had her arms full of material to be copied and her mind on the coming science fair when she entered the main office. Science fairs were always hectic, but fun. Naturally, Kayla wanted to do one on animals. Which reminded her that they needed to stop by the store to pick up the supplies for Kayla's project. Thank goodness the last hour of the day was her planning period and she could work on getting the never-ending paperwork done.

She smiled at the secretary and clerk as she passed

the curved desk counter. Neither acknowledged her. Their gaze was fixed on the door leading into the school clinic. Puzzled, she glanced in that direction to see the broad-shouldered and hulking build of a man, and a petite woman.

"You're just stupid!" yelled the man.

Naomi froze, clutching the books and papers to her. The angry voice hurtled her back into the past.

"I'm sorry, Jessie. I just forgot to give the school the new phone number."

"Forgot!! You're as useless as they come!" the man continued. "You don't work! All you have to do is keep the house and take care of one child, and you can't even do that!"

"Your daughter only had a slight temperature elevation," the school nurse said soothingly. "I have your new phone number now, so if anything else comes up, I should be able to reach you. I'll also give it to Lisa's teacher and place it on her record. It shouldn't happen again."

"Damn right!" the man yelled.

Seconds later, a man in slacks, a blue shirt, and a tie rushed out of the office with a small child shivering in his arms. A woman half his size and a foot shorter, dressed in a long-sleeved blouse and jeans, followed. Her head down, she barely managed to catch the closing door before it hit her in the face. She glanced back toward the desk, then hurried after her husband and daughter.

"Scumbag!" the secretary said when they were out of sight. "He wouldn't talk to me that way."

"She should have put him in check long ago," commented the clerk. "She allows it."

The school nurse came out of the clinic. "She probably doesn't have a choice since she doesn't work. Their daughter appears well cared for. This is the first time I've seen her in the clinic, and she knew her grandmother's phone number, which is a good sign."

The secretary grunted. "I'd be in jail if Frank had treated me that way."

It was on the tip of Naomi's tongue to ask them if they knew what it was to live in fear—how the man you thought you loved could destroy your self-esteem, your courage.

"Mrs. Reese, I see you're just as shaken," the nurse commented.

Naomi was, but not for the reason they thought. They knew she was divorced, but not the shameful reason. "She needs help," Naomi finally managed.

"God helps those who help themselves," the secretary quipped, then reached for the ringing phone.

"Until she asks for help, there's nothing we can do." With a wan smile, the nurse returned to her office.

"You want me to run those copies for you, Mrs. Reese?" the clerk asked.

For a long second Naomi stared at the young clerk. The altercation between the woman and her abusive husband was forgotten. It saddened Naomi as much as it angered her that no one in the office felt the need to help the terrified woman. None of them had ever been in a position where they felt helpless and alone. The secretary was a widowed grandmother. Her desk was crowded with pictures of her children and grandchildren. The clerk, as far as Naomi knew, was single, but looking. The nurse was happily married to a fireman. They had five happy children.

Naomi didn't think any of the three women knew what it felt like to be scared and ashamed because the man you once loved, a man you thought loved you, thought more of the dirt on his shoes than he did of you. You didn't reach out because you were scared and felt trapped. Worse—you had done it to yourself by falling for the wrong man.

"Mrs. Reese?"

"Thank you." Giving the clerk the material, Naomi hurried back to her classroom. Closing the door after her, she took a seat behind her desk, something she seldom did while teaching. Her legs couldn't support her any longer.

She was trembling and she wasn't sure if it was due to anger at the man, pity for the cowed woman, annoyance at the staff's dismissive reaction, or the harsh reminder that she had once stood in the woman's shoes.

Naomi hoped she would have finally gotten the courage to leave, but if Gordon hadn't been so jealous of Kayla and posed a very real threat to her, Naomi wasn't sure. She'd wanted too badly to be loved, to make her parents proud that at least they could say their daughter had a good marriage like the children of their friends and associates.

Even when she and Kayla reached Santa Fe and needed help, she'd been too scared, too prideful to ask. Thankfully, Catherine had understood that fear. So had Richard. Neither had judged her.

Life had given her some hard knocks, but it had

also given her good friends and a beautiful daughter. She'd forever be grateful for both.

The strident sound of the alarm clock on her desk startled her. She always set it five minutes before the dismissal bell rang. She and the other kindergarten teachers walked their students from gym to the front of the school for dismissal. There were too many children for the coach to supervise, plus the teachers knew the parents or siblings and made sure they didn't leave with the wrong person.

Shutting off the alarm, Naomi rose from her chair and left her classroom. Deep in thought, she almost bumped into Bess Hightower, Kayla's teacher.

"I'm sorry, Bess. I wasn't looking where I was going."

The usual sunny smile didn't appear on Bess's pretty face. This was her first year teaching. She loved her students, and was always trying to come up with innovative ways for them to learn.

Naomi was immediately concerned. Bess had a peer partner, but Naomi wanted to help if she could. No matter how much you loved teaching, it could be daunting at times. "Bess, what's the matter?"

Bess glanced around the hall, then took Naomi's arm and led her back into her classroom. "It's about Kayla."

"Kayla?" Fear clutched at Naomi's heart. "What is it?"

"She's changed from the bright, outgoing child she was since the day after the interview. At first I thought it was because she missed being the center of attention, but I soon dismissed that. She's always ready to help other students," Bess explained.

"She doesn't participate in class, mopes during recess. The only times she eats is when you come over during lunch."

One fear receded, but another took its place. Naomi should have been more watchful.

"Then yesterday she was her old self. This morning she's back moping." Bess folded, then unfolded, her arms. "She's one of the brightest and most outgoing of my students. I hope you realize I'm not prying, but has there been a change in her or your personal life?"

Richard. Naomi's stomach knotted.

The dismissal bell sounded, giving Naomi a reprieve. "Thank you, Bess. We need to pick up our students." Not waiting for an answer, Naomi hurried out of her room and down the hall to the gym. The other kindergarten teachers were already there.

Naomi's gaze searched the row of students lined up until she located Kayla. Her head was lowered, her small shoulders slumped. Usually she watched for Naomi and gave her a discreet wave and a huge smile since they were supposed to remain quiet and at attention.

Not today, and Naomi knew exactly the reason. Her heart ached for her daughter.

Not even the strident whistle of the coach caused Kayla to lift her head. Row by row, the students came to the door to meet their teacher. Naomi positioned herself so she'd be closer to Kayla when she passed.

"Kayla?"

Her daughter's head came up, a pitiful excuse

for a smile on her face. "Hi, Mama. I'll wait with Ms. Hightower."

Her teacher was right. How had Naomi missed her daughter's unhappiness that morning? The answer was painful to admit. She'd been too busy thinking about herself. All she could do was stand aside when she wanted so desperately to hold Kayla and tell her how much she loved her.

Her students were called next. She led them outside, her mind in a whirl. Her daughter was hurting. The thought made her throat sting with unshed tears, her stomach knot. It was difficult to keep her own smile as she released her students to siblings, sitters, or relatives.

When the last student was released to her grandmother, Naomi quickly went to Kayla. She ached to pick her up. Instead she placed her hand on her shoulder and lifted her troubled gaze to Bess. "Thank you."

"Bye, Kayla. See you tomorrow."

"Good-bye, Ms. Hightower."

Naomi and Kayla walked in silence back to her classroom. "How was your day?" she asked, trying to find her way.

"Okay." Shrugging, Kayla stared down at her feet. "Mama, could we go see the puppies? Maybe they're awake."

Her daughter hadn't mentioned the puppies since yesterday. Naomi squatted down in front of her daughter and gently placed her hands on her shoulders. "You want to see Richard as well, don't you?"

Kayla glanced away, an evasive action that wasn't lost on her mother. She'd done the same thing when faced with a situation she wasn't sure how to handle. "You said we shouldn't bother him."

"I'll let you in on a secret. Mommies aren't always right," Naomi said, trying to smile and put her daughter more at ease. "Do you want to see Richard?"

Kayla's head slowly lifted. "The last show-and-tell is next week and I thought I could ask him to come. Maybe . . . if . . . if he wasn't too busy."

Naomi's heart ached. She'd promised to keep her daughter safe and happy. She'd broken that promise. Again.

Never again, if she could help it. She wasn't going to make her daughter suffer because of her unwanted response to Richard. Regardless of how scared she was of what was developing between them, Richard was a good man. "I think I might like to see the puppies again myself."

Kayla's head lifted. Her eyes were huge in her face. "You do?"

"I do," Naomi told her, happy to see Kayla smile for real. "And you can ask Richard about the show-and-tell."

"You think he'd come?"

"If at all possible, he'll come." Naomi came to her feet and reached for her tote. "Let's go see the puppies, and you can ask him."

Chapter 9

No more, Naomi decided on the drive to Richard's clinic. She wasn't going to let her fear take any more from her daughter. Somehow she'd get Richard to understand that anything more than friendship between them was out of the question.

She frowned and bit her lip as she recalled that yesterday he hadn't seemed to pay any attention to her. Perhaps she had misread him. Her ex was the only man she had seriously dated—and look where that had gotten her.

Her hands clamped and unclamped on the steering wheel. She might have jumped to the wrong conclusion. Her face flushed with embarrassment at the thought. But a quick glance in the rearview mirror at Kayla's happy expression and she stiffened her shoulders. She had to be strong enough to face her doubts and fears if she wanted Kayla to have a normal, happy childhood, and for now that meant having Richard in her life.

Putting on her turn signal, Naomi pulled into

the parking lot of Richard's clinic. There were several cars already there. "Looks like he has a lot of patients."

"He always has time for us."

Kayla said the words with such surety that Naomi smiled. Richard and Sierra might be right. Kayla could be stubborn, but that was all right with her mother—up to a point. No one was going to run over her daughter.

Unbuckling her seat belt, Naomi got out of the SUV. Kayla almost beat her out of her seat in the back. She reached for Kayla's hand. "Remember, we're just looking." Kayla nodded, and they started for the front door.

Richard was having one of those nonstop days that tested his patience. Besides his scheduled appointments, he'd had to work in emergency cases. He usually didn't mind, but today he was having a difficult time being the calm, unflappable doctor. At least this was his last emergency patient—unless another patient came in. He wanted to vent his anger, brood because Naomi had made it clear she didn't want him in her life any longer. Still, his hands were gentle and steady as he examined the Lab's foreleg.

"I don't think it's broken. An X-ray will tell for sure."

"What a relief, Dr. Youngblood." Tears filled Mrs. Sams's eyes. "I didn't know his paw was under the rocking chair."

Richard curved his arms around her thin shoulder. King had been a patient of his since he was a puppy, and the companion of his eighty-year-old owner, a widow of ten years. The thought of causing injury to her beloved pet was heart-wrenching to her. "It's not your fault. Accidents happen."

"That won't be happening again. I've already moved the chair into the guest bedroom." Her arthritic hand smoothed over the dog's shiny coat. "Dr. Richard is going to take care of you, and then we're going to stop by the store and get you a nice steak."

Richard didn't try to dissuade her. King and Mrs. Sam needed to do a bit of celebrating. "I'll get my assistant for the X-ray." Opening the door, he stepped into the hallway and came to a dead stop.

"Dr. Richard!" Kayla took off running.

Richard dragged his eyes from Naomi long enough to catch Kayla as she wrapped her arms around him as best she could. Her eyes wide and happy, she looked up at him.

"We came to see the puppies. Mama said she'd like to see them again, too."

Richard lifted his gaze to see Naomi slowly make her way toward him, as if she wasn't sure of her reception. "Hi."

"Hi," she said. Her smile kept sliding away. She had a death grip on the ring of her car keys.

"Naomi?"

She realized on seeing him how much she'd missed him. She could relax around him. He'd given her so much, and she had given little in return.

"I have a patient."

She felt a stab of disappointment and wondered if that was how he felt when she pushed him out of her life. "Oh."

"If it wasn't important, I'd go with you. I was about to do an X-ray."

He read her too well. She was so flustered, she didn't know how to respond.

"You have to take care of the animals that are sick," Kayla said.

"We can come back," Naomi quickly said.

Richard absorbed her statement, and wondered what had happened that she was no longer running from him. "Not necessary. You know the way, and Kayla knows she can't reach inside the cage." He stared down at Kayla. "Right?"

She nodded, then straightened. "I remember."

His hand swept over her head. She was so easy to love and so accepting of affection. He wished her mother was the same. Naomi's smile slipped as he stared at her, and she bit her lip. She reached for her daughter.

"Come on, Kayla. Richard has a patient to see."

Kayla's gaze went from her mother back to Richard. "Before we go, I want to ask you something."

Richard had to smile. Kayla was certainly persistent about having a puppy. "Sure, but the final decision rests with your mother."

"Oh. All right," she murmured, her head falling.

Richard frowned. Kayla usually bounced back.

"His patient is waiting." Taking Kayla's hand, Naomi passed Richard on the way to the back.

All Richard could do was stare after them and wonder what he'd missed.

Kayla sat cross-legged in front of the cage and stared at the sleeping puppies.

Naomi squatted beside her. "They're pretty cute."

"Yes, ma'am."

Polite and disinterested. Naomi had seen the change come over Kayla the moment Richard said Naomi had the final decision. Naomi could protect herself, but the price was too high. Clearly Richard ranked over a puppy. High praise indeed.

"You were going to ask Richard about the show-and-tell."

Kayla leaned over farther. "You said we shouldn't bother him."

Translation: You'd say no. Her arm went around Kayla's small shoulders. She was too young to have gone through so much, then Naomi remembered the children—babies actually—who had gone through so much more. "I might be wrong, but I think Richard was talking about my having the final decision on you having a puppy, not about you asking him to come to your show-and-tell."

Kayla's head snapped up. Naomi's heart squeezed on seeing the hope in her daughter's eyes.

"For real?"

"For real." Naomi pulled Kayla closer. "You can ask him before we leave."

Kayla was quiet for a few seconds, as if absorbing the information. "All right."

Naomi gazed down at her daughter, then noticed movement in the cage. "The puppies are waking up."

Kayla straightened and scooted closer on her knees, her small hands wrapped around the bars. "Mama?"

"Yes, honey."

"The brown one trying to lie on his mother's face sure is cute. He's the same color as Teddy."

Naomi laughed. She could almost hear the wheels turning in Kayla's head as she tried to think of ways to get that puppy. She was her happy self again, and Naomi planned to keep her that way.

Richard paused before opening the door to the kennel. He didn't know what to expect. Worse, he wasn't sure he could help make it better for mother or daughter. Kayla might be a child, but she often took her cues from her mother. Naomi probably didn't even realize how much Kayla watched her. Both had been through a lot. He'd do anything to keep them happy—anything but bow gracefully out of their lives. They needed him as much as he needed them.

It was clear by the strained smile earlier on Naomi's face that she hadn't wanted to come. It had to be more than Kayla's desire to see the puppies. Whatever it was, he just hoped and prayed he could help.

Finally opening the door, he was surprised to hear the joined laughter of mother and daughter. For a moment, he simply stared at Naomi, her pretty face animated and carefree. He'd seldom been able to watch her without worry of making her nervous or, worse, letting her see how deeply he cared for her.

He wasn't used to hiding his feelings or being secretive, but he had little choice. Naomi had already showed him that she didn't want anything more than friendship. He wasn't about to mess up.

He wasn't aware of making a sound, but he

must have. Naomi's shoulders tensed, her laughter abruptly stopped. Slowly her head turned. When their gaze met, he saw uncertainty, and breathed a sigh of relief that he didn't see fear. He let the door close. "The puppies are showing off."

Kayla giggled and pointed to the cage. "They're playing over their's mother's head."

"As long as they're near, she doesn't mind." Richard squatted on the other side of Kayla. "A mother's love is a strong bond. She'll do anything to make sure they're safe and happy."

"Daddies don't," Kayla said softly, her smile fading as she lowered her head.

He heard Naomi's gasp, saw the regret, the sheen of tears in her eyes. She'd put the blame on herself as usual instead of the bastard who had abused her and didn't want his child. He ached for both of them. "It's never the mother's or the child's fault. It's his that he can't appreciate what a wonderful gift he has." Richard circled Kayla's shoulder with his arm.

She leaned against him. His arm tightened.

Unlike her mother, Kayla reached out for love and acceptance. Her father's violence hadn't made her afraid to trust as it had her mother. Naomi had told him about the abuse, but he was sure she'd left out a lot of details. Out of the corner of his eye he saw Naomi blink back tears. He wished he could pull her to him as well. They'd both feel better.

She needed hugs. She needed him. The hard part was convincing Naomi.

"After I finish here, why don't I pick you two up

and we go to grab a burger at Brandon's restaurant?"

"I don't—"

"Please, Mama," Kayla interrupted, scooting over to her mother. "I haven't asked him yet."

Indecision flickered in Naomi's eyes. Love won. "It's a school night. We'll meet you there."

He'd accept her decision. "I'll call Brandon and get reservations." He stood, not wanting to give her time to suggest a fast-food place. Regardless of it being a Thursday night, the restaurant was usually packed. He held out his hand to help her up. "I'll walk you to the front."

He could tell she wanted to ignore his hand, and thought she might. He felt like shouting for the small victory when she lightly placed her fragile hand in his. He released her as soon as she was upright. He wasn't taking any chance that he'd do something to make her uneasy again and she'd back out.

"Thank you," she said, meeting his gaze

"Anytime." For some reason, he felt he'd won a major victory. "I'll make the reservations for six thirty."

Naomi reached for Kayla's hand. "Good-bye."

"Bye, Dr. Richard." Kayla took a step with her mother, then pulled away to stare up at Richard with wide, questioning eyes. "You won't forget, will you?"

Frowning, he hunkered down in front of Kayla until they were eye level. Naomi might question people's word, but never her daughter. "I'll always tell you the truth no matter what. I keep my word. If I can't make it because of an emergency, I'll call like I did Saturday. You can always count on me."

She threw her free arm around his neck and squeezed. His arms went around her, and he felt her tremble. What was going on? It couldn't be Naomi's ex, but whatever it was, it must be super important. His questioning gaze went to Naomi, but she glanced away. He straightened. "See you at six thirty."

Naomi nodded. "Come on, sweetheart."

Richard followed them out and watched Naomi's SUV pull off. Before the night was over he was going to find out what had put that shattered look in Naomi's eyes, and the miserable one in Kayla's.

"Kayla, what did you do to your hair?" Naomi asked on entering Kayla's room and seeing that her daughter had unplaited her neat hair; it was now sticking up all over her head.

Her daughter turned from the small floor mirror in the corner, her lower lip trembling, her hairbrush clenched in her small first. "I'm sorry. I tried to fix it the way you do. I wanted to look nice so Dr. Richard would say yes."

If he didn't, Naomi would . . . Her thoughts halted as she saw a tear glisten in Kayla's eyes. "Of course he'll say yes." Crossing the room, she brushed Kayla's hair into neat ponytails.

"I thought I could do it."

"That's all right. I like combing your hair." Tying yellow ribbon over the rubber bands securing

Kayla's hair, Naomi stared down into her daughter's face. "You look very pretty."

"You think Dr. Richard will think so?" Kayla asked, the worry still in her face.

"I do," Naomi answered, trying not to feel hurt that she wasn't enough. "Why don't you get Teddy and we can leave."

Kayla picked up Teddy, then adjusted his yellow tie. "We're ready. Mama. You only had to help us a little."

"Because you're growing up to be a big girl." Naomi went to her room for her handbag and car keys. Kayla was with her every step. "We can't stay long."

"But I have to ask him tonight. We have to turn in the name tomorrow," Kayla said, her eyes huge.

"I know, honey." Kayla's section was the last one in the kindergarten class to have show-and-tell. "Let's go before we're late."

Naomi had to circle the block twice before finding a parking space near the entrance. Each time they passed Richard's car, Kayla became more anxious. She was practically running when they reached the restaurant. As expected, there was a line of people waiting to get inside.

Naomi took Kayla's hand and went to the hostess stand. "I'm with Dr. Youngblood. He had reservations."

"Certainly. He's already seated. This way."

They followed the pretty young hostess to a small table near the back of the restaurant. Richard rose when they neared.

"Hi." He pulled out Naomi's chair, then helped Kayla settle Teddy in a waiting booster seat, then held the chair for her. "You and Teddy look extra special tonight."

Kayla beamed. "Mama helped with my hair, but I did the rest."

"You both did a good job." He retook his seat. "I was going to give you a few more minutes, then go out and let you have my space. Parking is worse than usual."

"We managed," she said, feeling nervous and off.

Richard picked up his menu. "I already know what I want. How about you, Kayla?"

She opened her mouth, then sat back in her chair. Instantly concerned, Richard and Naomi both asked in unison, "What is it?"

"I got ketchup on my top the last time we were here and I had french fries with my hamburger." Her lower lip trembled. "I want to ask you something and I want to look nice."

A lump lodged in Naomi's throat. Tears crested in her eyes as Richard rose and crouched by Kayla's chair.

"Pumpkin, you'll always look nice to me. I spill things on my clothes, too. But if you had ketchup on your head and mustard dripping from your chin, it wouldn't change how much I care about you, always remember that. Now give me a hug and ask me whatever you want."

Kayla threw her arms around him and just held on for a long moment before straightening. She glanced at her mother, who nodded, then looked at Richard. "My class has show-and-tell next week. It can be a relative or an important person in your life. I wanted to ask you if you'd come."

Richard fought the lump in his throat to get the words out. "I'd be honored."

Kayla's eyes widened with happiness. She threw her arms around him again. "I know you're busy like Mama said, but I thought you could come during your lunchtime. It's Monday morning at eleven. Right before my class has lunch. Mama wouldn't mind packing you a lunch, would you, Mama?"

Naomi sniffed. "No, I wouldn't."

"Would it be all right if I ate lunch with you and your class?" he asked. He remembered that the times his parents had eaten lunch with him in elementary school were pretty amazing.

Her eyes rounded to the size of saucers. "No one has ever eaten lunch with me before."

"Then I'd be honored to be the first," Richard said.

"Wow!" Almost jumping in her seat, she turned to Teddy. "You hear that, Teddy? Dr. Richard is going to eat lunch with me and everything."

Chuckling, Richard took his seat. He glanced over at Naomi, who mouthed *thank you*. For some reason, it annoyed him. Did she honestly think he'd say no? "Kayla, ready for that hamburger with mustard and french fries with ketchup?"

"Yes, sir," Kayla said.

Richard signaled the waitress. He knew it was rude not to ask Naomi if she had decided, but at the moment he wasn't too thrilled with her. "We're ready to order. This pretty young lady and I will have the Kobe burger medium-well with mustard on the side, and lots of french fries. She'll have orange soda. I'll have Pepsi." He closed the menu.

The waitress's attention shifted to Naomi. "And you, ma'am?"

"House salad with vinaigrette."

"But Mama, you always get the hamburger, too," Kayla said.

Naomi's smile felt stiff on her face. "I'm not very hungry." She handed her menu to the waitress.

"Now, Kayla, tell me more about the show-and-tell." Richard said, shifting his attention to Kayla. He would not be moved by the wounded look on Naomi's face. It was about time she learned to trust him. If she didn't, there was nothing to build on and he was wasting his time.

Naomi had never felt so conflicted or unsure of herself in her life the next day at work. She was in a pensive mood and couldn't shake it. She should be happy instead of moping. Her daughter was ecstatic. Sierra had called that morning excited about a house that had just come on the market. She wanted them to see it early Saturday morning before anyone else snapped it up. Naomi's evaluation scores earlier with the principal were the highest possible, and she had been recommended for her contract to be renewed.

Her life was moving forward, so why did she want to put her head down on her desk and bawl?

Even her students noticed she wasn't her usual self. They worked quietly in their groups, didn't jump to get in line for lunch, and marched like little soldiers to the cafeteria . . . which just reminded her that Richard was coming to lunch with Kayla next Monday, and she wasn't invited.

She'd already called Fallon, Catherine, and Mrs. Grayson and asked if they might drop by school to eat lunch with Kayla before school was out for the summer. She wasn't going to beat herself over the head for not thinking of it before. She'd done enough of that. Kayla didn't have grandparents who cared, but she had friends who did.

With that thought in mind, Naomi checked her watch. Ten minutes before the dismissal bell. Shutting off her alarm clock, she left her classroom. Just outside the double-door entrance to the classrooms, people waited to pick up the students. She saw the abusive husband. He was laughing and talking to other parents as if he didn't have a care in the world. Her ex had been well liked and gregarious. Their smiles hid the ugliness beneath.

Naomi continued outside, hoping to see his wife. She had thought badly of the women in the office for not helping, but had realized that she had done nothing as well. She planned to correct that oversight.

A friendly smile on her face, Naomi went down the row of cars already parked in front of the school. It wasn't unusual for a teacher to come out to search for a parent they'd been unable to contact, so she was sure her actions wouldn't arouse the husband's suspicions.

She was almost at the end of the cars when she spotted the woman in a late-model Cadillac, her head bowed, the window partially rolled up although it was a hot, humid day. Naomi remembered her shame and having no one to talk with or help her . . . until she'd reached Santa Fe.

"Hello."

The woman jerked her head toward Naomi. Then she sat up to glance at the entrance of the school. Naomi recognized the fear. She's seen it numerous times in her own mirror.

She held a Women's League card out to the woman. "If you ever want to talk. Call. No pressure. Just someone to listen."

"I don't need to call anyone."

Her hand still outreached, Naomi showed her the scar on her wrist. "My ex-husband did that and lots more. I've known fear. I don't have to fear the door opening or footsteps any longer. You're not alone. Please take the card."

The woman shook her head. "Just go. He's coming."

Naomi slid the card back into her pocket. "The Women's League is listed in the phone book."

"What do you want?" the husband practically snarled. He set the little girl down and glared at Naomi.

She kept the easy smile on her face. "Looking for volunteers with the end-of-school activities. Your wife wasn't sure," Naomi said.

"She don't have time." Opening the back door, he placed his daughter inside, then he rounded the car and got in.

Naomi watched the car drive away, and slowly realized that she might have left her ex-husband, but he still influenced her life. Until she took control, she'd be the same frightened woman she'd always been.

Chapter 10

Naomi desperately needed to speak with Catherine. If ever there was a friend who would tell it to you straight—whether you wanted to hear it or not—it was Catherine.

Dropping Kayla off with Fallon with a promise to bring back dinner and a movie, she continued to Catherine's house. She'd already called. Catherine must have caught the desperation in Naomi's voice because she was waiting on the porch and met her on the walkway.

"Breathe." Catherine caught Naomi's trembling hands in hers. "You can handle anything."

Naomi let out a shaky laugh. "I'm not so sure."

Opening the front door, Catherine led her to the kitchen again. She placed a glass of lemonade in front of Naomi. "I know you might not want it, but it will be something to hold. Now tell me how I can help."

Blowing out a breath, she told her about the incident at school with the abusive husband, her self-righteous attitude, then her trying to help. "She was so frightened."

Catherine placed her hand on Naomi's arm. "She has to be ready. Until then, all you can do is give her the information and pray she finds the strength to leave."

Naomi's hands flexed around the icy glass. "I didn't want help at first. I didn't trust you or Luke."

"And look at you now," Catherine said.

"Yes, look at me." Naomi came to her feet. "I'm a wreck. I can't sleep. I'm missing signals about Kayla any mother would have seen." She told Catherine about Kayla's teacher and finished by telling her about the show-and-tell. "I don't think Richard likes me anymore." The words were hard to get out, but they had to be said.

"You don't believe that any more than I do."

"Yes, I do. I thought I was being so smart trying to stay away from him, and it turns out he couldn't care less." She swallowed. "I wish it didn't matter, but it does."

"Of course it does."

Naomi whirled, her fists clenched. "He ignored me during the entire dinner last night. If he cared, he wouldn't have done that."

Getting up from her seat, Catherine went to Naomi. "Have you ever tried to love someone and they kept throwing that love back in your face no matter how hard you tried, until finally you gave up?"

"My parents and Gordon," she said tightly. "I tried so hard to please them."

"And how did that make you feel?" Catherine asked softly.

"Worthless," she said slowly, then her eyes widened as realization hit her. "Richard."

"Love has to be accepted, nurtured for a relationship to flourish."

Naomi folded her arms and looked out the window to the landscaped backyard, the large barbecue grill, the hammock hanging from two stout trees. "I'm not a whole woman. I'm not sure I can function as one. My ex took more than my self-respect. He took my ability to feel comfortable around a man, to trust him."

Catherine turned Naomi to her. "Then get it back! Be the woman you were destined to be."

Naomi wasn't aware of the tears sliding down her cheek. "It's not that easy for some women. You don't have the physical or emotional scars I do."

"Don't I?" Catherine said softly. A brief flash of pain shot through her eyes, then it was gone. "I tried to run from Luke once, but I thank God daily that he came after me. When he did, I realized my mother was right when she said no one could love him as much as I could. I grabbed for him and I never looked back."

Naomi stared at Catherine. Beautiful, successful, and married to a man who worshiped the ground she walked on. She came from a loving, wealthy, and influential family, had achieved more wealth and influence on her own. "You have everything."

"So it would seem," she said, her smile unbearably sad.

"But—" Naomi began then snapped her mouth shut as things clicked into place. She remembered the comment she'd made at the dinner about Catherine making a wonderful mother. Catherine's strange reaction. Luke's anger at Naomi.

Naomi's eyes briefly shut as she felt her heart clench. It couldn't be, but she knew it was. Catherine, who loved children, had devoted her life to seeing them safe, loved, and well cared for, couldn't have them. Naomi swallowed, fought tears.

Catherine wouldn't want tears or pity. She was too strong for both.

"If you want Richard, you'll have to reach out to him and show him."

"And if he walks away?" Naomi questioned, trying not to think about the devastating revelation she'd just figured out.

"He won't." Catherine smiled, once again her old self. "Invite him over tonight after Kayla has gone to bed so you can talk honestly with each other," she suggested. "Kayla will feel the tension between you two until things are settled."

"All right." Naomi picked up her purse, her heart going out to Catherine. She was reminded all the time of what she couldn't have, saw heartless people abuse and abandon what she desperately wanted, and it hadn't made her bitter. It had made her more determined to help. Her bravery made Naomi ashamed.

"Catherine."

She held up her hand, her smile and her warmth and her love clearly written on her beautiful face. "Love is too precious to waste."

"If I'm ever a tenth of the woman you are, I'll be proud."

"I'm proud of you already. You could have stayed a victim; you didn't. All you have to do now is keep moving forward."

Naomi blinked rapidly. "If I hug you, I'll cry."

"Tears are good, but you have to drive." Catherine smiled and caught Naomi's hand, squeezed it. "Take control of your life. Don't let your ex win."

Naomi squeezed back. "I won't." They wouldn't talk about it then. "I'll let you know how it comes out tomorrow. Sierra found a new listing she's taking me to in the morning."

"We'll be at the cabin, but I'll have my cell on."

Naomi had to hug her, forced herself to not cling. "I'll call." Hurrying out of the house, she got in her SUV, but stopped as soon as she was out of sight of Catherine's house and made a call.

"Man Hunters."

"Luke." She swallowed. "How did you get so lucky to marry a woman as strong and wonderful and compassionate as Catherine?"

"I'd walk through hell for her," he said, the words moving and deep.

"I know," Naomi said, trying to choose her words carefully. "I just left Catherine's. Nothing was put into words and nothing ever will be. She loves you an awful lot and might need a hug."

"Is she all right?" The words were sharp and insistent.

Tears flowed down Naomi's cheek. "She was trying to help me. It's not fair," she sniffed. "I'm so sorry I made her remember. I'd give anything—"

"Then forget the conversation. Don't treat her differently."

"Please. Just go to her."

"I'm on my way. And, Naomi?"

"Yes?" She sniffed, ready for him to blast her.

"Thanks for caring and being her friend."

Naomi dried her tears, then put the car into drive. But the tears kept coming back. She couldn't imagine the pain Catherine must be going through, yet she never dwelled on it, never let it make her not want to help others. Naomi's marriage had been hell on earth, but from it she'd had Kayla.

She'd always been thankful for her daughter, had called her a gift, but until that moment she hadn't realized what that entailed. Not only had she been able to conceive, Kayla had kept her going through the darkest moments of her life.

Naomi didn't realize she was headed to Richard's clinic until she was a block away. She didn't think, she just reached for her cell phone and called him on his. He kept it on vibrate when he was at the clinic. He might see her name and—

"Naomi?"

"I . . ." She swallowed. "Can I come in through the back door?" She didn't want to go through the front office, and he could cut off the alarm for the emergency exit.

"Are you and Kayla all right?" he asked, worry in his voice.

"It's not us." She pulled into the parking lot, turned off the ignition and placed her forehead on the steering wheel. "Oh, Richard."

"Where are you?"

"Here."

"I'm coming for you."

Naomi fumbled to open the door, wasn't sure how far she'd gotten before strong arms pulled her against a hard body. *Richard*. She clung. "Richard."

"I got you." He picked her up and went back into his office though the back door.

"Oh, Richard."

She was trembling. She wouldn't cry over her ex. "I got you, honey. It's all right."

"I feel so bad for . . . it's my fault."

Somehow he managed to open the back door without letting her go. Once inside his office he snagged a tissue, heard the box hit the floor, and continued to the sofa. He sat with her in his lap, tucked her head against his shoulder, and did his best to dry her tears. "Easy, honey."

She sniffed, clung to the lapel of his lab coat with one hand "I thought I was so brave. I didn't know what real bravery was. I don't want to be afraid any longer. I have to trust and accept . . ." She paused again. "I shouldn't be crying all over you. Men don't like tears."

That last statement was the first that he understood and could answer. "Bull. I, for one, like knowing I can offer comfort. Tears don't bother me."

"I don't want us to be at odds anymore. Kayla needs both of us. I want things to be as they were before."

He stiffened. "I don't."

She went still in his arms; her choke hold on his lapel loosened. She didn't move out of his lap, but that didn't mean she wouldn't.

"I can't pretend to just be your friend any longer. I care about you too much. Either we move forward or . . ." He didn't like ultimatums, but he didn't see any other way. Remaining silent and being old dependable Richard certainly hadn't worked.

She sat up and placed her hands in her lap. "I can't be the woman you want."

He would have cursed if he thought it would do any good. "Let me be the judge of that."

She looked up with such misery that he had to kiss her, just a gentle brush of his lips against hers. She trembled like a hummingbird, then went soft in his arms. He thought he heard a sigh, and fought to pull back before he frightened her.

She blinked as if awakening. And perhaps she was.

"That wasn't so bad, was it?"

She shook her head. Wonder in her eyes. "You think we could do it again?" she said softly.

He laughed, then sobered and hugged her. "Let's save it for later." He came to his feet, bringing her with him. "How about I take you and my best girl to dinner tonight?"

"Oh! I was supposed to bring Mexican food back to Fallon and Kayla. I forgot."

He pulled out his wallet. "Then buy enough for me and I'll see you later."

"If you don't put that away, I'm not inviting you to dinner tonight or to go look at the house with me in the morning."

Richard quickly stuffed the billfold back into his pocket. "Done."

"We'll see you when you can get there. Kayla has something to show you."

"I guess you know I'm pretty crazy about your daughter," he said. At least he could get that out front.

"She likes you better than puppies."

He grinned, delighted to the tips of his boots. "Yeah."

She kissed him on the cheek. "We'll see you when you can." She went out the back door again, leaving Richard with a big grin on his face.

Naomi couldn't tell who was more excited, Kayla or Fallon, when she told them Richard was coming over later. Kayla could hardly eat. Fallon had given Naomi a thumbs-up and tried to leave. Naomi had to threaten not to invite Fallon over again if she left. Naomi was nervous, but it was a good nervous.

Every once in a while, she just had to touch her lips. From the grin on Fallon's face, she knew why. Naomi hadn't expected the gentleness, the softness of Richard's lips against hers. His hands were the same way. There's been no grabbing and bruising, hard hands to make her open her mouth or submit. She wanted to explore being held with tenderness. She wasn't sure about the intimacy. She'd just have to trust Richard and herself most of all.

This was a new beginning for her. If she didn't take it with a man she cared about and respected, a man who had shown her in every way that he cared for her and Kayla, there wouldn't be a next time.

She'd live her life. Each time she got scared, she'd think of Catherine's bravery.

The knock on the door startled her although she'd been waiting for it. Kayla was up like a shot from lying on the floor in the living room watching the Disney Channel. She'd wanted to save the movie until Richard arrived.

"I bet it's Dr. Richard." Kayla rushed toward the window.

Naomi stood and felt her knees tremble. Her stomach wasn't much steadier.

"I'll get the door," Fallon whispered. "Excitement looks good on you."

Naomi was excited and more. She was also extremely happy. As Kayla dropped the curtain and rushed to open the door herself, Naomi wished she'd had the forethought to have combed her hair, freshened her makeup, and changed clothes. Then the door was opening and Richard was walking in, and all she could do was smile.

"Dr. Richard," Kayla greeted, reaching up for him to pick her up.

"Hey, pumpkin." He scooped her up with one arm. "Hi, Fallon," Richard said, but he was looking at Naomi. The look so warm that she felt her cheeks heat.

"Richard," Fallon greeted with a grin and closed the door.

Richard crossed to Naomi and held out a small bouquet of yellow roses. "These are for you."

Her hands shook at they closed around the plastic wrapping of the roses, the scent wafting up to her. "Thank you." Her voice quivered. She wanted to hug the flowers to her, bury her nose in them. She'd commented months ago that she liked yellow roses. He'd remembered.

Her first flowers, and she had almost missed them. She'd almost missed the man watching her so tenderly by being afraid. "They're beautiful."

"Just like you," Richard said.

Naomi knew her blush deepened.

His attention shifted to Kayla. "Save me any food?"

"Uh-huh. I wanted to wait and eat with you, but Mama said we could eat dessert together."

"Sounds like a plan."

"I'll go put these in water and fix you a plate." Naomi hurried to the kitchen.

"Good to see persistence pays off." Fallon grinned at him.

He smiled. "Should I tell Lance what you said?"

Her smile cooled. "I'd tell you what I thought if we were alone."

Richard sat Kayla down. "You mother said you had something for me."

"I'll get it." She took off running.

Richard knew he didn't have much time. Lance deserved a break. "He's the best there is. Life hasn't always been kind to him."

Fallon folded her arms. "So now he takes pleasure in shafting others?"

A shadow cross Richard's face. "He's as honest as they come. He used to be trusting as well. I bet so were you. He's had to learn to move past his anger. I don't think you have."

"You don't know me," she said tightly.

"You're honest, intelligent, hardworking, loyal," he said. "So is Lance. You two might have more in common than you think. My guess is there is another reason that you're so hard on him."

"Here it is." Kayla handed him her art book.

Richard hunkered down and stared at the pencil drawing of the man and the little girl. "You did a good job."

"That's you and me." She placed her arm around his neck. "I bet if I got lost and the guardian wasn't around, you and Mama would find me."

Richard felt his throat tighten. He hugged Kayla to him. Her trust and love were priceless. "We certainly would."

Kayla leaned her head against his. "You can have it if you want. Mr. Rodgers already gave me a grade. I asked if you could take it out and he said it would be all right."

"Tomorrow, we'll take it to a shop to have it framed, and then I can put it up in my office," he told her.

"For real?" The little girl's eyes rounded.

"For real," he said. "I'll always tell you the truth. Remember that."

"I do. It's just sometimes . . ." Her voice trailed off.

He hugged her. Adults didn't always keep promises. She'd learned that lesson much too soon. "I know, pumpkin. I know."

Naomi heard her daughter, and some of her happiness faded. Kayla didn't trust because, in her life, people didn't always keep their word. Her mother was at the top of that list.

Naomi's old habit would have been to drop her

head, berate herself. This time she accepted that life hadn't always given her a choice. Correction, she hadn't always made the right choice. Her gaze went to Richard, saw his unshakable faith in her that had never wavered. There was nothing she could do about the past. She just had to make the best of the future.

Her head up, she walked farther into the living room. "Your food is ready."

Richard came to his feet. "I'm starved."

Kayla grabbed his hand. "I'll show you. I helped Mama put a place mat and everything on the table for you."

"I'll let you eat and get out of here." Fallon headed for the door. "Thanks for the meal. Good night, everyone."

"Kayla, please show Richard where to sit." Naomi hurried after Fallon to remind her about staying or no more meals; then she saw her friend's unhappy expression. "What's the matter?"

Fallon shook her dark head of hair, then looked at Richard and Kayla heading for the kitchen. "Richard doesn't pull his punches."

"I think I wore out his quota of patience for the next ten years," Naomi said with feeling. "But he likes you."

Fallon wrinkled her nose. "He thinks I'm too hard on his cousin."

"Are you?" Naomi asked, then shook her head. "You don't have to answer that. I'm the last person to try to analyze another person's feelings when I'm having trouble with my own. I just know that I want to . . . live, for want of a better word."

Fallon finally smiled. "You certainly picked the right man."

Naomi grinned back. "I think so, too."

Fallon hugged her. "Then get back to him. Good night."

"Good night." Naomi closed and locked the door, then started for the kitchen. She'd been looking inward so much that she never realized that women like Catherine or Fallon, who appeared to have it all together, might have problems of their own. But they never let this deter them from what they wanted.

Entering the kitchen, she saw Richard eating and Kayla talking nonstop about her day at school. Naomi smiled. She was taking this chance.

They cleaned up the kitchen together. Richard insisted on helping, and because Kayla, who didn't like washing dishes, wanted to be with him, she'd helped. Both of them stared at Richard as he swept the floor.

He smiled at them. "After cleaning kennels, this is a walk in the park."

Naomi's lips twitched. "I bet."

Chuckling, he put the broom and dustpan away, then went to the sink to wash his hands. "Ladies, you want to go for a drive?"

"Mama got us a movie to watch." Kayla took his hand again. "It's about secret-agent dogs saving the world against some bad cats. Crystal, in my class, said it was funny. She likes dogs, too."

"How can it miss?" Richard held out his hand for Naomi. "Coming?"

She reached out her hand to his, then clenched it.

He frowned, disappointment clear in his eyes.

"I forgot to lotion them," she explained, then quickly went to the bottle by the sink, a gift from Fallon, another person who disliked washing dishes. After rubbing the lavender scent into her skin, she reached for his hand.

He gently squeezed. "Lead on, Kayla."

In less than a minute, Kayla had the movie in the DVD player, the control in her hands, and was scooted back on the living room sofa with Richard next to her. As movie trailers started to play, Naomi felt herself in a quandary. Usually she sat on the other side of Kayla as she did at the movies. She didn't want to sit there tonight.

Richard patted the space beside him. "I saved you a spot."

Naomi's gaze went to Kayla. She didn't like variations in their routine. And Naomi wasn't sure how to explain the shift in her and Richard's relationship.

"Better come on before the movie starts," Richard urged. "I don't want to miss any of the action of the dogs taking down those nasty cats. Although I wouldn't say it in front of my cat owners."

Naomi sat next to Richard, leaving a good two feet between them. The look he tossed her said it wasn't close enough. She inched over a bit farther. He reached out and tugged her arm, bringing her closer still, until only a scant space separated them.

Kayla snuggled against Richard, the control still in her hands because she enjoyed rewinding scenes she liked. "I'm glad you're here."

He leaned his head briefly against hers, then curved his arm around Naomi's shoulders. "So am I, Kayla. So am I."

So was she, Naomi thought, and gave in to the urge to take a cue from her daughter and lean into the warmth and strength of Richard's body. She barely caught back a sigh at how good it felt just to relax and not to be afraid. Then her mind went in an entirely different and new direction. Once Kayla was in bed, Richard would kiss her. She thought of the pleasure of the kiss in his office and snuggled closer.

"I can't wait another second." Richard pulled Naomi into his arms the moment she entered the living room, his mouth finding hers. He wanted the kiss to be warm and tender, the passion to slowly grow. It took all of his willpower for that to happen when she melted against him, a little whimper slipping past her lips.

The woman packed a wallop and had no idea how she got to him, how much he wanted her naked and willing in a big bed. Lifting his head, his breathing off kilter, he reached for control.

"I—no—I didn't know a kiss could be like this," she whispered, her splayed hands trembling on his chest.

"With the right person, a kiss can take you under faster than a riptide." He lifted his head, palmed her face, and stared down at her. "You make me ache."

Her eyes widened in wonder. "Me? I do?"

He would have laughed at the pleasure pushing

its way through the wonder if need hadn't been clawing though him. "You do." He kissed her on the lips, then took her hand and sat on the sofa, pulling her back into his arms. "This is nice."

"Everything with you is nice."

She tucked her head. His finger lifted his chin. "Never hide from me. Promise me."

"I don't want to disappoint you, say the wrong thing," she confessed.

"I didn't want to disappoint *you*, say the wrong thing either," he confessed. "It made me second-guess myself. It wasn't a good place. Let's make a pact tonight that we do what comes naturally."

"That's what I'm afraid of." She shrugged. "I don't think I'm very good at this."

"Any better, and I'd be chewing nails." He stared into her eyes. "Another pact. No comparison and no looking back at the past."

"I want that more than you know," she said. "Moving forward is the only way I'll ever be happy. I finally realized that."

"And that's just what you're doing."

"With you."

He smiled. "And the house. What did Sierra say about it?"

Naomi looked a bit embarrassed. "I was thinking about something else when she called so I didn't ask any questions, but apparently a house just came on the market that she thought would be perfect for us. I called her while I was waiting for the food order and told her that I thought you'd come with us—if you could make it."

"You told her right." He came to his feet pulling her with him. "Sleep in. We'll go eat breakfast after we see the house, then go find the frame shop to have my drawing framed."

Naomi's smile trembled. "You're a good man."

He wasn't sure he liked being called good. "What time should I pick you up?"

"Eight forty-five, and thank you."

"Thank you for trusting me." He gave her a quick kiss on the mouth to reward her and because he couldn't help himself.

She twisted her head to one side to study him. "I'm not sure you gave me a choice."

"Desperate times." His arms circled her waist. He liked that she was expressing her feelings more and more. "And I was past desperate." His mouth found hers again, taking and giving pleasure. "Dream of me." Turning, Richard left the apartment aware exactly of what he was going to dream about.

Chapter 11

"We're coming up on the house address," Richard said, slowing down.

Naomi leaned forward in her seat, reading the house numbers. The houses were all well kept, single-level adobe and wood with manicured lawns and rear-entry garages. They passed a man in a straw hat cutting his yard. A few houses farther, a woman worked in her flower bed. A couple of children raced down the street on their bikes.

"Looks like a good neighborhood," Richard said.

"And out of my price range." Naomi nibbled on her lower lip. "Sierra must have made a mistake."

"Not a Grayson failing. Sierra knows her business. That sharp brain of hers as a Realtor is what got her and Blade together," Richard reminded her. "Let's wait and see. Should be the next house."

Naomi's gaze had already moved ahead. She straightened on seeing the overgrown yard. Sierra's SUV was already there. Richard pulled to a stop in front of the walk.

"It's on a corner lot," Richard said encouragingly.

"I've never seen a garden like that," Kayla said.

Because it isn't one, Naomi thought as she unbuckled her seat belt and slowly got out. Through the tall grass to the left and right of the house were wooden arches. The white paint on each was chipped and faded, but what made Naomi not lose hope were the unruly yellow roses climbing up the structure.

Sierra, in a slim-fitting black skirt and a ruffled white blouse with black piping, got out of the SUV, her high heels clicking on the pavement as she came to meet them on the sidewalk. Her long black hair hung down her slim back. Aaron and Paul were behind her.

"Good morning, everyone," Sierra greeted cheerfully.

"Good moring," Naomi said, but she couldn't keep the frown from her face.

"Hi, Mrs. Sierra."

"'Morning, Sierra," Richard said from beside Naomi.

"Naomi, please keep an open mind. It's thirty thousand off the listed price because of the outward appearance, but it has great bones and loads of potential. It's sixteen hundred square feet with an updated kitchen, and the backyard has a sturdy eight-foot fence."

The thirty thousand off eased a bit of Naomi's worry about the cost, and she had said to look for a house that needed a little work. The fenced backyard was good. Sierra understood Naomi was on a budget, wanted safety for Kayla *and* what she needed in a house. "All right."

"Excellent. Shall we?"

"What about the previous owners?" Naomi asked as she followed Sierra up the sidewalk. At least there were no cracks in this one.

"Martha and Greg Allen moved to Denver almost a year ago to live with their son when she became ill. They thought they'd move back, but now realize that that's not going to happen," Sierra explained, continuing up the walk.

"Wait," Richard said from behind them.

Sierra looked back with a frown. "Yes?"

"Has Aaron already been inside?" Richard asked, holding Kayla's hand. "Sometimes transients move into abandoned houses."

Sierra rolled her eyes. "He's already been in yesterday when I first got the listing, and again this morning. I told him if he wanted to be sure of my safety, he should have cut the grass."

Naomi smiled. Richard's lips twitched.

"Come on, I can't wait for you to see inside." Sierra stepped on the porch. "I love the arched door, and the little courtyard off the front porch. You can plant cacti or put a water sculpture there that you can view from the living room."

Naomi reached out to take Richard and Kayla's hands as she stepped inside. She wanted to like this house. She wasn't sure if it was the yellow roses or just the desire to keep moving forward.

Early-morning light bathed them. She glanced up to see a skylight.

"I had them cleaned, and the French doors in the master bedroom as well," Sierra explained, then leaned closer. "Despite what I told Aaron, I would have had the yard cut as well, but I didn't want to alert any other Realtors or homebuyers."

Releasing Kayla and Richard's hands, Naomi stepped down into the open living area. Beneath her feet was badly scuffed wide-plank flooring.

"The open area allows for entertaining or just enjoying the family. The breakfast bar has enough space for three or four chairs, and on the other side there's lots of hidden storage space for kitchen and home needs. I love the window seating in the kitchen." Sierra nodded to the padded seat just off to the right. "Kayla and Teddy can sit here and keep you company or do her homework."

Kayla promptly plopped down on the faded material. Dust wafted up.

"The rods and curtains are custom for window shades, but I have a guy who can change out the rods to a simple draw or transverse rod. You can use a matching material to cover the chair seats or you could contrast." Sierra stared at the lighting fixture. "The reindeer chandelier has to go."

"Agreed," Richard said, his mouth a bit tight.

Naomi walked over to the curtain treatment and looked beneath. "It looks stylish and simple. Roman shades aren't that complicated, if you know what you're doing. I used to do a little sewing."

Richard and Sierra joined her. Sierra spoke first. "Try it out with an old sheet first."

"We can pick up a board and material after—"

"Whoa." Naomi laughed, but it was high-pitched and nervous. "It was just a thought."

"Let's look at the bedrooms." Sierra headed toward a short hallway. "While we're just talking, Richard, don't you think these floors can be stained a dark brown to hide the scuff marks? The color would also hide any future spills and scuff marks."

"I was thinking the same thing," Richard said.

"Painted a light blue-green, the walls would give the place a restful, open look," Sierra went on to say. "I'd keep the white trim. Here we are. The master bedroom." She waved Naomi inside.

The master bedroom had nothing in it except an upholstered headboard. The material matched the Roman blinds at the two windows on either side of the headboard, and the pole draperies at the French doors.

"A custom headboard makes a room feel luxurious." Sierra trailed her fingers over the nail heads on the curve of the headboard. "The slate-blue material held up well and wouldn't have to be redone. They probably didn't take the headboard because it wouldn't have matched. Isn't your bed a queen, Naomi?"

"Yes." Her heart was beating fast. She who couldn't decorate a box could actually see her things in this room. It had a real fireplace, not a kiva. There was one problem. "The house has a lot of windows."

"Security system and double-paned windows," Sierra told her.

Naomi could see her dream slipping away. "Those

would be costly, and before you say you know someone, I want to do this on my own . . . at least as much as possible. I hope you understand."

"I do. That's why I was glad to find out that Mr. and Mrs. Allen had double-insulated windows installed two years ago, which, while not unbreakable, will give anyone trying to break in a lot of trouble and enough warning for the home occupants and certainly the alarm system company."

"I can't ask Rio to do the alarm," Naomi told her.

"You won't have to," Sierra told her with a smile. "I checked yesterday. The installer, quite a reputable company I might add, will be only too happy to restart service. Because you're a new customer, and the fact that they don't have to go through the trouble of rewiring the house, they will give you a special monthly discount."

Richard chuckled. "Told you she was good."

"I'm not sure why I doubted," Naomi said, but she was smiling.

"Let's take a look at the second bedroom, which has its own bath for a very special young lady," Sierra said.

"Like me?" Kayla said.

"Exactly like you." Sierra took her hand and stepped into the room next door.

"Look, Mama, it has shelves for my books and toys," Kayla said.

Naomi noted that, but also that it only had one high window. "Yes, I see."

"Mrs. Allen liked to collect crystal and ran out of room, but wanted to keep it where she could see it every day," Sierra explained.

"Did you know them?" Richard asked.

"No. They contacted me when their last Realtor didn't work out for them," she said. "Their exclusive contract with him expired early yesterday and I was able to change the lockbox on the door and see the place without his permission. Other Realtors can show the house, but they have to ask my permission first."

"Do you think that other Realtor might have a buyer already?" Naomi asked, worry creeping in. She liked this house. She just hoped that she could afford it.

"Highly unlikely. We'll pop into the small guest bedroom and then we'll go back though the kitchen to the outside. The previous owners liked to entertain so they had a bricked patio and a small built-in barbecue grill, and the rest of the yard has motion lights."

The guest bedroom was small, but adequate. Naomi was anxious to see more. They followed Sierra back to the kitchen. She opened the back door.

Naomi couldn't believe it. Her amazed gaze swung back to Sierra. "The yard has been mowed."

"I knew how important the back was to you and Kayla, so I wanted you to be able to see its appeal." Sierra glanced down. "With the bricked patio, no matter how much it rains, you won't track in mud. The grass is struggling, but the two golden rain trees are beautiful by themselves with their yellow flowers, or you could plant a mixture of green and flowering plants beneath. In the morning, you could come out here and relax with a cup of coffee before work. In the evenings, return to wind down while you grill and watch Kayla play."

Naomi walked to the edge of the bricked patio. She could easily visualize everything Sierra had just said—with one addition. Richard. The yard stretched at least seventy-five feet both ways. A few steps away, a Chickasaw plum tree was loaded with fruit. She could try her hand at making preserves. This could be their home.

"I bet a doghouse would look real good out here," Kayla said, going to stand by her mother and slipping her hand into hers.

There was certainly room enough for a doghouse—and the swing set she'd already set aside money for. She glanced around the patio again. She could probably buy some secondhand patio furniture, paint it, and make some throw pillows out of brightly hued fabric scraps.

"Naomi, is this your house?"

Naomi opened her mouth to answer, but before she could she heard loud, angry voices coming from the house. Instinctively, she pulled Kayla closer. Richard and Sierra both moved toward the kitchen door.

"No!" Naomi cried.

"It's all right," Richard soothed, stopping to look back at her.

"Please excuse me." Sierra never paused. Entering the house by door they'd left open, she started to swing it shut only to have Richard catch the door and enter behind her.

"Touch me and I'll have you arrested," yelled a slim, middle-aged man in a tailored suit.

"Mrs. Navarone is the exclusive Realtor of this property as of eight yesterday morning," Aaron said, blocking the man. "You have to have her permission to be on these premises."

"I haven't seen any papers to that effect, and until I do, I'm still the exclusive Realtor, so get out of my way."

Sierra's eyes narrowed. "Richard, please go back with Naomi and Kayla. I'll be with you in a moment."

The man's fuming gaze zeroed in on Sierra. "You won't get away with this."

"George, I personally sent you a certified copy of my agreement with the Allens, plus his son said he was going to call you. Since you're here this early in the morning, I'd say you were lying about not knowing you were fired," Sierra told him.

George Bryant tried to go around or shove Aaron aside. It wasn't happening. George wasn't smart enough to realize he'd only gotten that far because Aaron allowed it. He didn't want neighbors to see the scene that was going to play out

"Don't you dare insult me. I've been in this business twenty years," Bryant snarled. "Isn't it enough your husband owns God-knows-what without you trying to cheat and undermine the rest of us? You probably badgered *my* clients. They're old and easily influenced. I'm reporting you to the board. I'll have your license. You won't get away with this."

Sierra's temper spiked. She was not taking another insult from this fool. "Stand aside, Aaron."

"Mrs. Navarone."

"I'm not asking," Sierra said, her voice precise and cool.

Aaron moved to stand between her and the angry man. That was as good as she was going to get. She stepped closer to the incensed man.

"I don't have to undermine. I simply do my job better than you." She placed her hands on her hips. "You're lazy and sloppy, and your abysmal sales records show it. You're a disgrace to our profession. Good people depend on you and you don't even try to do a first-rate job. I should report you to the board for your ineptness and unprofessionalism. You couldn't sell ice water in hell."

With each word, the man had become more enraged. "You take that back." Hands raised, he lunged for her.

Sierra slipped out of her backless heeled sandals and raised her hands palm-out.

Richard, who had remained, moved to intercede, but Aaron was faster.

The livid man found his path blocked by two hundred pounds of coiled muscle. "You do not want to make that mistake."

"She can't talk to me that way," he shouted.

"Aaron, get out of the way," Sierra ordered. "I'm not afraid of him."

"I'm trying to protect him," Aaron said easily. "If you take him down, he'll have to deal with Blade, and your brothers will take care of what's left. Then Rio will want to know why I let it happen and our loudmouthed friend here will then have to deal with me."

"You forgot Mrs. Grayson," Richard supplied.

Aaron grinned. "Yeah. You really stepped in it this time."

"I—I'm not afraid—"

"Then you're a fool." A cold voice cut the Realtor off.

The man spun around to face the newcomer, then took a step backward. All eyes in the room watched Rio as he silently crossed to them, his gaze never leaving the now quaking man.

"Did he touch her?"

"He's breathing, isn't he?" came Aaron's matter-of-fact answer.

The man staggered back. "You—you can't threaten me. I know people."

"Rio, I—"

He held up one hand.

Sierra pressed her lips together. Rio only took orders from Blade, and then only to a point. "I should have snuck out this morning. I could have taken care of this," Sierra muttered.

"And Blade would have become involved and none of us would have liked the consequences, least of all Mr. Bryant," Rio answered without looking at her.

Sierra groaned inwardly. She'd forgotten that nothing much got past Rio's keen hearing.

"You—you know my name?"

"A better question is, what don't I know?" Rio said, his voice void of inflection, his black eyes emotionless.

"You—you think—"

"Shut up and listen," Rio said quietly, again cutting the man off. "You can't reason with incompetence or stupidity, so I won't waste my breath. You will apologize to Mrs. Navarone and then leave. Don't get in her way again."

"You—"

Rio moved so quickly the man didn't have time to evade the unrelenting hand holding his suit jacket. Rio whispered something in his ear, then released him. The man's eyes were huge as he staggered back, then turned and ran out of the room. Aaron followed.

Rio faced Sierra. "Please excuse us, Dr. Young-blood."

Sierra saw Richard hesitate, then he left as well. She was on her own. She folded her arms. If she could stand up to her brothers and Blade, she could do the same with Rio. Although, she usually could tell what they were thinking, with Rio you never knew, which put the other person at a distinct disadvantage.

As silently as a cat on the wooden floor, he came to within a foot of her. He simply looked at her.

She lasted for only three seconds before unfolding her arms. "Don't give me that look. It wasn't my fault."

"I've heard that before. I'd like not to hear it again."

"It's not my problem some men are cowards and fools. Bryant is both. You were right about him."

"Knowing that, you should have let Aaron handle things. Instead, you provoked him."

"It's a gift." She grinned. She didn't expect him to grin back. He didn't.

"What you do affects Blade. Let Aaron and Paul do their job."

"I don't need—"

"True, so you shouldn't be so quick to try to prove it and put Blade in jeopardy."

Her mouth opened, then she snapped it shut. You couldn't argue against the truth. Blade wouldn't allow any man to touch her, no matter the provocation, and not pay him a visit.

Rio wasn't finished. "Use that brilliant brain of yours for purposes other than having your way."

She took immediate exception and stepped to him. "You calling me spoiled?"

"Headstrong. Courageous. Unpredictable. Loyal. But those same qualities made Blade fall in love with you."

The fight went out of her. "I was ready to take you on."

"Learn to think with your heart and make life simpler for all of us," Rio said.

"Another woman would make it easier, wouldn't she?"

"But no other woman would make Blade smile for no special reason." Rio turned and walked away.

Sierra grinned. "I'll be good for the rest of the month—better make that all next week." Pleased with the way things had turned out, all things considered, Sierra went back outside. Richard was trying to distract Kayla with a butterfly. Naomi's eyes were huge. Sierra wished Aaron had let her hit Bryant at least once for scaring Naomi.

"Are you all right?" Naomi bit her lip. Initially, she'd tried to distract Kayla when the shouting grew louder, but she hadn't been able to stop looking. She couldn't believe Sierra actually wanted to confront the man. "Richard said Rio wanted to speak with you alone."

"He just wanted to remind me that what I do affects Blade." Sierra sighed. "Loving a person brings responsibility."

Naomi's frown didn't clear. "You couldn't possibly regret your marriage."

"Never. Blade is the only one for me. He's not going to be too happy with me if he finds about what happened here today, though."

"I bet you can put him in a good mood," Naomi suggested, then her eyes widened and her cheeks flushed in embarrassment. She would have never thought about such a thing before kissing Richard.

Sierra whooped. "Count on it. Now let's get back to talking houses. Do you think this could be the one?"

"What's the price?" Naomi asked, hoping, praying it was within her price range.

"One thirty, but they might take a little less since they're ready for this to be over," Sierra told her.

Naomi's heart was racing again. She liked the house, thought it had potential. She could almost visualize them living there.

"Have you had a chance to look it over?" Richard asked Sierra.

"It's sound and a bargain." Sierra folded her arms. "If you don't buy it, I might. I can't let Blade think he's the only one who can wheel and deal in real estate."

"Kayla, come here, please," Naomi called.

Her daughter came running to her. "I saw a lizard."

Naomi caught her hand, felt hers tremble. "Do you think you'd like living here?"

Kayla nodded and grinned. "I do, Mama. I like it here. The yard is big enough for a doghouse. If you decide I can get one."

Naomi glanced back at Richard. He nodded. She took a deep breath. "I'd like to make an offer."

She was actually going to buy a house. The excitement Naomi had felt earlier faded into nagging doubts a few hours later. Perhaps she should have waited a little longer and saved up more money. What if she got sick or her car needed major repairs? What if there was some underlying structural problem with the house that Sierra hadn't seen? What if—

"Stop worrying."

Her head lifted. She stopped clutching her purse strap and stared into Richard's strong face as he stood next to her at the park. They'd ended up there after breakfast and a visit to the frame store. He knew her better than anyone. The thought was comforting rather than scary.

"You can do this. I'll be there to help."

Naomi watched Kayla playing with the other children on the slide, and tried to find a way to tell him how she felt, then decided to just say it. "Don't take this the wrong way, but I don't want to depend on anyone."

"You won't be dependent on me. I'll be there to help, and if you slack off, you'll hear from me."

A smile curved her lips. "You aren't going to let me start having doubts, are you?"

"Nope." He caught her hand. "But I do think Kayla is going to wear you down on getting her puppy."

"You think?" she asked, smiling up at him. Somehow her gaze drifted to his lips, strong, sensual, and inviting.

His gaze narrowed. "Stop tempting me."

She was just learning that she could and it was . . . exciting. "You shouldn't be so yummy."

His jaw dropped.

She laughed, enjoying the naughtiness of shocking him. "Well, you are."

"I'm going to get you for that," he promised, his voice dropping to a suggestive purr.

Her body heated even more. "Since you're a man of your word, I'm going to hold you to that later."

Regret crossed his face. "I have to work at the animal hospital this weekend."

She frowned. "Work? I thought you volunteered there sometimes."

"I had to rearrange a few things, get a couple of vets to cover for me, to be able to spend as much time as I wanted with Kayla on Monday," he told her slowly. "I didn't want an emergency taking me away in the middle of my presentation or our lunch."

She didn't know what to say, so she hugged him and blinked back tears. No man had ever been there for them the way Richard had. "You're a wonderful man."

He grunted. She lifted his head. He looked a bit annoyed. "I guess you don't like being called wonderful, either."

"I just don't want you feeling grateful," he muttered, obviously displeased.

"Well, I do, and I can't help it. You've been there for both of us so many times since we came here. I don't know what I would have done without you. I don't want us at odds again," she told him, misery creeping into her voice. "I told you, I'm not good with words."

"It's not you, it's me," he said slowly. "I said I wouldn't push, and I'm doing just that. Ignore me."

"I tried. It's impossible," she said softly.

"Because I'm yummy," he said, obviously trying to get them back on an even footing.

"Exactly."

Saturday night, Naomi's apartment was quiet. Kayla had gone to bed earlier than usual, giving Naomi a chance to finally finish the novel she'd stated weeks ago. It wasn't happening.

She kept having to reread pages. She couldn't concentrate on the plot. She missed Richard, wanted him there with her. He might not like her calling him a good man, but he was in every sense of the word. He was going out of his way for her daughter, had gone out of his way for both of them. He was a man you could count on, and his kisses left her breathless and yearning for more.

She hugged the book to her chest. A poor substitute for what she really wanted.

Naomi could mope or do something constructive, like call Catherine. For a moment, sadness almost overwhelmed her as she thought of her friend's plight. She had so much love to give to a child. The thought had no more than formed than Naomi realized Catherine was doing just that. She hadn't let her inability to have children dictate how she lived her life. Just as Naomi couldn't let her abusive marriage overshadow her life.

Sticking a bookmark between the pages, Naomi picked up the phone on the nightstand and dialed. Catherine answered her cell on the third ring.

"Hi, Naomi."

"I'm buying a house," Naomi said without preamble.

"Naomi, that's wonderful. Tell me all about it."

Scooting back against the headboard, she did just that, her excitement building all over again. She ended by saying, "The house is just about perfect. It has everything we wanted and then some."

"Sierra is good at what she does. There aren't many better."

Naomi thought of Sierra's altercation with the angry Realtor and wondered if she had been able to keep what had happened from Blade. Naomi certainly hoped so, and she wasn't going to mention it. "I can't wait for you to see the house."

"Me, either."

"I hope you keep saying that when I'm bugging you to help me decorate."

"I will, and I'd love to help," Catherine told her. There was something else she wanted to say. "I also stopped running from my feelings for Richard. We talked yesterday after I left you. He came over last night and this morning he went with us to see the house."

"He cares about you and Kayla. For what it's worth, you made the right decision."

"It means a lot to hear you say that. Thanks for not letting my fears get in the way."

"Thank yourself. I could talk until I'm eighty, but unless you had the courage, you'd still be trapped by the past. I bet it feels good."

"You can't imagine." Naomi laughed for the sheer pleasure of it. "I know I have a long way to go, that fear might still catch me unaware, but I also know I can handle those moments and get on with my life."

"I'm proud of you, Naomi. I know it wasn't easy."

"No, but it helps to have friends like you," she said. "I better let you go. I just wanted to let you know how well things are going for me. Bye."

"Bye."

Naomi hung up, snapped off the light, and pulled the covers over her shoulder. She was going to be a homeowner. There was a special man in her life. All in all, it had been an eventful day.

And she could hardly wait to see Richard again.

Chapter 12

Monday morning Naomi got out of bed the moment the alarm went off. For once on a Monday morning, she didn't linger. She hadn't seen Richard since he dropped her and Kayla at their apartment around two Saturday afternoon. They'd only talked briefly Sunday afternoon. She was anxious to see him again.

She took a little more time with her makeup, even put on a light touch of blush and mascara. Taking a cue from Sierra, she wore a crisp white blouse, black skirt, and black skimmers.

She and Kayla were out the apartment door ten minutes earlier than usual. Kayla was bubbling with energy and excitement. Naomi couldn't leave her class to hear Richard's entire presentation, but she had a teacher assistant who'd stay with her class while she went to hear part of what he said.

She knew something was up when she entered Kayla's classroom later that morning and saw the counselor and the office clerk. Both seemed to hang on Richard's every word when he was speaking.

She left five minutes later and passed the other counselor and a first-grade teacher on their way to Kayla's class. There could be only one reason: Word had spread, and they were trying to scope Richard out. Naomi wasn't sure how she felt about that.

Less than an hour later Naomi might not be sure of her feelings, but she was sure of one thing: Richard was a hit. Not only did the schoolchildren enjoy his presentation, but the teachers, especially the single ones, seemed to be just as taken with him.

Naomi had initially been proud of him, then as the teachers kept going over to him and Kayla in the cafeteria, Naomi had to work hard to keep the smile on her face. She hadn't known she could be possessive or jealous.

Kayla's teacher, Ms. Hightower, usually a bit timid except when it came to championing her students, was actually humming with excitement. "I can't believe he's not married."

"Neither can I," added the office clerk.

"He was so patient with all of the students asking him questions," Ms. Hightower said. "Good father material."

"I wonder if he's seriously dating?" asked a second-grade teacher who had joined them.

Yes, Naomi wanted to say, but when they all looked at her for an answer, she couldn't get the word out.

"What's all the excitement?" Principal Crenshaw

asked. "Teachers have been buzzing in the office for the past hour."

"Kayla has done it again," her teacher said, nodding toward Richard and Kayla sitting in the lunchroom. "Her show-and-tell is Dr. Richard Youngblood, a local vet. I'm seriously thinking of adopting a dog."

The office clerk laughed. "I was thinking the same thing."

"Good thing I'm happily married, but it wouldn't hurt to welcome him to our campus," Principal Crenshaw said. "He would be an asset for career day next year."

"Since I'm on the committee," said Elaine Smoothers, the counselor, "I'll just walk over with you."

Naomi hugged her arms tighter to her body as the two women started for Richard and Kayla.

"We just lost out," Kayla's teacher muttered. "Elaine is tall, chesty, and gorgeous."

"Yeah," agreed the office clerk. "Well, if she nabs him at least there's always the possibility he'll come to school functions and we'll get to drool over him once in a while. I better get back to the office."

Naomi was left alone as the women moved away. She barely noticed. She was trying to see if Richard reacted to Ms. Smoothers the entranced way some men did on seeing her. The UPS guy had walked into a door. She even had a time limit during parent conferences because some of the fathers lingered too long. But if she thought she was getting Richard, it wasn't happening.

Richard had been sized up by women before. Some of them had even tried to get to him by bringing to his clinic pets they obviously didn't want and had no clue how to care for. He'd tried to be as tactful as possible to discourage them from keeping the animals, even going so far as to tell them he'd find them a good home if they felt they weren't a good match.

More often than not, they'd taken him up on his offer. He'd like to think it was because they were nice women and not because, as Brandon had suggested, it gave them another chance to try to seduce him. A few times he'd let himself be tempted for a while, but it never lasted and he liked it that way.

This time, however, he wasn't interested in the long looks, the suggestive smiles. He only had to glance at Naomi to know she wasn't too pleased. He could have shouted with joy.

He came to his feet when the principal and the woman with the greedy eyes approached. Kayla had happily introduced both women. He was proud of her. Naomi had done a good job. He'd dutifully thanked the principal for having him and gave his card to both women for next year's career day. "Kayla is going to be a vet."

"I'm going to be just like Dr. Richard and take good care of all the animals in my care," Kayla told them.

"What kind of pet do you have?" Principal Crenshaw asked.

"I don't have one yet, but Mama might get me a puppy soon," Kayla told them.

The women's eyes narrowed speculatively on Richard. He knew the "soon" had piqued their interest. Naomi probably hadn't mentioned she was looking for a house, so they'd made the giant and incorrect leap that the puppy was to attract his attention. He wasn't sure if Naomi wanted them to know they were dating or about the house.

A whistle blew. "Five minutes to finish eating, then line up," announced the cafeteria monitor.

"Nice meeting you, Principal Crenshaw, Ms. Smoothers." He picked up his and Kayla's trays. "We better dump this and get you in line."

Ms. Smoothers placed her hand on his arm, let her fingers slid down. "Thank you again. I'll be in touch."

He nodded and continued to dump the trays. It wouldn't do her any good. He already had his eyes on the woman he wanted, but when he looked up Naomi and her class were gone. She hadn't come over to say good-bye. He had a feeling that he might be in the doghouse.

Richard left a message on Naomi's answering machine that he'd drop by later that night. He had no idea at the time "later" would be almost nine. He'd shifted some of his appointments to be able to spend time with Kayla, had a fellow vet take his emergency calls. He'd often had to reschedule if there was an emergency that took him out of the city or was prolonged. His patients didn't seem to mind.

He knocked softly on the apartment door. He loved Kayla, but he wanted her mother all to himself tonight. He was about to knock again when the door opened. Naomi wasn't smiling.

"Is everything all right?"

She folded her arms across her chest. "Have you changed your mind about us? Elaine is a beauti—"

His mouth stopped her flow of words. He needed the kiss as much as she did. She clung to him, her tongue sliding against his driving him to the breaking point. He pulled her tighter, enjoyed the warmth of her body, the soft fullness of her breasts against his chest, and he kissed her deeper until his head was spinning.

"You're the woman I care about, the only woman I want to be with."

Her hands clutching his shirt trembled. "I was jealous."

He tried hard not to show how smug he felt hearing her say that. "You have no reason."

"I know that, it's just . . ." Her head twisted to one side. "You smiling?"

"A little. Maybe," he confessed, pulling her back flush against him. "I never thought I'd get to hold you like this, knowing you're a bit jealous makes me want to strut."

"You were the talk of the campus. One woman, who has never spoken to me, just happened to drop by my classroom to try to pump me for information about you."

"You tell her I'm taken?"

The half smile on Naomi's face slid away. "The words wouldn't come."

He might want to tell the world, but she wasn't ready. "They'll come one day. In the meantime—" His mouth covered hers, taking, giving, his tongue relearning the sweetness of her mouth. He couldn't help kissing her, especially when she surrendered so sweetly to him.

He didn't intend to, but somehow she was in his arms, and then he was following her down on the sofa. The moment his weight covered hers, his sanity returned briefly as he thought that being pinned beneath a man's body might scare her. He was about to shift his weight when her arm tightened around his neck, her mouth and body straining against his.

His mind emptied until there was only the pleasure. His hand cupped her small breast, his thumb raked across the distended nipple. The buttons of her blouse came undone: He parted it to reveal her white bra. His fingers touched her bare skin, felt her heartbeat quicken, felt his own body quicken and stir with hunger.

He wanted their clothes gone, his body pumping into hers. His hand moved down her flat stomach, then slid over the slim skirt that had him thinking naughty thoughts all afternoon. He was going to strip her naked and take her to bed and—

His head jerked upward; his hand released the skirt he'd been tugging up. Sanity slowly returned. His eyes closed. It took a moment or two to realize her hands around his neck had gone slack, that she was still beneath him.

Blowing out a breath, he tried to gracefully climb off her. Aware she might be embarrassed, he picked her up and placed her in his lap. He thought about buttoning her blouse, but decided he wasn't quite that noble.

"I'm sorry. I should have had more control." He leaned his head against hers. "Kayla could have walked in here."

"I share the blame." Her voice didn't sound any steadier than his. She shivered. "I've never felt like this before."

"That makes two of us."

Naomi lifted her head, a smile playing at the corner of her mouth. "I'm glad. I like it being new for both of us."

Tenderly, he brushed her hair away from her face. He wanted to tell her so much more, but she wasn't ready. "I'll be doing some night clinics until this weekend."

Her pretty mouth tightened; outrage sharpened her voice. "They're taking advantage of you."

"I would have given up a lot more not to disappoint Kayla or you." One day soon, he hoped he could tell her how precious she was to him.

"You're a . . . wonderful man."

He grunted, hugged her, then stared down into her face. "Let's go out on a real date Friday night. We won't tell Brandon, but I'll get dinner reservations at the Casa de Serenidad. Henri is a great chef."

"Since I've heard from a few of the teachers how wonderful the restaurant is, I'll live dangerously and go with you," she told him, finding she was more excited than embarrassed by the bulge beneath her hips.

He chuckled. "I'll protect you."

He would, too. There wasn't a shred of doubt in her mind.

"Afterward, we'll go to Phoenix's opening at the art gallery."

"I'd like that. Kayla has her first sleepover Friday and I'm a bit anxious about it." She shook her head ruefully. "I'll hope I won't make a nuisance of myself calling the poor mother."

"Kayla will have a great time, and it will be my pleasure to keep your thoughts occupied."

"Mine, too."

He kissed her. She let herself be seduced by his mouth and hands and enjoyed every wicked second.

The next day at school Naomi found herself questioned about Richard's availability. With a straight face she'd told them she thought he was seeing someone and let it go at that. If a few women looked at her with suspicion, that was their problem. She had other things to think about, like what to wear to dinner. She called the hotel and spoke to Faith, who assured her a step above casual was fine.

Since all Naomi had were casual clothes, she invited Fallon over to get her opinion. Afterward they went to her closet. She nibbled on her lower lip as Fallon went through her meager wardrobe once, then started going though her clothes again.

Naomi sighed. "I was afraid of that."

Fallon kept pushing hangers aside. "You haven't had any use for anything other than casual clothes. Women even wear jeans to church."

Naomi placed a hand on Fallon's shoulder. "You're not going to find anything. I have until Friday. Maybe there's a good sale."

"We'll go tonight," Fallon suggested. "I'll search the Internet to see who's having a sale." She glanced down at the flat or low-heeled shoes with toes neatly lined up on the bottom of the closet. "You're going to need a new pair of shoes as well. You could borrow a dress or shoes from me, but you're smaller."

Naomi bit her lips again. "Thank you, but I want to wear something new. I hope that's not vanity."

Fallon grinned. "Nothing wrong with a little vanity and wanting to look special for a man you like."

"Maybe I should ask Richard to just go to a casual restaurant. I wouldn't mind spending the money if I planned to wear the dress and shoes again, but I can't see it for one night." Naomi glanced at her clothes.

Fallon rolled her eyes. "It's your first official date with Richard. You want to make his eyes pop. For him to wonder what's beneath that sexy dress, to groan when he sees how your hips sway in those strappy, high-heeled sandals."

Naomi couldn't deny it. "Maybe we'll find a dress and shoes tonight."

They found plenty of shoes and dresses on sale, but either the price was still too high or they didn't like the dress or shoes. An hour later, Kayla was tired and bored. The excitement of helping Mama find a dress had faded. They'd left the mall and stopped at a fast-food place for takeout and then gone home. Fallon was sure they'd find what they were looking for the next day. They didn't.

By Wednesday night, after another fruitless search, Naomi was beginning to panic. When Richard called Naomi, she had been trying to come up with a reason to ask if they could go someplace else . . . until he'd said he'd made reservations and asked for a special table.

"I want the night of our first date to be memorable for you."

She wanted that as well, and she wasn't going to spoil it for either of them. "With you, it will be."

There was a slight pause. "I wish I was there with you."

"Me, too." Sitting on the sofa, her hand lightly grazed over the cushion next to her. Erotic images of her and Richard filled her mind. She hadn't been afraid. Far from it, she had been excited and aroused. She wanted that again, and more.

" 'Night."

" 'Night." Naomi hung up. There had to be a dress and shoes in her price range, and she was going to find them. She couldn't drag Kayla out again. For the second night in a row she was so tired she hadn't protested about going to bed. She didn't want Kayla so tired she couldn't enjoy her first sleepover. She had to find a sitter.

Mrs. Grayson taught class on Thursday night, and that left Catherine. Since it was nine fourteen, Naomi would call tomorrow.

Naomi stood and went to check on Kayla before going to her bedroom. She couldn't resist going to her closet. Clothes had never been high on her list of things to buy. For so long she hadn't cared because Gordon would accuse her of trying to entice a man. Now that she wanted to, she couldn't find anything to wear.

She glanced down at her shoes. They were comfortable and dependable. Nothing remotely close to sexy. Her thoughts stumbled to a halt. If there was one woman who knew beautiful and sexy clothes and where to find them at a discount, it was Sierra. Naomi went to her purse and found Sierra's card. If Sierra couldn't help her, Naomi wasn't sure who could.

Not only did Sierra agree to help, she picked up Naomi and Fallon at Catherine's house Thursday evening in the big black Lincoln, explaining she didn't want them wasting time searching for a parking space or worrying about talking and driving. "If we have time, I'm thinking a quick trip to the salon is in order."

Naomi touched her shoulder-length hair. She did it herself to save money.

"You have beautiful hair," Sierra said. "Anita can do a quick dry shampoo and show you how to style it for tomorrow night. We want Richard's eyes to pop."

Naomi smiled. "That's the idea."

"Then we're going to make it happen. Looks like we've arrived at our first stop."

They went to three stores before Sierra zeroed in on a straight black dress with pink piping and a little pink bow at the sleeve at a specialty shop with lots of glass, space, and clothes on padded hangers in single file. The store shouted *expensive*.

"Demure and sexy. This is the one."

Naomi wanted to look at the price tag, but she didn't dare. Sierra was helping her. In the dressing room, she searched for the tag and didn't find one and recalled the old saying: *If you had to ask, you couldn't afford it.*

The dress fit like it had been made for her. The shoes Sierra found made her feel almost pretty.

"You look beautiful, Naomi," Fallon said. "Sierra, you certainly have an eye for clothes."

"My family would say I shop enough." Sierra nodded. "I think we're done here."

It had to be said. "How much are the shoes? The dress didn't have a price tag."

"Must have fallen off the dress. You change and I'll go ask," Sierra said.

Naomi turned, then turned back to Sierra. "You wouldn't have helped it fall off, by chance, would you?"

"Me?" Sierra's dark eyes widened in innocence. "I shop here too much to destroy their property. They have cameras."

Naomi wasn't convinced then or later when she saw the price tag of the shoes and dress. It was a little more than she'd planned, but considerably less than a couple of other dresses she'd managed to see the price tag on.

From there, they went to the beauty salon to get her hair styled. By the time they arrived back at Catherine's house to pick up Kayla, Naomi was a bit overwhelmed and so eternally grateful to Sierra.

"Thank you doesn't seem enough."

"Just have fun," Sierra told her. "By the way, you never did tell me which restaurant you were going to."

Naomi bit her lip. "The Pueblo at Casa de Serenidad."

Sierra laughed. "If I were you and Richard, I wouldn't mention that to Brandon."

Richard slammed out of his car and quickly went to Naomi's front door and knocked. He couldn't wait to see her. Now that he knew what she tasted like, how good she felt in his arms, he didn't want to be apart from her if at all possible. This weekend he was free for the first time in months and he fully intended to enjoy being with Naomi.

He heard the locks disengage, the smile already forming on his face as the door opened.

"Hi, Richard."

He felt his mouth become unhinged, his blood heat. She'd always been pretty to him: Tonight she was stunning in a little black dress that skinned over her small body and stopped above knees he was going to enjoy kissing behind. She was taller. He noticed the black heels that had a little bow at the toe, the same as on the short sleeve of the dress. Her hair was different as well. Soft curls framed her face and made him want to run his hands through and muss it up. But it was her eyes, direct and knowing, that captured him and drew him again and again.

"Aren't you going to say anything?"

"Wow," he said, finally entering the apartment and closing the door after him. She was in his arms before the door closed, his mouth on hers an instant later. "You taste and look incredible."

"Thank you."

"I'm not sure we should go out. I don't want to have to fight off men," he said, only half teasing.

"I only want to be with you." She went to the sofa to pick up her purse. Richard's gaze dropped to the enticing sway of her hips. His body stirred. She turned and caught him staring. She smiled.

Richard knew when he was in trouble. Naomi trusted him enough, cared enough to flirt with him, entice him. He wanted to slide that dress off her and make love to her until they were too weak to do anything except breathe. But he understood women. Naomi might want to tempt him, but she also wanted to show off a bit.

"All I can say is that if a man tries to hit on you, I won't be responsible." He took her arm and started for the door.

"Men don't notice me that way," she said matter-of-factly.

"They notice all right. You just don't notice them that way." He opened the door. "But it won't do them any good, because you're with me and I'm not letting you out of my sight."

It had happened just the way she had hoped and dreamed. Richard had actually been stunned speechless when he first saw her. Naomi had wanted to stop time and savor the moment.

After she'd taken Kayla to her sleepover and come back home to shower and dress, she'd worried that perhaps Sierra and Fallon had been wrong. They weren't. And when he'd kissed her, she'd felt the tenderness and something else she couldn't put her finger on.

She glanced at him as the maître d' led them to a secluded table for two with fresh-cut white roses on top. Richard held her seat for her. She smelled his crisp clean scent and a citrus cologne. He smelled as good as he looked.

"Would you care for a glass of wine or do you prefer the sommelier?" the man asked.

"Naomi?" Richard asked.

Her hands clutched the oversized menu. Her knowledge of wines was limited. "You decide."

"Two sweetened iced teas for now," Richard said.

"Certainly, sir." He moved away.

"I hope that's all right. I seldom drink alcohol," Richard said.

"Neither do I," she confessed, then glanced around the restaurant. "It's lovely."

"You look even more beautiful in candlelight."

She glanced back at him, saw the admiration in his dark eyes, and felt her body quicken.

He held up his menu. "What looks good? I think I'll have a porterhouse."

Naomi glanced at the menu and gasped at the prices. Everything was à la carte. A meal would cost more than her dress and shoes.

"Naomi?"

Her menu lowered. Richard was successful, but . . . "I'm not that hungry."

Richard gave her a long level look. It was all she could do not to hide behind the menu.

Their waiter appeared with their drinks. "Good evening, are you ready to order?"

"Yes," Richard said and ordered house salads for both of them, the sea bass for her, and the porterhouse for him with asparagus and mashed potatoes. "We'll decide on dessert later."

"Very good, sir." The waiter moved away.

"What if I didn't like sea bass?" she asked, making herself relax. Richard was too self-assured to try to impress her or anyone else by dining at a restaurant he couldn't afford.

"You had it at Catherine's birthday party." He picked up his glass of tea.

Shock crossed her face. "That was months ago."

He placed the glass aside and stared across the table at her. "You wore a pretty blue dress, and ate crab legs for the first time."

Naomi's eyes widened. "You remembered what I wore." If he remembered that clearly, he'd also know she had a limited wardrobe. Embarrassment tinted her cheeks.

"Probably because I like blue and you looked so determined to crack that crab leg yourself." He chuckled.

She relaxed. "You kept showing me how to use the lobster cracker, not eating. You've always been there for me. For us."

"And I always will be."

Something about the intensity of his gaze, the way he said the words, warmed her as nothing else could, but they also gave her pause. After Monday night she knew they were going to be intimate. She trusted him enough to give him her body, but not anything more. As she'd told him, she wanted her independence. Never again did she want to be tied to a man in marriage.

Chapter 13

"If you hit the guy talking to Naomi, Morgan isn't going to be happy you ruined Phoenix's opening," Brandon said casually as he stood next to Richard.

"If he keeps leering at her, Morgan will just have to be unhappy," Richard said tightly. Ever since they'd arrived at the art gallery forty-five minutes ago, men had been coming up to Naomi. Since she was having a good time and talking with Catherine, Richard was trying to be cool.

"Ease up." Brandon sipped his sparking water. "I admit she looks different tonight, prettier, happier, but you're not dating her or anything."

Richard tossed his friend since grade school a look of annoyance. "We're dating."

Brandon almost spewed his drink. "You're lying."

"If his hand moves anywhere except near her shoulder . . ."

"You're not the possessive type." Brandon wiped his mouth with a napkin. "If you're dating, she'll tell the man to back off."

"Faith just joined them, and he's looking at her," Richard said.

Brandon whirled around so fast, his drink sloshed over the side of his wineglass. Faith had indeed joined them, but the man was still grinning like an idiot at Naomi. "Dirty, but I see your point. I'll explain to Morgan."

"Thanks." Richard worked his way through the milling crowd. Santa Fe had over three hundred galleries that had openings regularly, but a showing by Phoenix Bannister Grayson, the nationally renowned sculptress, was an event. Collectors from around the country were there or had sent a representative. Nine of the fifteen bronze pieces were already sold and it was only an hour into the opening.

"Hello, Richard," Catherine greeted, looking beautiful as usual in an apricot-colored dress. "I was wondering when you'd join us."

"Brandon detained me." Smoothly Richard placed himself between Naomi and the overly attentive man. He caught her hand. "Good evening," he said casually, but his gaze said *Back off*.

Relief crossed Naomi's beautiful face. She squeezed his hand back.

Brandon curved his arm around Faith's shoulders, kissed her on the cheek. "Hi."

Used to Brandon's possessiveness, Faith leaned into him. "Hi."

The man blinked as Luke joined them to stake his claim on his wife. "Hi."

"Hello," the man finally said, his mouth pursed. Clearly he wasn't pleased by the men joining them.

"Mr. James is the rep for a buyer in New York," Catherine explained. "He's waiting on a call from his client."

James smiled warmly at Catherine and missed Luke's glare. "His collection of bronzes is one of the foremost in the country. If he decided to purchase one of Bannister's bronzes, she'll find herself in some very esteemed company."

"Since Phoenix's last three showings have sold out opening night, and she's been featured on the cover of several premier art magazines, I'd say your client would be the lucky one," Catherine said. "Please excuse us, I'd like to go congratulate my husband's sister-in-law on another successful opening."

"Same here," Faith said, leaving with Brandon.

"A close friend," Naomi said as Richard led her away.

Richard's hand slid up her arm to curve around her waist. "Snob."

"Yes, he was." Naomi stopped in front of a two-foot bronze of a woman and man embracing. You could almost feel the intensity of their love and passion. "Thanks for the rescue."

"The way he was leering at you, I should have hit him." Richard shot the representative a menacing look. Since he was on the phone, the man missed it entirely. "If his client is as dense as he is, he doesn't deserve to have one of Phoenix's pieces."

"They're beautiful." Naomi ran her hand over the sculpture's entwined arms. "Phoenix is very good."

"She is. But everyone has some kind of talent.

You just have to dig deep sometimes to find out what it is."

"If you don't mind. Please don't touch the bronze," Mr. James said. "I've just been instructed by my client to purchase this."

"He's too late. I own the bronze," Lance said, joining them.

"What? You can't," the man sputtered. "I spoke with the gallery owner and told him I was waiting for a call."

"As a seasoned rep, you should know that interest doesn't pull a piece. If you wanted the bronze, you should have purchased it." He turned to Richard and Naomi, ignoring the angry man. "Is Fallon coming?"

"I don't think so," Naomi said.

"Pity. I think I'll go home. 'Night."

"Good night."

" 'Night, cuz," Richard said, feeling sorry for his cousin. "I hope Fallon changes her mind about him."

Naomi gazed up at him tenderly. "We both know it is entirely possible for a woman to change her mind."

"We do." Suddenly he wanted to be alone with her. "Let's get out of here."

"All right."

After they congratulated Phoenix on a successful showing, Richard was steering Naomi toward the door when Sierra asked to see her for a moment. He waited impatiently as they talked. Sierra laughed, then escorted Naomi back to him.

"Enjoy the rest of your night," Sierra told them.

Richard didn't know why he felt his face heat. That was a lie. He'd been thinking of taking Naomi to bed ever since she said Kayla was sleeping over. "Thanks, good night."

Richard ushered Naomi out to his car and pulled off. He usually preferred to drive his truck, but tonight he'd wanted a bit more luxury. They were silent on the drive to her apartment. Not a good sign. He parked in front of her apartment and switched off the engine.

"I had a wonderful time tonight." Naomi fiddled with the clasp of her small purse.

He prayed she wasn't about to brush him off. "So did I." He got out of the car and opened her door. They weren't going to be necking in the car when there was a comfortable sofa inside . . . if he got that far.

He watched her fumble with her key, trying to open the apartment door, before taking it from her hand to unlock the door and gently helping her inside since her head was down and she wasn't moving.

He closed the door, saw her jump. Looked like cold showers and erotic dreams again. He held out the key.

After a long moment, she took it. "Would . . ." She cleared her throat. "Would you like something to drink?"

He stepped closer, tilted her chin up so he could see her face. "What I'd like is an explanation why you're nervous all of a sudden. You know I won't push you."

She swallowed, licked her lips. "I . . ."

"Remember the pact." He took both of her arms. "Just say it."

"The kissing was nice, but I'm not sure about the other." Her gaze skittered away. "I don't want to disappoint you. I don't expect much—"

"Whoa," he said cutting her off. "If we do make love, we'll both derive pleasure from it. I don't want a sacrificial woman in bed with me. I want one who gives and takes pleasure, just as I will."

"Don't you see, that's just it. I don't know how. He said . . . I don't know how," she murmured softly.

Richard would gladly kick her ex's butt if he ever saw him. "You ever think the inadequacies were his? You ever think he belittled you because he was the dud?"

Her gaze lifted to him. Clearly she hadn't.

"Trust yourself, trust me." His thumb grazed her cheek. "Forget about the past."

"I want to," she said.

His hands fell. "Then do it."

Seconds ticked by and she said nothing, her gaze on the center of his chest. He was about to leave when she looked at him.

"Why are you so patient with me?" she asked.

"Because I see the woman you don't."

She went into his arms, hugged him. "I don't want you to go."

"Then I won't." His arms firmly around her, he brushed his lips across hers, felt her lips tremble, then open.

He carried her to her room and stood her by the bed. The covers were already drawn. She blushed.

"I'm glad you want me, Naomi. Never be ashamed of that."

Her head lifted. "I'm not. At least not anymore."

He kissed her with the barest of pressure, letting the heat and desire build before drawing back. Grasping the zipper in back of the dress, he slid it down, then pushed it off her shoulders and over her hips.

His breath caught. She was as exquisite as he knew she would be. His fingertips grazed over her delicate skin between her breasts, felt her shiver. He looked at her face, afraid he'd see fear. What he saw was desire.

"We'll take this as slow as I can make it."

She nodded, her eyes huge in her beautiful face.

He unbuttoned his shirt and tossed it aside. His shoes and pants came off next. Palming the condom package, he shoved it discreetly beneath the pillow.

He was aware she was watching him, and it added to his arousal. He wanted her to know he wasn't going to rush her. Kneeling, he picked up one dainty foot to remove her shoe, then the other foot.

He had to grit his teeth to keep from whimpering as he pulled off her sheer stockings. His face was so close to her stomach he couldn't resist kissing her there, running his tongue across the indentation of her navel.

Her trembling hands clenched on his shoulders. "Richard." His name was a shaky thread of sound.

Standing, he kissed her, long and slow. He wanted tenderness for her, he thought as he lowered them to the bed. Tenderness and passion.

One kiss drifted into another. She'd never felt so . . . cherished. Exquisite sensations rippled though her. She felt his damp, hot mouth on her bare nipple and wondered when he'd removed her bra. A scant second later she could only think of the desire heating her blood and making her move restlessly beneath him. She wanted something . . . more.

His relentless hand swept down over her stomach and found the essence of her desire. He stroked her there while his tongue laved her nipple. She had no defense against him, wanted none. Her hips moved, seeking, finding.

While she was still coming down, he entered her, pushing past the slight resistance, the pleasure so intense she moaned and arched again. He began to move, slowly in and out, stroking her, filling her.

Wrapping her arms around him as much as she could, she met him stroke for stroke. Soon she was falling again. His hips pumped faster. They went over together. Smiling, she closed her eyes and was asleep within seconds.

Hearing Naomi's even breathing, Richard pulled her the tiniest bit closer. How he loved this woman, would do anything for her, except walk away. And after making love with her, that was no longer an option. He wasn't going to fool himself that it would be easy to get her to open her heart and mind to him all the way. The task ahead was convincing her that they belonged together.

Naomi drifted on a soft cloud of contentment and happiness. She smiled without opening her eyes, enjoying the feather-light brushes against her skin. Half asleep, she snuggled deeper into the covers and came against the muscled warmth of another person. Before fear could choke her, she remembered the night before and finally realized Richard was kissing her awake.

Angling her head up, she smiled. Last night had been beautiful. She was glad she'd trusted Richard. "Good morning."

"Now it is." He kissed her again. "I was beginning to think I'd have to take drastic measures to wake you up."

"I'm sorry. I haven't been sleeping well lately." She started to rise, blushed, and caught the sheet when it began to slide over her naked breasts.

"Why?" he asked, tilting her chin up.

For just a moment, she thought of evading. "Because I had shut you out of my life. I was miserable and so was Kayla."

He kissed her. "I'm here now and I'm not going anywhere."

Perhaps in time he would, but he was here now and that's what mattered. She smiled up at him. "You want breakfast?"

"You. Just you." He rolled over on top of her, his hands stroking her body, his lips nibbling on her skin. "You're more incredible than my fantasies and I have a very active imagination."

Naomi's breath shuddered out of her as his hand swept over her stomach, going lower. "Y-you touch me and I for-forget to think."

"Then don't. Just close your eyes and enjoy." His mouth drifted over her body with incredible tenderness before closing over her breast and taking the turgid peak between his teeth and tongue to lave and suckle as his hand trailed down her stomach to her woman's softness.

She moaned deep in her throat, her hips lifting against his hand. She was so responsive, so giving, and his. His mouth and hands paid homage to her exquisite body.

He sheathed himself, then lifted her hips with his hands and entered. The fit and feel were mind-blowing. He gritted his teeth to maintain control. She twisted beneath him, her nails biting into his shoulder. He stared down into her face, taking immense pleasure on seeing her eyes glazed with desire.

She wrapped her legs around him and he was lost. He flexed his hips, moving in and out of her, taking her, and being taken in return.

Pleasure engulfed her. It came in waves, her body riding on a crest of ecstasy. Each stroke took her higher and higher. She strained closer, her hips lifting to meet his. She wanted to give him as much pleasure as he was giving her.

She felt the coiling of her body, tried to hold back, but she was helpless against the orgasm that swept through her like a tidal wave. She spasmed, her hips lifting as he plunged into her one last time before he was riding with her as the wave took them both over and under.

He held her to him. Each time they made love it was more amazing than the last. She was all that he ever wanted. She snuggled against him, kissing his shoulder.

He nuzzled her cheek, rolled over so she was

draped on top of him, and nipped her shoulder. "I can't get enough of you."

She shivered. Every place he touched was sensitized to him, craved more. She hadn't known her body could want this way. She realized she was naked, the sheet kicked off the bed, and she was too content to care. She felt a peace she'd never experienced before and it was all due to the man holding her so tenderly. "Now I know why the Grayson women are always so happy."

"The right woman can put a smile on a man's face and keep it there."

Her head lifted to study his face. He was so handsome—gorgeous, actually—and he wanted her. Unpopular, mistake-driven Naomi. He looked as happy as she felt, and she was responsible. She felt powerful for the first time in her life. "I think they'd agree that it's the right man."

Chuckling, he picked her up. "Let's discuss it in the shower, and then I'm cooking you breakfast."

"This is delicious." Naomi cut into her omelet stuffed with ham and oozing with cheese.

"Some men who aren't chefs can cook." He smiled at her and sipped his coffee.

"I know that." She leaned back in her seat, her face intense the way it became when she was trying to find the right words. "It's just that a man has never cooked just for me."

He frowned and sat his mug down. "Surely your father cooked sometimes?"

She shook her head. "My mother was a stay-at-home mom. I never saw Daddy cook a single dish. I'm not sure Mama would have let him. She took pride in a spotless house, balanced meals, and a happy husband."

Richard heard himself ask, "And what about a happy daughter?"

A shadow crossed her face. "My parents tried, but I was an oddity to them. I preferred to curl up with a good book rather than go out or be on a sports team. My mother was captain of her tennis team in college, and my father loved basketball and coached at the college level. They neither loved nor understood me."

Instantly he was out of his chair, kneeling by her side and taking her shivering hand. His heart ached for her. Her ex wasn't the only one he wanted a moment with. "I'm sorry."

Her smile trembled. "I'm over it now."

No, she wasn't. The happiness in her eyes was gone. She deserved love, needed it, and he was going to make sure she received so much there'd never be any doubt how much she was loved.

The phone on the counter rang. "Kayla." Naomi shot out of her chair to grab the phone. "Hello. Hi, Carol. Is Kayla still having fun?"

Richard eased back in his chair, noting Naomi kept her back to him. It could be a coincidence, but his gut was telling him that wasn't the case.

"Yes, thank you. I'll be on my way to get her." Naomi hung up the phone and slowly turned to face him. "I have to go get Kayla."

He studied her, noted that her gaze kept slipping

away. The world had intruded, and she was probably embarrassed. "I don't suppose I could drive you?"

Arms straight, she linked her fingers together. "You'd look at me the way you're looking at me now and they'd know."

"Are you ashamed or concerned?" he asked.

"Neither." She unlinked her hands, but she didn't move away from the counter. "I just don't want to be the subject of gossip. The mother is the PTA president. Another teacher's child was invited as well. I don't want Kayla to hear things about us she doesn't understand."

He wasn't sure it wasn't more than that. Pushing her now, when she had to pick up Kayla, wasn't the time. "All right. I'll be at the ranch if you want to come by once you pick her up."

Finally, she smiled and came to him, dropping a kiss on his mouth before straightening. "I think it's a safe bet to say you'll see us this afternoon."

Richard was worried. Making love with Naomi had, as he'd told her, far exceeded his fantasies. It was astonishing. Even now, hours later, he'd just stop at times and shake his head in wonder. Good thing the horses didn't mind his strange behavior as he cleaned the stalls and put in fresh hay.

Yet intimacy hadn't brought him and Naomi closer as he'd hoped. She trusted him with her body, but he wanted more. He wanted to be there for her to comfort her, help her fight her problems, share her life. Despite the wonderful night together, she still held back.

She still thought she couldn't let him into her heart and life, and keep her independence. She only had to look at Catherine—or Sierra, for that matter—to know that marriage to the right person made life richer, fuller. Sure some marriages failed, but others succeeded and flourished. His parents were immensely happy. His mother loved his father, but she didn't put up with any of his "foolishness," as she called it. His father might act tough, but he'd bend over backward to keep Mama happy.

"Richard, are you in here?"

"Dr. Richard?"

Hearing Naomi and Kayla call him, he propped the pitchfork on the wall of the stall and stepped out. Mother and daughter were silhouetted at the opening of the barn. He'd seen few sights that were prettier. Certainly none that made his heart race, made him glad to be alive.

"You're just in time to help clean stalls."

"We found you!" Kayla cried and ran to meet him.

He scooped her up. "You have a good time at the sleepover?"

"Yes, sir. We played games and ate pizza and hot dogs and soda." She looked back at her mother. "When my birthday comes, I want to have my friends over and do the same thing."

Richard turned his attention to Naomi. The happy smile on her face made him breathe easier. "Hey."

"Hey yourself."

He wanted to kiss her. He saw the desire in her eyes. He simply held out his hand to her, and when

she took it, he pulled her closer. He intended a simple brush of his mouth against her cheek, but apparently she had the same thought because her head
turned at the same time, their lips met, clung. He
inhaled her sigh; his tongue touched hers, tasted the
sweetness. He fought to lift his head and finally won.

He stared down into her face, soft and warm,
then saw her eyes widened in alarm. He simply
turned to look at Kayla's wide-eyed stare. Looked
like they had some explaining to do.

"You kissed Mama."

"Yes, when a man and a woman like each other,
they kiss," Richard explained.

Kayla's face scrunched up. "Rose's mommy and
daddy kissed like that last night. Are you going to
be my daddy now?"

Naomi was too stunned to speak. Her heart
clenched at the hope in Kayla's eyes. She wanted a
daddy so much. Just the thought of marriage made
Naomi's stomach tense. How could she have for-
gotten for an instant and kissed Richard in front of
Kayla? She was trying to find the words when
Richard released her and stood Kayla on her feet.
He knelt in front of her.

"I bet Rose's mommy and daddy went out on
a lot of dates before they ever talked about getting married," Richard said. "Do you know what a
date is?"

"No, sir."

"Well, a date is when a boy and girl, or a man or
a woman, go out together, just the two of them to
get to know each other better," he explained. "It
can be to the movies, to dinner, or just a walk."

Kayla looked at her mother, and then at Richard. "Children don't get to go?"

Richard hugged her. "Sometimes, but sometimes they go by themselves. Your mother and I had our first date last night while you were at the sleepover."

Naomi's face heated. She barely kept from squirming.

"You did?"

Naomi finally found her voice. "Dating doesn't mean getting married."

"But if you or your mother need me for anything like the show-and-tell or to help get the house ready, or anything else, I'd be there," he said.

"Did you and Mama have fun?" Clearly, Kayla wasn't ready to let the dating go.

"The best time ever," Richard said.

"I wore the dress I showed you." At that, Richard glanced up at Naomi with a knowing look, and her body quickened.

"She was beautiful. We went to dinner and then to see Phoenix's art showing."

"I went with her to look for a dress," Kayla said. "Are you going on another date?"

Richard curved his arm around Kayla's waist and looked up at Naomi. "This is our second date."

Kayla frowned. "But I'm here."

He picked Kayla up with one arm and curved the other around Naomi's waist. "Which means, I'm a lucky guy to have two beautiful women for a date. I might even grill us burgers and hot dogs after we go for a ride."

"Mama's not very good at riding."

Since it was the truth and Kayla said it with a

smile and appeared all right now, Naomi didn't take offense. "You and Richard can show me again what I'm doing wrong."

Kayla grinned. "I'm going to like my first date."

Naomi hugged Kayla and thought, just as she'd liked her first date with Richard. She was a fortunate woman.

A little after nine that night, Richard followed Naomi in his truck to her apartment. They'd had a fun day. Somehow it was better than the ones they'd spent together before. He thought it was because Naomi wasn't as wary of him and he didn't have to keep reminding himself not to get too close, not to look at her as if he could eat her alive. They were both probably more relaxed. Kayla must have sensed it as well, because she'd been as lively and as playful as he'd ever seen her.

Naomi had done only marginally better with her riding skills. She never seemed to be able to completely loosen up on the horse, whereas Kayla was a natural. She had good instincts about animals and people. She was going to grow up to be a strong woman just as Sierra had predicted.

Kayla wanted him for a father. Just the thought made Richard proud, his heart joyful. They'd both have to work on Naomi. He had to park a short distance away. By the time he got to her car, she was reaching in the backseat for Kayla.

"Let me have her. You get the door." Picking her and Teddy up, he followed Naomi inside her apartment and to Kayla's bedroom.

"She should have a bath after riding and playing

all afternoon, but I'm not sure she'd wake up enough." Naomi turned back the covers of the bed.

"Then do what my mother used to do, wash her face and hands and leave the rest until the morning." Placing Kayla on the bed, Richard slipped off her tennis shoes and socks, and placed Teddy beside her.

"Your mother is a smart woman. I'll be out shortly. There's soft drinks and iced tea in the refrigerator."

"I'm good. I'll go channel-surf on the TV."

Leaving the bedroom, he picked up the controls of the TV and sat on the sofa. He wasn't interested in watching TV, but it would make things less awkward for both of them. He wasn't sure how Naomi felt about them making love with Kayla in the apartment. He wouldn't dream of spending the night, but even given that concession, he figured it was too soon for that to happen. Kayla had awakened to find him there in the past, but it had been innocent.

"She's all tucked in."

He looked up to see Naomi across the room. Ten feet away, and it might as well have been ten miles. She was nervous, and probably thinking he wouldn't understand she wanted him to leave. One day she'd realize he'd always do what was best for her and Kayla, and always put their welfare first.

He shut the TV off and came to his feet. "I'll pick you and Kayla up around two." They were going on his and Kayla's "second" date to the Children's Museum. Neither of them wanted her to feel left out because they were dating.

Naomi followed him to the door. "Thank you for a wonderful day."

She was so polite it set his teeth on edge. He should probably keep walking, but he was already turning and drawing her into his arms. His hungry mouth cut off her gasp of surprise. He wanted her to remember the passion they'd shared, the heat. One hand wrapped around her waist; the other pressed her hips against his growing erection.

Need trampled though him. The little moans Naomi made in the back of her throat drove him on. When he lifted his head, they were both breathing hard. He'd remembered as well and it had been worth it.

"I need to get out of here."

Her fingertips gently swept across his lips. "I want to be with you, but her room is next to mine. She's never woken up once she goes down for the night, but . . ."

He kissed her. "You're a good mother. Kayla has to come first."

She leaned her forehead against his chest. "I should have known you'd understand." Her head lifted. "You're a very special man, Richard Young-blood."

"With you I feel that way." Palming her face, he kissed her long and deep. "See you at two tomorrow."

"We'll be waiting. 'Night, and thanks for everything."

"The pleasure was all mine." He left with a huge grin on his face. By the time he reached his truck he was whistling.

Chapter 14

Naomi could do nothing but smile at the enthusiasm of Kayla on her "date" with Richard at the Children's Museum. She hardly wanted to leave his side to do the hands-on activities. What warmed her heart even more was that he seemed to understand this new turn of events. He was as patient with her as ever.

"Don't get 'the look,' and I didn't expect you to act any other way, but thank you for being so wonderful with Kayla," Naomi told Richard, who was standing beside her.

He curved his arm around her shoulders. "Told you, I sort of like her."

Naomi leaned into him before she could stop herself and straightened. "I believe you did."

Richard dropped his arm and slid his hands into his pockets. Naomi felt badly, but she wasn't sure she wanted other people to know about them.

"Why hello, Mrs. Reese."

Naomi jerked around. Her eyes widened on seeing her principal. "Mrs. Crenshaw."

"Hello, Mrs. Crenshaw," Richard greeted. "How are you doing?"

"Fine. Thank you, Dr. Youngblood." The middle-aged woman nodded toward the children's activity of painting. "I'm here with my two grandchildren, who are visiting from Albuquerque. I see Kayla doing the same project."

"Yes," Naomi said slowly. She wanted Mrs. Crenshaw to move along before Kayla returned, but her boss seemed in no hurry to leave, especially since her husband joined them.

"Naomi, you know Mr. Crenshaw. Bill, this is Dr. Youngblood, the wonderful veterinarian who came to our school last week."

The men shook hands. Out of the corner of Naomi's eyes, she saw the children stand with their artwork.

"I better get the twins," Mr. Crenshaw said. "They'll take off and we'll never find them."

Mrs. Crenshaw patted his arm as he passed. "They're eight and a handful. I can't believe my quiet, studious son has two girls who test every limit we've set."

"And you wouldn't take all the gold in the world for them," Richard said knowingly.

She laughed. "You're right, of course. I love Derrick, my son, but the love for grandchildren is different. You'll understand one day."

Naomi moved her shoulders restlessly. Principal Crenshaw was looking at Richard. Naomi didn't want to get married, but she discovered the possibility of Richard marrying another woman and having children didn't set well.

"Look what I painted," Kayla said as she ran up to them. "Hi, Principal Crenshaw."

"Hello, Kayla. That's a nice watercolor," Principal Crenshaw said.

Kayla smiled as she looked at the picture of three people on horses. "It's me, Mama, and Dr. Richard on our first date. Today is our second."

Mrs. Crenshaw lifted her gaze to Naomi. "Oh."

Naomi opened her mouth, but nothing came out.

"Good job, Kayla." Richard hunkered down. "You're becoming quite the artist. I'll have this one framed for you to put in your room."

Mr. Crenshaw joined them with the identical twins dressed alike in white shorts, pink T-shirts and ponytails tied with pink-and-white ribbon. "I just caught them."

"Exploring is good for developing the mind, Grandfather," they chorused.

Apparently this wasn't the first time their grandfather had heard this. He knew them well because his hand remained on each of their shoulders. He shook his head. "I don't need any more gray hairs."

"Gray hair is distinguished looking," one said.

"Very," said the other.

Mrs. Crenshaw's lips twitched. "We'd better be going. I'll see you Monday morning."

"Good-bye," Naomi said, wishing she had had a moment to ask Principal Crenshaw not to mention the date. She wasn't a gossip, but it might come out when she was talking about her grandchildren . . . which she always did when they visited.

Richard came to his feet as they walked away. "You all right?"

It didn't take two guesses to know what he was talking about. "I won't be able to work Monday for all the questions, not to mention the sly looks and whispers."

"Will you be all right?" he asked.

Naomi studied him as closely as he was studying her. As usual, he was sensitive to her mood and concerned. No one had ever been so in tune with her feelings. "How did Kayla and I get so lucky?"

A smile took the worry from his face and caused her to sigh. He was so handsome, beautiful in fact, and for the time being he was theirs.

"Luck had nothing to do with it." His arms circled her waist. "So, I'm officially off the market?"

Kayla squeezed in between them and looked expectantly from one to the other. "You gonna kiss her again?"

Naomi blushed. Richard picked up Kayla and kissed her cheek before setting her on her feet. She giggled.

"Kayla, you shouldn't say things like that in public," Naomi told her, glancing around to see who might have heard. Kayla hadn't been quiet when she asked.

"Why?" she asked

Naomi leaned down and answered in a hushed whisper. "Because kissing is private."

Holding the painting with one hand, Kayla promptly pointed to a couple. "I saw Mrs. Catherine and some of the other women kissing at the table after the program I was on with Mrs. Catherine. And they're kissing over there."

A young couple was indeed kissing, her hands still on the stroller.

"Always knew Kayla was smart. Can't fight facts." Richard smacked Naomi on the lips and caught Kayla's free hand. "Let's see what else they have here."

Walking beside Richard, who was talking quietly with Kayla, Naomi decided she could be uptight about the change in her and Richard's relationship or take another cue from her daughter and just enjoy. She looked at Richard, who happened to glance at her. Her heart thumped. Her body heated.

The choice was easy: Enjoy.

Naomi didn't know what to expect Monday morning at school, so she was thankful when everyone acted normally on seeing her. Richard had already had a talk with Kayla about dating being "private." She liked the idea of something special between them and promised not to tell. He was coming over that night to help with her homework.

Naomi loved her daughter, but she hoped she went to bed early that night. Last night she had been too keyed up and hadn't fallen asleep until almost nine. She and Richard had watched a movie. His hands didn't move anyplace they shouldn't have, and not a piece of clothing was discarded. Since she didn't have a satisfied smile on her face the way she did after they made love, it was probably for the best.

"Naomi, are you all right?"

Naomi straightened and glanced around in the cafeteria at Ms. Hightower and hoped her face wasn't flushed. "Yes. Just thinking."

Kayla's teacher's frown didn't clear, then her eyes widened. "Oh, my. Isn't that Sierra Navarone? I've seen her in magazines and on the Internet news with that gorgeous husband of hers. That's one lucky woman."

"Blade would say he's the lucky one. Excuse me." Naomi crossed to Sierra, who was standing on the landing of the steps leading down into the cafeteria. She looked stunning, and completely at ease in a beautiful cream-colored suit that probably cost three months of Naomi's salary. In her arm was a notebook.

"Hi, Sierra." Naomi stopped in front of her. "I have lunch duty this week and can't leave."

"No problem. I thought you'd want to know that the Allens accepted your counter-offer. Congratulations."

Naomi gasped, then hugged Sierra. She had taken the hint from Sierra and taken another seventy-five hundred dollars off the asking price. "Thank you."

Smiling, Sierra handed her a notebook. "Mr. Allen called me yesterday, and I had my inspector go out at six this morning. As I thought, the house is in excellent condition despite having been left vacant. They were smart enough to leave the water on and have a neighbor water the foundation. This is your copy."

"I still can't believe it."

"Perhaps this will help." Sierra held out a gold

heart-shaped key ring with two keys. "The same key opens all doors."

Naomi's trembling hand closed around the key ring. "I get them now?"

"I told them you were a teacher with a small daughter and since your credit score was excellent and the down payment good, the sale should go through without a hitch. I added that you were anxious to move in and have the house ready by the time school was out," Sierra told her. "By the way, a locksmith reset the locks; those are new keys. I have one, but I'll turn it over to you as soon as you sign at the mortgage company. It can be Kayla's when she's older."

"I don't know how to thank you," Naomi said.

"That smile on your face is enough." Sierra looked behind her. "And here she comes."

"Hi, Mrs. Sierra. The monitor wouldn't let me go until I finished my corn." Kayla screwed up her face. "I don't like corn."

Sierra leaned down to her. "I dislike green peas and brussels sprouts."

"Yuck!" Kayla said.

Naomi squatted down to her daughter. "Can you keep another secret?"

"Yes, ma'am."

She held up the keys. "We got the house."

Kayla hugged her. "Can you start thinking more about the brown puppy now?"

"Your daughter will go far in life." Sierra chuckled.

"That's definitely a possibility." Naomi came to her full height. "Thank you again."

"My pleasure. I better go before we have a visitor." She checked her watch. "I promised Rio a full week of no problems."

Frowning, Naomi glanced over Sierra's shoulder. "Where are they?"

"One's at the school's entrance and the other is just off the hallway. The things I do for love." Sierra leaned over and whispered, "Your and Kayla's names are engraved on the key chain. There's room enough for another name. Good-bye."

She meant Richard. Some of Naomi's happiness faded. Their relationship wasn't forever.

"Mama, you look sad," Kayla said.

Smiling, Naomi scooped her up to hug her before putting her down. She needed that hug. She'd just enjoy the time with Richard with no regrets. "Just thinking. How about we invite Richard over tonight and celebrate?"

"Yeah," Kayla shouted. Her mother put her finger to her lips and smiled back at her.

"I can't believe it." Holding Richard's hand, she walked though the house that afternoon. She'd driven there straight from work. She hadn't been able to wait. She'd called him and he'd met her there.

On arriving, she was happy to see that the front yard had been mowed, the rosebush trimmed back, all the windows washed. Sierra was as efficient as usual.

"You did it." Richard kissed her on the cheek. "I'm proud of you. What do you want to tackle first?"

She held her hand to her chest and laughed nervously. "I don't know."

"Let's start at the top with painting and move down to the floors. Once that's done, you can make the draperies. I can seed the backyard to get the grass growing. Luckily that type doesn't need much water."

Naomi looked out the patio door. Kayla was jumping, trying to grab a plum from the fruit tree. "I think she likes it here."

Richard's arms went around her waist and he pulled her back against him. "She's a wonderful little girl. Anywhere you are, she's happy. You're a good mother. It wasn't easy, but she's proof it was worth every sacrifice."

He understood that so well. And she'd been alone until she came to Santa Fe. She angled her head and kissed his chin. "Despite my talk of being independent, I like having you to talk to, be with." She grinned. "Among other things."

"Yeah. I better go say good-bye to Kayla and get back to the office."

"Will I see you tonight?" she asked as he started out the door.

"Count on it."

Laughing, Naomi watched Richard lift Kayla so she could finally reach the fruit. Taking it from her, he went to the outside faucet and washed it, then gave it back to her. She took a bite and then offered the plum to him. Together they shared the fruit. Kayla loved him so much. He was easy to love. He—

With a jolt, Naomi realized she loved him as well. She staggered as if that would take the thought back. It didn't. How could she have let this happen?

She'd promised herself she'd never be vulnerable again. Not even to a good man like Richard.

Her fingertips covered the lower half of her face. He must never know. She was too vulnerable where he was concerned. If he knew, he'd push for a deeper relationship. This was all she could handle now, perhaps forever.

Richard must never know she had fallen hopelessly in love with him.

The next evening, Naomi was humming to herself, cleaning out the cabinets beneath the sink of her new home. The uncertainty of the night before was gone. She was going to take one day at a time.

She reached farther back under the cabinet. A lizard darted close to her hand. She screamed, barely missing hitting her head when she jerked back. Without thinking she ran, screaming Richard's name. He'd been painting Kayla's room. He met her in the hallway. "What is it?"

"A lizard!"

Trying not to smile, he pulled her into his arms and gently brushed his lips across hers. "It won't hurt you, and he's probably long gone by now. I'll put an organic deterrent out tomorrow."

Once her heart stopped racing, she stared up at him. Another man might have been angry or called her foolish. Richard had comforted and reassured her. She placed her head on his chest again. If she had to be foolish and fall in love, she'd picked good, as Sierra would say.

"You all right?"

She sighed and relaxed against him even more.

"Just thinking. If I saw another lizard, would I get another kiss?"

He lifted her head and kissed her. "Answer your question?"

"Yes."

"Then why are you still standing here?"

"Guess." She liked teasing him, liked flirting.

Pulling her more securely into his arms, he kissed her until her toes curled in her tennis shoes. Slowly she opened her eyes. "You amaze me."

"You inspire me. Now back to work."

She had to ask. "How can you be so calm?"

"Because I've had practice and, if I kiss you again, we'll end up on this hard floor making love." Dark passion swirled in his beautiful eyes. "Your skin is too delicate and I treasure you too much to hurt you in any way."

Her heart and body quickened. "There's a blanket in the emergency kit in my car. "

"Where are your keys?"

Naomi hummed as she painted the walls in the open area. She felt good. It felt good getting the house ready for them to move it, but it also felt good working beside Richard. She stopped, smiled, and looked across the room at him. He was painting as well.

For the past two weeks they'd worked together whenever they got the chance. They'd gone shopping for paint, material for the draperies, and to secondhand stores looking for patio furniture. He never seemed to care how long she took or how indecisive she was. He was patient and understanding.

They'd been on dates with just the two of them, and with Kayla. He made sure she never felt left out. He'd even taught her his private cell phone number in case she needed to call.

He'd slipped effortlessly into their lives. Once she'd dreaded the sound of a man's heavy footsteps, the sound of his car door closing, a man touching her. She welcomed them now.

"I think someone is loafing," Richard said, still painting. "The walls won't paint themselves."

Dipping the roller in paint, she rolled it against the wall. "I'm almost finished and you're not."

"Because you got a head start on me." He glanced over. "Looks good."

Naomi stared at the wall. She'd been afraid to try at first. She'd recalled too well her ex-husband's humiliating words. With Richard she'd try anything. And had. She giggled. Richard had purchased an air mattress to go with the blanket.

"What's so funny?" He picked up his paint tray and roller and went to the kitchen sink.

Naomi followed with her things. He reached for them when she stopped beside him.

"Are you going to tell me or do I have to guess?"

She looked up at him through a sweep of her lashes. "You've made me shameless and I sort of like it."

He kissed her on the lips. "I love it."

Her smile trembling, she turned away. "I better go put the lid on the paint."

His hand closed around her arm before she had gone two steps. "I thought we agreed to talk."

"Isn't that what we're doing?"

His brows arched. She wasn't fooling him. "I mention love and you take off. Now you won't look at me."

Her head lifted. His eyes were so intense, she could get lost in them. "This is all I can give."

His hand flexed on her arm. "If I want more?"

She fought the misery sweeping though her. If she lost him . . . "This is all I can give."

His fingers uncurled. He went back to the sink. "You better close that paint."

She'd hurt him. Going to him, she circled his waist from behind, tightened his arms when he shifted, and placed her cheek against his back. "I know it's selfish, but I don't want to lose you, to lose this."

"Marriage would make it better."

Although she knew what he was thinking, she flinched. Her eyes shut tightly. "To you marriage is love and honor and commitment for a lifetime. To me it's pain and humiliation and embarrassment."

He turned then and took her arms in his damp hands. "You've seen Catherine and Luke, and the others. You know it doesn't have to be that way."

"Don't ask me for more than I can give," she whispered. "Please. Don't leave me. Us."

"Never." He held her at arm's length. "A man can't walk away from his heart."

Her heart stumbled. She loved him so much. She kissed him, giving with her body what she couldn't say with words.

A little after seven Thursday night, Naomi pulled the baking dish out of the oven and placed it on top of the kitchen stove. She'd been home less than an hour after stopping by the house again to remeasure the windows for the draperies. Mrs. Cruz, a fourth-grade teacher, was the unofficial director of all of the school plays and made their costumes. She was letting Naomi borrow her portable machine this coming weekend. The house was coming together, and the side benefits weren't bad.

She paused and thought of her and Richard's discussion on marriage. Thank goodness the subject hadn't come up again. Hearing the familiar knock on the front door, she checked her reflection in the toaster and hurried to the front door. Richard was coming over for dinner. Unlocking the locks, she opened the door with a smile. It slowly faded. She began to tremble.

"Honey, it's all right," Richard quickly said.

No it isn't. She knew it the moment she saw the anger on Richard's face. She'd have known something was wrong even if Catherine and Luke hadn't been standing directly behind him. Dread clawed at her throat. "Is he in Santa Fe?"

"No, baby," Richard said, stepping inside and pulling her into his arms. She clung.

"Dr. Richard. Mrs. Catherine. Mr. Grayson," Kayla greeted happily as she came into the living room from her bedroom.

"Hello, Kayla," Catherine said, stepping past Richard and Naomi. "How was school today?"

"It was good, but I'm glad tomorrow is Friday," she said. "I'm going to a birthday party and, when I come home, we're going to a movie."

"Sweetheart." Naomi tried to keep the smile on her face, her voice normal. "I need to speak with Richard and Catherine alone. Why don't you finish your homework in your room?"

"Dr. Richard, you won't leave, will you?" she asked.

He placed his hand on her small shoulder. "No way."

Picking up her books from the living room floor, Kayla went to her room.

Naomi whirled to them the instant Kayla was out of sight. "Tell me."

Richard curved his arm around her waist and started for the sofa. "Why don't you—"

"No." She resisted, hating that fear was making her skin cold. "Please."

"He was fired three days ago from his security job," Luke said. "That same night he had a fight with his live-in girlfriend. Someone called the police. She had a busted lip, but she said she fell."

Naomi momentarily closed her eyes, remembered her fear and her lies out of shame, and then to protect Kayla. She looked from one to the other. If that was all there was, they wouldn't be here. "What's the rest of it?"

"His credit card popped up yesterday in Amarillo," Richard said.

Her hand covered her mouth. "That's on the way here."

"And a lot of other places," Luke said. "There's been no other activity on the card. His checking account has less than a hundred dollars in it. He won't receive his severance check for a couple of weeks. He didn't strike me as a man who kept a lot of cash on hand."

"She could have given him the money." Naomi's arms wrapped around her waist. "You do anything to keep him happy. Anything."

Richard pulled her into his arms, felt helpless as she shivered. "You're safe."

She wanted to believe that, but she'd thought that before. "Kayla." Pushing out of his arms, she started for her daughter's room.

Richard held her. "She's all right."

Logically she knew that, but the fear remained. "I need to see her."

"No. Not until you calm down," Richard told her.

She pulled away and was surprised when he didn't release her, but feeling afraid or threatened never entered her mind. "Please."

"Naomi, he's right." Catherine gently touched her arm. "As long as you keep your head, keep control, you don't let him win. You said it yourself. He doesn't want you happy. He'll do anything to rattle you. Make you live in fear. Don't let him win."

Closing her eyes, she buried her head against Richard's chest. "In my head, I know you're right, but . . ."

"I'll put a guy outside the apartment tonight and tomorrow night," Luke said. "He'll follow you to school and back home."

Her head lifted. "Thank—"

"I'll take the shift tonight and see that they get to school," Richard said. "I'd appreciate someone seeing they get home."

"You are not going to watch over us, then go to work."

"I've pulled all-nighters before. This is important. Until you feel safe, I want to be here as much as possible."

And she wanted him there. "Thank you." She turned to Luke and Catherine. "Thank you both."

"This is what friends do." Catherine took her hands in hers. "I'm going to go get Kayla. We'll only stay for a little while."

"No. You'll stay for dinner," Naomi said, her control slowly returning. "I made enchiladas because I thought Fallon was joining us, but she's working on a deadline. There's enough."

"Naomi's a good cook." Richard said proudly.

She blushed at the compliment. "Afterward, we can ride over and I can finally show you the house."

"Oh, I'd love to. Sierra said you got a good deal."

"Thanks to her." Naomi faced Luke and discovered that his size didn't intimidate her any longer. "Your sister is amazing at what she does."

"And like Brandon, she is as competitive as they come," Luke said. "Marriage has helped settle her a bit, but she has a long way to go."

Naomi didn't dare look at Richard. Luke knew his sister well. "Catherine, if you'll get Kayla, I'll go set the table."

Through dinner and showing the house to Luke and Catherine, Richard watched as Naomi conquered her fear and relaxed more and more. By the time they'd said good night to Luke and Catherine, and they'd put Kayla to bed, she was almost her old self.

"You sure you'll be all right sleeping out here?"

He pulled the pillow from her hand. She'd already put a sheet and blanket on the sofa. "I won't be sleeping."

She bit her lower lip and hugged her arms around her waist. Tossing the pillow aside, he took her into his arms. "He won't get to you."

She pressed against his hard length. "I knew he wouldn't like seeing us happy. Why won't he leave us alone?"

"He's a coward and a bully, but you're not the same woman anymore."

Her head lifted. "How can you be so sure?"

His hand palmed her cheek. "Because you're standing here with me, trusting me to keep you safe instead of in your car leaving." She didn't deny it. "You won't let him win."

"Because of you and Catherine. Mostly you. You made the difference."

"I'll always be here for you," he said, wishing he could say more. Now wasn't the time to bring up marriage again. "Now go to bed. I'll see you in the morning."

"It's barely nine," she protested.

"I'm sure you have lesson plans or something to do." He sat on the sofa, picked up a magazine on the table, and began flipping through it. He was weak where she was concerned. " 'Night."

"Can I get you anything else?"

"I'm good. 'Night."

"Good night."

Richard placed the magazine back on the coffee table and leaned back on the sofa. He'd wanted to hold her some more, but he wasn't sure of his control. She didn't deserve to have that bastard disrupt her and Kayla's life again. If he showed up, Richard was going to take great pleasure in kicking his good-for-nothing ass.

Chapter 15

Stepping out of the shower the next morning, Naomi smelled coffee. Thanks to Richard, she'd been able to sleep. She'd peeped in on him earlier, saw the bedding neatly folded and him entering data on his cell phone.

In her robe, she got Kayla up, helped her with her bath, combed her hair, and left her to get dressed while she did the same. Finished, she went to get Kayla and found her room empty. More and more she wanted to do things for herself. Yesterday she had gotten her box of cereal, spoon, and napkin out. She couldn't reach her bowl or lift the jug of milk.

Halfway to the kitchen, she heard Kayla and Richard's shared laughter. For a moment she thought of Gordon out there someplace wanting to harm them, then she pushed him from her mind. She wasn't going to let him destroy her life again.

"Good morning."

"Mama, Dr. Richard came over for breakfast,"

Kayla said. "I helped pour the juice and I didn't spill any on the table or my dress."

"Of course you didn't. But even if you had it would have been all right," Richard said, then pulled out a chair for her. Kayla was already seated. "Pancakes and pan sausages."

"It looks good. Thank you." Naomi blessed the food, then started to help Kayla. She saw Richard place a pancake on her plate. Naomi gave her a sausage, and watched Kayla pour her maple syrup before preparing her own plate. She was about to take a bite when there was a knock on the back door. She froze, then reached for Kayla.

"Too small." Richard rose and answered the door. "Hi, Fallon."

"Oops." She started to leave, but Richard caught her arm. "Coffee is made and so are the pancakes and sausages. Come on in."

"Since I'm hungry as usual, I'll be rude, grab a plate, and leave." She stepped inside. " 'Morning, Naomi, Kayla."

"Hi, Fallon," Kayla said. "Dr. Richard cooked breakfast and I helped, but it's our secret. I can tell you since you're here."

Fallon's lips twitched as she filled her mug with coffee. "Good job, too."

Naomi prepared her a plate. "You can stay."

"I'm rude, but not dense." She went to the door Richard was holding open. "See you later, and thanks."

"You're welcome." He closed the door. "Were those bunny slippers she had on?"

"They're her favorite." Kayla forked in pancakes.

"She's going to buy me a pair, too, if she ever finds them again. She's nice."

"I think so." Richard picked up his fork. "After school, why don't you and your mother come to the clinic and visit the puppies. Later we can go to my ranch and watch some movies."

"Can we, Mama? I bet the brown puppy has really gotten big by now."

Richard was watching over them, and Naomi found she liked it. "I don't see why not."

"Reese's credit card popped up yesterday at a gas station and this morning at a restaurant in San Antonio," Luke said on the phone.

"About time." Late Sunday evening, Richard paced in his home office. Naomi and Kayla were on the patio. One of Luke's men had followed them to his clinic Friday after school. Richard had been with Naomi and Kayla since then. They'd spent the day at his ranch. "I'm not sure how much more of this Naomi can take."

"Or you," Luke said knowingly. "It's hard when the woman you love is in danger."

Richard didn't even think of denying it. "She's had a rough life."

"Having you in it will make it better."

For how long, Richard thought. She wasn't thinking in those terms. "Thanks for the call. She and Kayla are outside. I'll let her know he's back in San Antonio."

"But tell her to still be cautious. It bothers me that there was no activity between Amarillo and San Antonio," Luke said.

Richard was instantly alert. "You think he's trying to fake us out?"

"Could be. He certainly knows how to leave a trail if that was his intention. I have a guy there, trying to get a visual."

Richard looked out the window to see Naomi and Kayla playing patty-cake. Darkness was fast approaching. "In the meantime, I'll keep watch over them."

"Thought you might. Someone will follow her from work tomorrow. I'm assuming you'll take the night and the morning shift again."

"I feel better if I'm with her and Kayla."

"From what I've seen, they will as well. I'll call you if and when I hear anything more."

"Bye, and thanks." Richard hung up and went outside. He hated the fear that quickly came into Naomi's eyes. She'd known he'd gone inside to speak with Luke.

"Kayla, we can play hide-and-seek now if you want." Naomi came to her feet, her eyes on Richard. "You can hide in the house."

"I bet you won't find me." Kayla rushed inside.

"Tell me quickly."

His hands clenched in impotent fury. "His credit card showed up twice in San Antonio yesterday and this morning, but Luke thinks it could be a trick. He wants us to remain cautious."

Her eyes closed, then opened. She started past him. He caught her arm.

"I won't let him near you or Kayla."

"Kayla is waiting."

His hand flexed, then loosened. He remembered

too clearly the last time her husband had come for them in Santa Fe. Richard had offered his help and she'd refused out of fear for Kayla. It made his gut twist that she didn't trust him enough to keep her safe, and there was nothing he could do to convince her.

It was all Naomi could do to keep standing and search for Kayla when all she wanted to do was sit down and bawl. She realized with a sinking heart that Gordon would never leave them alone. He'd come for them, and when he did this time, he'd come ready for trouble. Luke's men had guns. Richard didn't. If he tried to stop Gordon—

She stumbled. The thought of Richard being hurt while trying to protect her made her physically ill. She couldn't, wouldn't let that happen. She swallowed.

She heard giggling. How she wished she could always keep her daughter this happy.

"I hear a sound." Richard had followed her. "Perhaps it's a lion or maybe a tiger."

More giggles, muffled this time.

Naomi tried to join in the game, but couldn't. Richard's understanding smile somehow made it worse. She had brought this danger to his door when all he had ever done was love them.

For him it had never been just about intimacy. Finally, she'd found the love she'd always dreamed of having, but the price was too high. Initially she hadn't wanted to accept his love because of her fear for herself. Now the fear was for him.

"Naomi?" Richard took a step toward her.

If he touched her she wouldn't be strong enough to send him away. She quickly stepped back. "I think it's neither." She started around his desk. "I think it's Kayla Reese and here she is."

Giggling, Kayla crawled from under the desk. "You found me, Mama."

"Yes, I did." She took her daughter's hand and made herself look at Richard. Her heart twisted at the wounded look on his face. She'd done that.

His cell phone rang. He ignored it.

"Maybe it's Luke again," she said, hoping they'd located her ex.

"It's the ring tone for the answering service," he said.

"You gonna go help a sick animal, Dr. Richard?" Kayla asked, going to stand in front of him. "We have to help them get better."

He stared down at Kayla for a second longer, then answered the call. "Dr. Youngblood." His gaze went to Naomi, then back to Kayla. "Call Anderson."

"You're not going?" Naomi asked.

"You and Kayla will always come first," he told her, the words sinking deep in her heart and soul. She understood because Kayla and he would always come first. "Excuse me, I need to find my purse. Kayla, you and Richard can play another game. I bet you can find a real good hiding place."

"I bet I can, too." Kayla took off and Naomi went to find her purse. She'd protect her daughter and Richard.

Late Sunday Richard pulled up in front of Naomi's apartment and turned off the ignition. He'd barely opened the door before Jake Creed, one of Luke's men and the one who had followed Naomi and Kayla from school Friday, was there.

"Good evening, Dr. Youngblood, Mrs. Reese, and Kayla," he said, touching the brim of his black Stetson. "Just wanted you to know I'm here. Mrs. Reese, you have my cell if you need to call."

"Thank you," Naomi murmured and got out of the truck.

Richard was supposed to have the night shift. For Creed to be there Naomi must have called Luke. She didn't trust him enough to protect them. He clenched his jaw to maintain control.

They were barely inside before Naomi said, "Kayla, please go to your room. I'd like to speak to Richard in private."

Kayla looked from Richard to her mother and began to giggle. Obviously she thought they were going to kiss. "Come on, Teddy. Let's go play."

"You trust me that little," he asked when Kayla was out of sight. He could hardly get the words through the constriction in his throat.

"I trust you that much. You'd do anything to keep us safe, including putting yourself in danger." She swallowed. "I don't want to see you hurt."

The tight band around his heart eased. He pulled her into his arms. "I can take care of myself. More important, I can take care of you and Kayla. He's not getting near you again."

He believed that. She wasn't so sure. "I won't let him win by being afraid. The doors are solid with good locks. We're inside. He can't get in easily except through the windows, and that would give

Kayla and me time to get into the bathroom and call Creed. So go take care of the emergency. We're safe."

"I don't want to leave you," he protested.

"Help me to be strong," she said, trying to smile. "I don't want to be afraid any longer."

"That's not fair." His worried gaze never left hers.

"When I called Luke at the ranch tonight while you were playing with Kayla, he said he and Catherine would stop by later. We'll be well protected." She kissed him, then stepped back. "Go do what you do best."

He shook his head. "Loving you and Kayla is what I do best."

She trembled because she realized it was the truth. No matter what, he'd always be there for them. Tears crested in her eyes. She and Kayla were safe. She had to make sure he was as well.

He stared at her, almost as if expecting her to say something, and when she didn't, a shadow crossed his face. Then he was gone.

Naomi stared at the door. He'd wanted her to say she loved him. She loved him to the depth of her soul, yet had been afraid to say the words. If she had, he wouldn't have left.

"Where's Dr. Richard?" Frowning, Kayla came farther into the living room.

"He had to leave," Naomi passed Kayla on the way to the bedroom. "We need to get you ready for bed."

"But since you started dating, he always helps tuck me into bed if he's here. Maybe he hasn't left," she reasoned.

"We forgot, sweetheart. I'm sorry." Naomi held out her hand to her daughter.

A light knock came at the back door. Kayla took off running. "I knew he wouldn't leave."

Naomi ran after her. "Kayla, wait!"

She didn't listen. She quickly unlocked the door and swung it open. "Dr. Ri—"

Her word abruptly stopped. She stood frozen as Gordon rushed inside, almost knocking Kayla over.

For a split second, Naomi didn't recognize him. He'd lost weight, looked slovenly when he'd always taken pride—too much at times—in his neat appearance. The baseball cap shadowed his whiskered face. He'd always been clean-shaven.

Naomi put herself between her ex and Kayla. "Get out!"

"You don't tell me what to do. I own you." His mean gaze cut to Kayla. "You better keep that brat quiet if you know what's good for her."

"It's okay, Kayla," Naomi tried to soothe her. Kayla was holding her as tightly as she could. She wasn't making a sound. She'd learned early that tears and words made things worse around her father.

"Because of your accusations, I lost my job as a policeman. The only job I could get after that was as a lousy security guard!" he shouted. "It's your fault and the brat's fault. My mother won't even speak to me. Says she's ashamed I let a woman destroy my life. I lost my friends on the force, my nice apartment, everything, because of you. It's payback." He pulled a small-caliber gun out of his pocket.

Icy fear shook Naomi to the core. She'd never been so terrified. Her heart raced. Her stomach clenched. He didn't sound rational. With difficulty, she loosened Kayla's arms and put her behind her. "I'll do whatever you want. Just leave Kayla alone."

"No, you'll only do what I say if you're scared for her. You never cared about me," he snarled.

"I promise. I'll do anything you say. Anything. I was about to cook. Let me fix you something to eat."

"You owe me more than food."

The implication made bile rise in her throat. "Let me take Kayla next door."

"You think I'm a fool." He aimed the gun dead center at her stomach. "You ruined my life and you're gonna pay."

"Please, Gordon. I'll do anything you want. Just give me another chance," she begged. He liked it when she begged. All she had to do was stall. Luke would be there soon, but then so would Catherine. She had to protect Kayla and Catherine. She had to get Gordon out of there.

"Please let me show you." With unsteady hands she opened the top button of her blouse. "I won't fight. I'll do whatever you want. However you want, for as long as you want. We can go to your place."

He licked his lips. The gun wavered. "You're not so uppity now. You'll be begging for it before the night is over." A predatory gleam came into his eyes. "Let's go."

Trembling, Naomi turned to kneel in front of a terrified Kayla. "Remember what Mama—"

A cruel hand snatched her upright. "Let's go unless you want her to come with us." Sticking the gun back in his pocket, he reached for the door.

"Mommy and Daddy need to talk. Go into my room and watch a movie."

"No," Kayla cried, wrapping her arms around her mother's legs, tears glistening on her cheeks.

"Be Mama's big girl and do as I say. Stay here with Teddy." Naomi wanted to hold her daughter so bad. One last time. There was no way she was going to let him touch her once Kayla was safe. Tears still falling, head down, Kayla left the room.

"Let's go!"

His arm moved around her waist. To anyone else they would appear to just be a loving couple. They walked down the path people had made in back of the apartment as a shortcut to the small store on the highway.

She just prayed Kayla wouldn't come after them, prayed she'd remember to call Catherine as Naomi had taught her if her father ever showed up, and thanked God Richard was safe. He wouldn't have backed down from the gun.

Reaching his car parked at the end of the dimly lit parking lot of the store, Gordon roughly shoved her into the passenger seat and placed his hand over the pocket with the gun. "You can't outrun a bullet, and then guess who's next?"

"Let's go." Naomi closed the door.

"Anxious, huh? I knew that vet didn't have what it took, but you're gonna pay for letting him screw you." Gordon went around to the driver's side, got in, and pulled off with a squeal of tires.

Naomi folded her hands in her lap. Kayla was safe. That's all that mattered. If she didn't come back Richard would take care of her, because there was no way she'd ever submit to Gordon again. She'd fight until her last breath.

Richard had gotten a block away when he called his service and turned around. He couldn't leave Naomi and Kayla. He wouldn't be of any help to the animal with his mind someplace else. Naomi would just have to understand. Getting out of the truck, he started for Naomi's door.

He answered his ringing cell without looking at it. "Hello."

"Dr. Richard, he took Mama."

Terror ripped though Richard. "Creed," he shouted, running the few steps to the apartment door. "Let me in, Kayla."

The door opened. He swept a crying Kayla into his arms. Knowing it was useless, he still yelled for Naomi and rushed to the back door. That was the only way they could have left.

"Call Luke. He must have had a car parked at the store." Creed passed Richard at a dead run.

Richard was shaking so badly he could barely call. Kayla clung to his neck, her small body trembling. "I have you, Kayla. Luke. He got her. The bas—" He bit back an oath. "I'm taking Kayla next door. Creed thought he might have parked at the store in the back. They couldn't have gotten far."

"We're pulling up to the apartment complex now," Luke told him. "Cath can watch Kayla. I'll call the police."

"Don't cry, baby. We'll find your mother and bring her home safely." Richard felt helpless as he closed the back door and went to the living room to look for Luke's truck.

Another car pulled up first. Fallon got out of the rental with a smile that quickly faded. "What is it? Is Naomi—"

"The bad man took her," Kayla cried. "I want my mama."

Richard held her closer, thankful when Luke double-parked and he and Catherine got out and rushed to them.

"Come here, Kayla." Catherine reached for the little girl. After a long moment, she went into her arms.

Richard kissed Kayla. "Don't worry. We're going to find your mother and bring her back."

"Cath," Luke said.

Catherine walked inside the apartment holding Kayla. "I know you're frightened, but can you tell us anything that will help? Did he say where they might be going?"

Kayla hiccupped. "He had a gun. Mama didn't want to go."

Richard swiped his shaky hand over his face.

"Mama told me to leave. She said, if he ever came back I wasn't to argue and to call for help." Kayla placed her head against Catherine's shoulders.

"You did good, pumpkin."

"The police will be here any minute," Luke's said. "Let's go see if Creed got anything."

Outside they saw Creed walking fast toward them, his cell phone to his ear.

"Make me glad I hired you," Luke said.

Creed disconnected the call. "Reese was busted a couple of months ago for a phony ID. A kid at the store remembered seeing a man and a woman get into a white Ford sedan with a car rental decal. Vince is calling the rental agency now to see who rented that type of car. From there we should be able to get a name and a credit card number."

"You redeemed yourself. Now go sit with Cath and wait with them." Luke was already walking quickly away. "They're holed up someplace. It's too dicey driving. I want the name of where they're staying and fast."

"You'll have it."

Gordon stopped at the last unit of a small motel on the outskirts of town. Naomi opened the car door to run, but Gordon pulled out the gun. "I'd hate to miss our time in bed. Your choice."

Standing, she closed the door and rounded the car. She'd bide her time. By now, Luke would be at her apartment. They'd find her. She just had to stay alive.

Opening the door, he shoved her inside and flipped on the light. The curtain was already drawn. The full bed dominated the small room with only one nightstand, a rickety desk, and a chair.

"Don't turn up your nose." He grabbed her by the chin. "This is what you've reduced me to, but tonight I get some of mine back." He shoved her away. "Strip. Slowly."

She reached for a button of her blouse, saw the hatred on his face. He wanted to humiliate her. Never again. Her hands fell.

"I'm not afraid of you anymore, Gordon. You need a gun against a defenseless woman. You're a spineless coward." She couldn't hold back her fury and contempt another second.

Enraged, he advanced on her. "Shut up and do as I say, or I'm going back and get the brat you're so crazy about."

"She's safe by now. You'll never get close to her."

"I've seen you with him. You're a slut." With one hand, he ripped her blouse. She stumbled and fell.

One-handed, he reached for the snap of his jeans. "You're going to be screaming for it, just like last time."

The bastard had raped her. Enraged, she came off the floor, reaching for the lamp on the night-stand as she did.

Surprised, he lifted his hands seconds too late. She brought the bottom of the lamp down on his head. He howled in pain, staggering back to hold his head. He dropped the gun.

Naomi rushed to pick it up. She tried to watch Gordon and get to the phone she'd knocked off the nightstand.

"Give me that gun! You're too much of a coward to pull the trigger," he sneered.

"Once, but not after you threatened my baby." Her hand flexed on the handle.

"Give me that gun! You haven't the nerve."

Behind them the door burst open. Gordon swung around, a snarl on his face.

"Yes, she does." Richard said from the doorway. Luke stood behind him. "But I want a piece of you first." He planted his fist in Gordon's face. He went down like a stone. Richard jerked him up by the shirtfront and hit him again and again.

"That's enough. He can't feel it anymore." Luke pulled Richard off the unconscious man.

Richard distastefully shoved the man away, stood and saw Naomi's torn blouse. Enraged he went for the man again.

"Richard, please take me to Kayla," Naomi said, her voice and body trembling. "I know you took care of her, but I need to see her."

The anger cleared. Richard pulled out his cell phone. "She's with Catherine and Fallon at your apartment. You can talk to her until we get there. Let's go."

Naomi and Kayla held each other a long time before either was willing to let go. Richard stayed close to them both. The police came and went, and then Fallon went home. Luke, Catherine, and his team were the last to leave.

"I owe you," Richard said.

"You owe nothing." Luke nodded toward Naomi and Kayla huddled together on the sofa. "Go take care of your family."

"Good night," Catherine called. "We'll talk tomorrow. "

"Good night," Naomi said, kissing Kayla on the top of her head.

Richard closed the door. He wasn't leaving.

"Can me and Teddy sleep with you tonight?" Kayla asked. "We won't be a bother or trouble."

"I'd like that, and why would you think it would be a bother?' Naomi asked.

Kayla looked at Richard and tucked her head before saying, "I heard some of the mothers at school say how much of a bother it is to take care of their children. They can't wait for summer to ship them to their grandparents. I don't have any grandparents who want me so you have to keep me."

Naomi's eyes stung. "I love you, Kayla. You could never be a bother or trouble. Never. I'd be lost and miserable without you. You're the most precious thing in the world to me. Remember that always."

Richard crouched in front of them. "Your mother loves you, pumpkin. As for the summer, I was hoping we could get in a little fishing, maybe some camping. The horses at my place would like to see you as well."

She perked up. "Really?"

"Really." Richard plucked her up in his arms, sat down beside Naomi, and picked up the remote control. "No school tomorrow for either of you, so we can stay up late. I called Principal Crenshaw and asked for a personal day for your mother."

The credits for *Finding Nemo* began to roll. Handing the control to Kayla, he put his arm around Naomi and drew her closer. *His family.* He wasn't about to have it any other way.

Kayla was asleep ten minutes later. Richard didn't want to release her or her mother.

"I didn't want you to stay because I knew Gordon would have a weapon. I went with him to keep Kayla safe, but I'd called Luke and knew Catherine was coming with him. He'd protect her with his life, but bullets stray."

Richard clamped his teeth together. She needed to get it all out. "I-I wouldn't have let him touch me that way. Not after us, and not after realizing I wasn't a coward any longer. You're the cause of both."

His eyes squeezed tightly shut. She was making him weak.

"I knew if I didn't come back, you'd be safe and you'd take care of Kayla. You'd be her father."

Moisture formed in his eyes, and seeped onto his lashes and down his cheeks.

"I realized weeks ago that I loved you, that you loved us. You went out of your way to ensure Kayla's happiness and made sure she never felt left out even before we were officially dating. You'd only tried to love me, and I pushed you away because I let my past fears get in the way.

"I finally realized tonight that committing to you won't make me dependent or vulnerable; it will set me free. I'm going to live my life without fear or looking over my shoulder or second-guessing myself. I want you to be a part of that life—if you can forgive me."

"You love me?"

"Hopelessly. Desperately. Endlessly. I love you will all of my heart." Lifting her head, she kissed the wetness from his cheeks. "I think we should get married as soon as possible. What do you think?"

"What took you so long?" he managed.

"I was waiting to be the woman you could be proud of." Standing up to Gordon had proven that she was woman enough for Richard.

"You always were." Lifting his head, he gently kissed her.

"You're all I ever wanted," she said, closing her eyes, feeling safe and loved. She and Kayla were going to have it all, thanks to the man holding her. She'd never have another doubt.

Epilogue

"Kayla is going to be so excited." Naomi sat on the side of her bed, waiting for her daughter to wake up. Richard had moved all of them last night into the bed so they'd be more comfortable. While she and Kayla slept, he'd held and watched over them. Naomi had never felt safer or more loved.

"Just like I am." His hands on both of Naomi's shoulders, Richard leaned down and kissed her on the cheek.

One hand on his, the other on Kayla's, Naomi leaned her cheek into his kiss.

"Mama."

Naomi looked around, praying she didn't see fear in her daughter's eyes. Kayla scrambled into her mother's arms. Naomi firmly held her daughter to her and thanked God she wasn't shaking, and her hold wasn't desperate as it was last night.

"Dr. Richard!"

They reached for each other at the same time. "Good morning, pumpkin."

Her face bright and unafraid, Kayla smiled up at him. "I'm glad you're here."

His hold tightened for a second. "Me, too."

Relishing the sight of them safe and happy, Naomi came to her feet. One arm went around Richard's waist. Her other arm went around Kayla's. "Richard and I have some exciting news for you." She swallowed and fought the tears of happiness. "We're going to be married."

"And I get to be your daddy," Richard said, fighting his own lump.

Kayla's eyes rounded. "For real?"

"For real," Richard and Naomi answered at the same time.

Kayla hugged his neck. This time she did tremble.

Richard had to swallow a couple of times before he could speak. "I called my parents. They're on their way back from Canada. They're anxious to see you and already planning to do a lot of fun things with their granddaughter this summer. I'll have to share you."

Naomi laughed. "They asked if they still had Grandparents Day at school. Richard's mother wants to be a classroom volunteer in your class next year."

"I get to have grandparents, too?" There was awe in Kayla's voice.

"And they get to have the best granddaughter in the world," Richard told her. "Just as soon as the minister marries us, you can start calling me Daddy."

"Daddy," Kayla repeated. "I was just practicing."

He kissed her on the forehead. "I like the sound of that."

Her smile growing, Kayla hugged him again. "Wait until I tell Teddy. We're going to have all we ever wanted."

Naomi smiled, felt Richard's lips graze her hair, and heard Kayla giggle. She no longer felt like a failure when Kayla indicated Naomi hadn't been enough. Loving Richard, and he loving her back, helped her to understand. "You'll have more family to love, and who will love you."

"Wow!"

"I'm going to cook my future family breakfast," Richard said.

"I wanna help," Kayla said excitedly.

"Not until you wash your face, and brush your teeth," Naomi told her

Kayla scrambled down and left at a dead run. Richard and Naomi smiled.

Richard curved his arms around her waist. "I love you."

"I love you right back." She leaned into his kiss, the shelter of his strong arms, feeling safe and loved and cherished.

Giggles sounded from the doorway.

They lifted their heads slowly. Kayla would see lots of kisses and gentle touches. She'd grow up watching parents who loved each other.

"I think my future daughter needs help," Richard said.

Her arm around Teddy, the toothbrush in her hand, Kayla's eyes widened. "Daddy."

Richard picked them both up and kissed Kayla on the cheek. "Perfect. Just like you. Come on, Teddy. Let's get our best girl ready for breakfast."

Naomi stared after them, ignoring the tears of happiness streaming down her cheeks. She couldn't agree with Kayla more. They had all they'd ever wanted.

Read on for an excerpt from

ALL THAT I NEED
by Francis Ray

Coming soon from St. Martin's Paperbacks

Fallon Nicole Marshall had always considered herself cool under pressure. After all, she was a well-respected travel writer for some of the top magazines in the country. She routinely dealt with tight deadlines, demanding editors, computer glitches and uncooperative people. She'd baked in 107 degrees and frozen in 6 below to get a story and just the right photographs. She had the patience of Job and the tenacity of a terrier. Nothing—if you didn't consider her need for two cups of coffee each morning—got the best of her anymore. She'd been there, done that.

Or so she'd mistakenly thought.

Slowing down on the highway, Fallon put on her signal and turned her rental onto the paved road three miles out of Santa Fe. Her slim fingers flexed on the steering wheel of the late model Taurus. She was only marginally pleased that they weren't damp with perspiration. She might be a bit nervous about obtaining information for her next story, but at least she wasn't showing her frayed nerves about meeting Lance Saxton again.

It was perfectly understandable that she felt apprehensive—after all, she had been, well, rather abrupt to Lance Saxton two weeks ago when they'd first met. She'd practically accused him of being a thief and walked away from him in self-righteous indignation. Although he had to share some of the blame for that crack about "not handling their financial responsibilities correctly," she had to take her share as well.

She freely admitted that since her mother was swindled by the unscrupulous owner of an auction house, and Lance owned an auction house, she had judged quickly and harshly.

And she'd been wrong.

She hadn't discovered her mistake until recently.

Now she needed Lance Saxton to gain access to the Yates' home for the article she planned to write. He might toss her out; then again, he might not. There was only one way to find out.

Moments later the red barrel roof of a house came into view; then as she rounded a curve, she saw the sprawling Yates house. She slowed and came to a complete stop. It was simply beautiful with the afternoon sun shining on the roof and the adobe exterior. She could easily imagine coming home from work or a trip and catching the first glimpse of the house. She didn't even live there and yet she felt a sort of calming peace. One day she'd have a house, a family, but for now she enjoyed her job. She loved to travel and was paid well to visit and write about some of the most exciting places in the world.

The last thought had her squaring her shoulders. She was good at what she did. Nothing had ever stopped her in the past, and she wouldn't allow Lance Saxton to be the first.

Putting the car into motion, she continued down

the mile-long road and parked on the circular drive-
way in front of the massive red double doors, reason-
ing if Lance threw her out, she wouldn't have far to
go to her car. Getting out, she again studied the
sprawling two-story house.

The home was originally built in the 1920s by oil
mogul Thaddeus Yates. He liked the Southwest and
chose Santa Fe as his base when he wanted to relax
and get away from Lubbock, Texas. After his death,
his only child and daughter, Colleen, expanded the
six-thousand-square-foot home another five thousand
square feet to include a loggia and pool house. Her
son did more renovation on the house plus extensive
landscaping, turning the usually parched grounds of
the area into a verdant paradise with lush green grass
and a rainbow hue of flowers.

Fallon realized she was stalling, and with good
reason. She wasn't looking forward to ringing the
doorbell and meeting Lance Saxton again. She didn't
mind admitting she was wrong so much as she didn't
like the idea of making that admission to a man she
had a mild attraction to. She'd like to think he'd
caught her at a weak moment, but that would be a
lie. She traveled so much she didn't have time for a
relationship, and she valued herself too much to have
meaningless affairs.

Yet her girlie antenna had zinged the instant she
looked into Lance's midnight black eyes. He had the
"Y" yummy factor in spades. At least six-feet-four in
sinful jeans and a white polo that delineated hard
muscles, she was almost fantasizing about the naughty
things he could whisper in her ear—until she learned
what he did for a living. And went as cold as an ice-
berg on the man.

Sighing, Fallon removed her camera from the case,

looped the strap around her neck, and grabbed her notebook. Standing there wouldn't get the job done. Closing the car door, she followed the paved path to the wide double doors, all the time telling herself that this was a story like all the hundreds, probably thousands, she'd written in the past.

Fallon realized she was stalling. Again. She hadn't called for an appointment. She honestly hadn't known what to say. *Hey, I'm sorry I accused you of being a thief, but I have this great idea for a story and two editors are interested so let's forget about our first meeting.* If the positions were reversed, she would have thrown him out. She had a bit of a temper— which had gotten her into this mess.

Blowing out a breath, Fallon rang the doorbell.

In the small library of the Yates house that Lance Saxton had taken for his office, he slowly lifted his head when he heard the doorbell. He'd been waiting for the sound since Richard called that morning to tell him that Fallon had asked if he would be there. To Richard's "Don't blow your second chance," Lance had said nothing.

Since Lance didn't have any other appointments and he wasn't expecting any deliveries, he reasoned it was Fallon Marshall. His hand flexed on the pen in his hand. It didn't take much to visualize the stunning woman with long curly hair, bedroom brown eyes, model cheekbones and lips to drive a man crazy. For some reason—perhaps because Richard was in such a great mood and Lance could tell his cousin was finally interested in a woman—the moment they'd met, Lance had found himself attracted to Fallon.

It was the first time in months he'd had more than a passing interest in a woman. He'd honestly thought he had written women off except for the occasional ones he took to bed. It was purely physical for both of them; easily had and easier forgotten.

The chime came again. This was the housekeeper's half-day off. The people he'd hired to help catalog the house's contents for the auction had driven into town for a late lunch. There was no one there but him. If he didn't answer, she'd leave and he wouldn't have to worry about forgetting his long-ago promise of steering clear of women he couldn't easily walk away from. Yet he found himself coming to his feet and leaving the study. Fallon was just a woman.

Opening the front door, he had to revise his earlier thought about Fallon. She was stunning in a raspberry knit top and white walking shorts. Her eyes were just as captivating as before, her mouth just as tempting. His hand clamped on the door knob as they continued to stare at each other. He wouldn't be the first to speak. She had called him a thief.

"Hello, Lance. I guess you're surprised to see me."

"That's putting it mildly."

Fallon ran her tongue over lips he'd dreamed about before saying, "I'm not sure if you remember or not, but I'm a travel writer."

Since his mouth was dry, he simply nodded. Fallon was too much of a temptation. As soon as possible, he was sending her on her way.

"I read about this place and the auction you're having. I came up with the idea for an article." She glanced around the yard. "This house might not be on the historical society's register, but it has a lot of history that will be lost once the auction is over. I'd like to preserve that."

"By doing a story," he said, unable to keep the derision out of his voice. Another person who wanted to profit from the misfortune of others. And she'd thought *him* heartless.

Her eyes narrowed briefly, then she shifted back to him, inadvertently making her breasts in the knit top jut forward. Lance gritted his teeth and opened his mouth to tell her goodbye, but she finally spoke.

"Not just a story. I want to bring the history of the house and the people who lived here to life. I also want to let readers know that it's all right not to plan every second of a vacation. Wonderful opportunities like this auction might present itself. I've done a bit of research on the house already."

"Don't you think that was a bit premature?" he asked, glad his voice was normal even if his heart rate wasn't.

"Yes, but knowledge is never wasted." She stepped back and looked up at the window overhead. "Do you know that some of the timber in this house came from Yates' grandparents' property in Louisiana? He was a bit of a sentimentalist." She sent Lance a quick grin. "The stained glass in the window overhead is from Paris and the chandelier in the living room is Waterford. They're his wife's selections."

"Women like the finer things." He'd learned that lesson the hard way.

Her brow arched. "So do men. Thaddeus spared no expense to build this house. It took three years. His daughter expanded it even more. From the little I was able to find, she doted on her son and wanted the house to last for generations. It's a shame that her dreams died with him." Fallon gave him her full attention, her expression so heartrending he had to lock his knees to keep from reaching out to comfort her. "It would be wonderful if that didn't happen, if the family history could be preserved, and be the impetus for other family dreams and legacies."

His gaze narrowed on her. So, she wasn't just beautiful and brassy. It was rare to meet someone not in the business who really understood the value and importance of beloved furniture and accessories being a legacy.

Even at thirty-six, there were times when he thought of his own mortality. He never planned to marry. What would he leave behind? Who would mourn him? The answers weren't comforting, so he continued to study Fallon. Unlike most people, his direct stare didn't make her fidget.

He'd been devastatingly wrong about women before, but something told him that Fallon was telling the truth. This was more than a story to her. Watching her hair dance in the breeze, her steady gaze, he came to a decision.

Stepping back inside, he watched her eyes widen, her mouth open. He realized she thought he was going to shut the door in her face. It annoyed the hell out of him that she believed he was that rude. "Come in."

Her mouth hung open for a second longer, before she snapped it shut. She quickly stepped inside. "Thank you."

"Would you care for something to drink?"

"No, thank—" Her eyes widened and she was across the room. Reverently her hand grazed the top of an oak-finished chest of drawers. "This is one of Thaddeus's pieces, isn't it? His daughter used this for her hope chest."

Lance joined her. "You did your research well, I see."

"I wanted to be prepared." She smiled over her

shoulder at him, then turned back to the piece that was as tall as she. "He was a furniture maker before they struck oil on his property. A picture of this chest was the only one I could find of the contents in the house."

"There are other pieces he made mixed throughout with the more famous makers like Chippendale," he said. "The house is a treasure trove of furniture, art work, and crystal."

Her eyes glittered with hope, one hand clamped on the camera, the other on the notebook. "Then you'll let me do the story?"

He was probably crazy considering he barely could keep his eyes off her lips. "You can do the story." He motioned toward her camera. "Feel free to take as many photos as you like. You seem to understand and appreciate the furnishings—that they meant something to the Yates—they aren't just things or possessions," he said.

For a second, her eyes darkened with pain. "Yes."

He wondered if she was thinking about the incident that caused her to brand him a thief. "Feel free to look around. I'll be in my office." He pointed to an open door to the left. "Just let me know when you're leaving."

"Thank you."

With a brief nod, he returned to his study, hoping he hadn't made a terrible mistake.